Island of the Dolls

The Real Story of the Muñecas Project

I0687389

By A.E. Hodge

A Fiction Fugitive Select Publication

Text, cover, and interior images copyright © 2016 by A.E. Hodge
Edited by J.P. Peters
Cover Design by M.F. Mueller

www.aehodge.com

ISBN: 0692661395
ISBN-13: 978-0692661390 (Fiction Fugitive Select)

Special thanks to the Find Carmen Foundation
For permission to transcribe and publish
EXHIBIT 001B ("Audio File, C. Benitez")

www.findcarmenfoundation.com

Dedicated to the ongoing search for
And loving memory of

Carmen Benitez
John Cavill
Larry Richmond, Jr.
Miguel Lopez Rosario

In 2012, three students left home to film a documentary on *Isla de las Muñecas*—an island deep in an ancient canal, haunted by a dark history and home to a thousand rotting dolls.

The student filmmakers were last seen Saturday, October 27, boarding a ferry bound for the Island of the Dolls.

They were never seen again.

Three years later, a digital audio recorder was recovered from a tree near the island. Forensic teams were able to salvage the last recording of the missing filmmakers.

The following is a transcript of their final audio log.

TABLE OF CONTENTS

PROLOGUE: THE CONFESSION OF CARMEN BENITEZ 1
CHAPTER 1: A MOTHER'S PRIDE... 2
CHAPTER 2: ARRIVAL..10
CHAPTER 3: XOCHIMILCO..19
CHAPTER 4: MIGUEL AND LA JUANITA 29
CHAPTER 5: JOURNEY TO THE ISLAND.......................... 37
CHAPTER 6: LA ISLA DE LAS MUÑECAS.......................... 47
CHAPTER 7: THE HOUSE OF DON JULIO...................... 57
CHAPTER 8: STRANDED 69
CHAPTER 9: NIGHTFALL 77
CHAPTER 10: BUMPS IN THE NIGHT 88
CHAPTER 11: UNINVITED GUESTS 95
CHAPTER 12: FORSAKEN 103
CHAPTER 13: FUEL.. 111
CHAPTER 14: THE CROSS AND THE COQUITA 119
CHAPTER 15: DARK WATERS..128
CHAPTER 16: VANISHED 136
CHAPTER 17: THE HEART TREE 141
CHAPTER 18: FIRST WATCH...149
CHAPTER 19: THINGS IN THE WATER 154
CHAPTER 20: THE WEEPING...163
CHAPTER 21: THE OFFERING 168
CHAPTER 22: OUT OF THE FRYING PAN.......................175
CHAPTER 23: ON THE CANAL..182
CHAPTER 24: RETURN..189
CHAPTER 25: THE SÉANCE..196
CHAPTER 26: DON'T GO 204
CHAPTER 27: ALONE IN THE DARK 211
CHAPTER 28: THE JOURNAL OF DON JULIO.................219
CHAPTER 29: THE BREAK-UP FOR REAL...................... 228
CHAPTER 30: PURIFICATION BY FIRE 236
CHAPTER 31: MOTHER OF THE DEAD 243
CHAPTER 32: LANDFALL 250
CHAPTER 33: THE LAST STAND.................................... 255
CHAPTER 34: A MOTHER'S LOVE 261

Prologue: The Confession of Carmen Benitez

—And I'm not sure how long it'll record or how much longer I can last, but it has to be said and I hope to God someone finds this, so my dad and everyone will know.

It was me. I killed them. They died because of me.

My name is Carmen Benitez, and I killed my friends.

It's getting dark now and I know I won't make it home. None of us will make it home. And I want you to know I'm so sorry for that. I'm so sorry, Dad. You warned me. Everyone warned me. But I didn't listen. I *couldn't* listen.

Now I can't stop listening. Can't stop... *hearing* it. I think it's just the water, just the sound of the canal—but God, it sounds like crying, and I don't know if she'll let me go, Dad. I don't think she'll let me go.

So I've got this voice recorder. All I have left, since I lost Mom's camera. Funny how that used to matter. How the *Muñecas* Project used to matter.

I've got this voice recorder, and I know I don't have much longer. The water's so cold here. So cold...

But I want to tell my story. So everyone will know.

Why we're not coming home.

How I killed them all.

So if... if someone finds this recording, please get it to my father, Orlando Benitez, in Middleton, Colorado.

And if you hear this someday, Dad... I'm so sorry. To you, to Mr. Cavill, to the Richmonds. To Miguel's mom and sister. To all our friends and family.

This is my confession.

Chapter 1: A Mother's Pride

You remember the night before I left?

It's very clear in my mind. I was so excited to leave in the morning on my big adventure. The trip of a lifetime, or so I thought. I'd been excited for months.

Yet for some reason I could barely keep from crying.

I was in my bedroom, in the attic of our old suburban townhouse—a small room with a slanted ceiling and a window on the north wall that never got any sun. Under the window sat the writing desk you found for me at some garage sale, years ago. It was too big for me in elementary school, too small for me now. My video camera sat on the desk, recording me as I packed.

I was kneeling over my battered suitcase, stowing away *Abuelita's* pretty topaz earrings—the one girly thing I was bringing to offset all the sweaters and jeans—when for no discernible reason, I found myself fighting back tears.

I wasn't sad. I wasn't scared. I wasn't feeling much of anything except excitement.

But the tears came anyway, and I had to stop packing and sit in my scuffed office chair to catch my breath. My big, clunky camcorder sat recording on the desk beside me. I could see my reflection in the camera's lens. I was wearing frumpy pink pajamas with dog print patterns, my brunette hair pulled back in a short, frizzy ponytail. My brown eyes were bloodshot, and tears traced the freckles on my round, tan cheeks. I hid my face from the camera as I broke down in sobs.

Then a knock on the door broke the spell, and I heard your big, reassuring voice on the stairs.

"Carmen? Everything okay in there?"

I grabbed a tissue and wiped my eyes. "Yeah, Dad. Just doing some takes."

"Can I come in?" you asked.

Leaving the camera running, I lurched out of my old, squealing office chair and went to the door.

When I opened it, there you stood—a burly Latino guy with short dark hair, full red cheeks, and deep laugh lines under a bushy salt-and-pepper mustache. You wore a white T-shirt and blue jeans, same as always. That's what I remember, anyway. How I always see you in my mind.

I did a bad job hiding my tears. Concern lit your eyes and you rushed to me, wrapping me in your arms.

"What's a matter, Maricarmen?" Your Mexican accent slipped, like it only does when you're worried.

I pulled out of the embrace. "Nothing, Dad. Really! I guess I had something in my eyes."

"Yeah, right. Listen, you know you don't have to do this. Lord knows I begged you not to."

I rolled my eyes. "It's not that."

"It's okay to be scared, honey. You never even left the country before. This whole thing is dangerous and stupid."

"I'm *not* scared," I insisted. "Honestly, nothing's wrong. I don't know why I'm crying. It's probably just, you know. Woman problems."

The words *woman problems* were usually enough to make you drop anything. Not this time. You scowled.

"It's *him*, isn't it? What he do this time? I tell you, Carmen, you just say the word and I go to town…" You swung an imaginary baseball bat in the air. *"Bam!"*

"Jesus, Dad! It's not John, either!"

"Hey, don't say the Lord's name in vain."

Rolling my eyes, I returned to the camera on my desk, looking at the old-school swing-out LCD screen in hopes you wouldn't press further—especially not about John.

After a moment, you said softly, "Is that your mom's old video camera?"

I stiffened, surprised. "Yeah. You don't mind if I take it with me? It's got some features I want."

You smiled. "I don't mind. She'd want you to use it."

I smiled back, looking down at the camera. Then, to my vast annoyance, fresh tears welled in my eyes—the traitors—and I covered my mouth to hide a gasping sob.

You crossed the tiny space to sit on my neatly made bed, which groaned beneath your weight. "Come on, Carm. Come here."

Exasperated with myself, I set the camera down and sat beside you, and you wrapped your arm around me.

"Really, now, what are you crying for?" you said. "I thought this film was your big thing. Thought it finally got you out of this whole *John* funk, you know?"

I frowned and looked across the room at my corkboard, where I kept the picture of Mom. You know the one. She's about my age in it. Right before she had me, I guess. The small, red lips and tiny pointed chin, the bright brown eyes, the delicate, doll-like features. She looks just like me, only lighter skinned.

As I studied that worn-out photograph, I started to wonder if maybe I *did* know why I was crying.

"My big thing," I repeated, in a creaky voice. "I wish Mom was here to see it."

You barely missed a beat. "She sees it," you said. "She sees you right now."

That did nothing to comfort me. "Do you think she'd be proud of me? For doing this film?"

"Is *that* what this is about?" Your strong, worker's hand squeezed my shoulder. "Listen, Carmen, just because your mom made movies doesn't mean you have to. All she wanted was for you to be happy. So if you want to be a big hotshot director, hey, more power to you. When you get your mansion, I'll be the first to live in your pool house. But do it because *you* want to. You do, don't you?"

I wiped my eyes. "Yeah," I muttered. "Hell, yeah! You know it's all I've *ever* wanted. To be respected as a serious documentarian, like Mom. I'd do anything to make this work. I think I really have a shot with this one, Dad."

Sliding out from your arm, I crossed the room to my desk and picked up a photo of my destination. The photo showed a reedy, muddy river bank, shadowed by leaning juniper trees and semi-tropical foliage.

At the center of the photo, mounted on a stick and rotting in the sun, was a child's severed head.

Not a real child, of course. It was just a doll's head, the mottled, ruined flesh only rubber, the sightless eyes only faded plastic. Still, it made for a disturbing image.

"I mean, you know I don't do spiritual stuff," I said. "But this island! Whether you believe in ghosts or not, it's compelling. This *Muñecas* project is more than just a film school assignment. This is our chance to break out big! If we tell this story right, we could win a festival, get a studio contract. Who knows?"

With a smile, you put a hand on my shoulder. "There's the enthusiasm! Nothing brings it out like your movies."

"People say it's the most haunted place in Mexico," I said. *"Isla de las Muñecas*, Island of the Dolls. Deep in the old Aztec canals, an entire island, filled with creepy dolls."

You looked over my head at the photograph, frowning skeptically. "Definitely gives *me* the creeps."

"They say the island's former owner, Don Julio, saw a girl drown in the canal back in the fifties. He tried to save her, but he couldn't reach her in time.

"The very next day, a doll washed up on his island. He was sure it must have belonged to the girl. So in his guilt and sadness, he pinned the doll up in a tree, as a kind of memorial to her.

"But he didn't stop there."

I studied the rotten doll's head in the photograph. It looked back at me with a vacant mockery of innocence.

"From that day on, those who knew him say Don Julio changed. For the next fifty years, he spent his life obsessed with collecting dolls, hanging hundreds, even *thousands* of them across his island.

"Now, long after he's gone, the dolls remain. Some say they come alive at night. Ferrymen who pass the island can hear the dolls, crying to them across the canal."

You shook your head and turned away. "Carm, I'm worried enough already."

I grinned, pleased with the effect I was having—proof of my subject matter. "But that's not the end. You want to know the creepiest part? Don Julio died in 2002. His cousin, Fernando, found him floating in the canal. He'd drowned, in the exact same place as the little girl."

Your eyebrows rose slowly with concern and dismay. Finally you forced a smile. "It's quite a story."

"And it's true." I crossed the room to my desk. "Or so they say. The place is a tourist trap, now. Don Julio's cousin, Fernando, runs tours there during the day, from what I've read. How much of the story is true and how much is publicity for the island…?" I shrugged. "But I'll find out what *really* happened. The truth about *Isla de Las Muñecas.*"

"Well. I'm just glad you're feeling better. You've been crying enough lately."

I averted my eyes. The damn walls in that house always were too thin.

"And honey," you added, "don't you worry if your mom would be proud. She *is* proud. A mother always loves her children. Not even death changes that."

By then, the crying spell was long broken, and I again felt nothing but excitement—and perhaps embarrassment at my tears. So I distanced myself. "Don't get sappy on me. Like I said, you know I don't do spiritual stuff."

You stepped back, and when I turned to face you, your smile had become somewhat stern.

"You're going to a spiritual place," you said. "Some say a haunted place. You best *respect* the spiritual, even if you don't *do* it."

I rolled my eyes and set the photo down, picking up my video camera again. "It had better be haunted. Think of the footage we'll get!"

As I looked through the black and white viewfinder at you, you smirked. "You filming this? I should've known."

"Don't worry, I'll edit you out in post. I told the other guys to take some footage tonight, too, before we leave. I'll splice it up into an intro or something."

You frowned, immediately suspicious. "Wait. *Guys?* I thought this was just you and Larry."

Realizing the Pandora's Box of trouble I'd just opened, I forced a smile and set the camera down. "No. I thought I told you. John's coming, too."

A fire lit in your flint-black eyes. In a low, deliberate voice, you said, "I thought you two broke up."

"No, no!" I said. "We patched things up. We're good."

"Really? You sure, after all he put you through?"

I felt my face tighten. "We talked things over, Dad. We're doing much better."

Now it was your turn to roll your eyes. "Shit! Well, I know better than to argue. But it seems like a pretty big change at the last minute. Does Larry know?"

"I'll tell him." I waved a hand. "He'll understand. I mean, we're just friends. Dad, trust me. John has his faults, but he can be useful, too. Especially on an adventure."

"If I didn't trust you," you said, "I wouldn't let you go *adventuring* at all. I mean, what kind of dad am I?"

I grinned, then stood on my tip-toes to kiss you on the cheek. "The good kind?"

You frowned under your mustache. "We'll see. Anyway, I packed some snacks for your trip."

"John's bringing all that stuff," I said dismissively. "I told you, he's useful."

You winked. "But is he bringing my homemade salsa?"

"Dad, I'm going to Mexico. Do I *really* need to pack salsa?"

You rubbed the back of your neck. "Okay, maybe not."

I relented with a smile. "All right, I'll take it. Hopefully I can smuggle it through the airport. I'm sure it's spicy enough to call it weapons-grade. Anyway, I have to leave early to pick up John. I might be gone when you wake up."

"Good." You shrugged. "Or I might try and stop you. Just remember what I told you. Be respectful. Of the land, the people, the customs. The spirits, too. Bad luck to disrespect them. It *is* the land of your ancestors, Carmen."

"Trust me," I insisted, a bit amused by his superstition, "I'm taking it seriously. I'll be fair and objective, like Mom. A biography of the local people, their culture and beliefs. Plus a few thousand creepy dolls. It'll be fun!"

You smiled. "I'm scared," you said from the door,

"but you know I'm proud, too. I love you, Carmen."

"Love you too, Dad."

You closed the door behind you, leaving me alone with the running camera and my thoughts. I found myself caught up again in excitement. I didn't give much deeper thought to what you said, to your misgivings, or even to my fit of inexplicable crying.

But I think now I know why I was crying that night.

And I know why it was so hard for you to let me go.

A parent's love is such a powerful thing. You must feel responsible for my well-being, even now—this person that was once your child, once a *part* of you.

I could see the worry in your eyes, weighing down your eyelids, as you spoke to me that night. The fear of a parent's ultimate failure: the failure to protect his own child.

But I want you to know you didn't fail, Dad. You were right to worry, but you were right to let me go, too. You couldn't have stopped me. And you tried to warn me.

There were so many warnings. If I'd been the voice of reason I thought I was, maybe I'd have turned back before it was too late.

So if this tape reaches you, I just want you to know I don't blame you, Dad. I hope you're still proud of me, and I hope you don't feel guilty. You tried to warn me.

I was the one who wouldn't listen.

Chapter 2: Arrival

In the morning, I left home before the sun came up, heading to John's place in my old Saturn. I picked him up around six from his dad's row house in west Middleton and we drove to the airport in Denver.

I was dressed in jeans and a tank top under an open hooded sweater, my hair pulled back in a ponytail. *Mi Abuelita's* topaz earrings swung lightly from my ears. The freckles on my cheeks were concealed by light, practical makeup—I'd be on camera, after all—and last night's tears were long-forgotten. Now I was bright-eyed, excited, and immune to John's attitude.

"Did you pack enough?" John said, through a forced smile. "It's a little cramped."

He pulled his camo hat low to keep the rising sun from his eyes. Under the cap, his dark hair was buzzed to the same length as the stubble covering his strong, angular jaw. He wore an orange Denver Broncos sweater and, in spite of the late October chill, a pair of frayed cut-off jean shorts that bared his long, muscular legs. Even with his seat shoved against the luggage in the back, his knees brushed the glove compartment.

"We could've taken your truck," I reminded him.

"Yeah, but parking an F150 in one of them tiny airport spaces is just *asking* for scratches, babe."

Not like my car has any value or anything. I rolled my eyes behind my sunglasses, but said nothing.

"Scratches at a minimum," John grumbled, pulling the bill of his hat even lower. "Could get stolen. Blown up by terrorists. I don't know."

"Yeah, go ahead and get all your *blowing up* and *terrorist* references out before we get to the airport, thank you."

He laughed, glancing my way. "You still mad at me?"

I frowned, considering. "I haven't decided if I believe you or not. My dad doesn't."

Larry didn't, either, but I left that unsaid.

Reaching out, John put his hand on my thigh and studied me with his handsome blue eyes. "I'm telling you, *nothing* happened that night. She was just some drunk freshman. She was pawing on everybody."

"Yeah, I bet."

"I'm serious, Carmen! Anything else you heard is a *lie.*"

I sighed. "Can we not talk about this now? I just want to make a movie, okay?"

"I know," he said. "That's why I'm here."

"Funny, I thought you were here because you didn't trust me alone with Larry."

"Should I not?" he said immediately.

I clenched the steering wheel and said nothing.

"Look, all I'm saying is I'm here for you, all right? For *you.* Because anything that's important to you is important to me, too. You're all that matters in the world to me, Carmen. I'll prove that to you."

We'll see, I thought. After a moment, I turned up the radio, and John looked out his window. We rode in silence down the narrow mountain road into Denver.

At Denver International, we met my partner on the film project, Larry Richmond, Jr. He was waiting for us in the lobby, wearing iPod earbuds. His green Jamaican-flag backpack and shaggy mane of dark, curly hair made him hard to miss, despite his small stature.

As we caught his eye, Larry's soft brown face fell in dismay at the sight of John pulling luggage behind me.

With a sinking feeling, I waved. "Hi, Larry."

Larry pulled out his iPod earbuds, his dark eyes not leaving John. "I thought he wasn't coming," he blurted.

I mumbled, "I meant to tell you…"

Setting the suitcase upright, John advanced on Larry, smirking, his hand extended. "Larry. Long time, no see."

The two of them were a study in contrast. John was over six feet tall, ruggedly athletic, pale and sharp-featured.

Meanwhile, Larry was short, only a few inches taller than me. His skin was dark, soft, and freckled. He wore stylish narrow-framed glasses, a stainless steel stud in his left nostril, and a small goatee that brought some character to his otherwise round, boyish face. Beneath his black leather vest, he was dressed in a gray short-sleeve Polo shirt tucked neatly into fitted blue jeans. As usual, he wore black Harley Davidson boots, though as far as I know he'd never so much as sat on a motorcycle. The boots, along with his big hair, gave him a few extra inches in height.

Like me, Larry was studying film at Middleton Heights College of Liberal Arts. His specialty was camera work and editing, while my focus was in directing. The *Muñecas* project would be our first collaboration.

Larry endured John's overly vigorous handshake, his low, radio-quality voice shaking with the force of it. "Hey, John. I didn't think you'd be here."

John released Larry from his iron grip. "Well, you know. Carmen wanted someone good for more than just camera work." His tone was friendly, but only barely.

"It's not a big deal, is it?" I asked Larry, donning my most endearing smile. "It's your project, too."

Smiling tightly, Larry shrugged. "I mean, he's already got a ticket, right? It's kind of a done deal. But," he said flatly, "it's cool. The more the merrier."

John started to fish around in the front pocket of his sweater. "Actually." He held his plane ticket out to Larry.

"You mind switching seats with me?"

"Do you mind?" I said, with another ingratiating smile. "He ordered at the last minute, so he's kinda far from me."

Larry took John's ticket in silence, his jaw clenched.

As we waited for the call to board the flight to Mexico City, we sat together in the tightly-packed lobby chairs, Larry to the left of me, John to the right. Larry fiddled with his smartphone in silence while John looked around the airport, hiding bored irritation behind a thin smile. The bill of his camo hat was pulled down to hide his eyes. I was certain he was checking out some bimbo across the lobby, but I couldn't catch him in the act.

I told myself not to think about it. I couldn't worry about John or our relationship or any of that—not until after this trip. The only thing that mattered was the film.

Yet I couldn't stop watching him, jealous of his gaze.

When they called our flight, the three of us took our seats on the plane. I'd bought two seats for Larry and me weeks ago, together in the center island. John and I sat there, while Larry took the seat John bought at the last minute when he decided to chaperone; it was a window seat several rows back.

As the flight attendants reviewed the procedures for takeoff, I twisted in my chair, searching for Larry through the sea of heads. When I caught his eye, I offered him a commiserating smile. He sighed and looked away.

I chewed my lip. I'd meant to warn him that John was coming, but in the excitement and frenzy before the trip, I'd simply forgotten. Larry was my best friend and I'd never known a more accommodating guy, but he'd never liked John, or surprises.

I hoped it wouldn't affect his work ethic on the film.

The flight took several hours. John listened to MP3s on his smartphone beside me and read his *Automotive*

Monthly. His hand rested on my knee, moving sometimes to caress my thigh through my jeans. After my short night's sleep and the drive to the airport, I mostly dozed.

We touched down in Mexico City around two o'clock in the afternoon on Friday, October 26.

The airport was crowded and noisy, and the signs were all in Spanish. Attractive young Mexicans in suits greeted us at the baggage claim. I did all the talking. Having a first-gen immigrant as a dad, I spoke almost as well as a native.

I had already booked a taxi in advance, since Dad warned me not to trust any old taxi in Mexico City. For a smile and a few American dollars, a young porter helped John with our bags and brought us to the departure area, where the taxi was waiting.

Finally, in the backseat of the cab, I had the chance to get out my big, clunky camcorder and continue filming.

"All right, we just touched down in Mexico City, and we're *en route* to Xochimilco. How we feeling?"

As I filmed him, Larry looked back from the passenger seat, raising an eyebrow at my old camera. "What the heck is *that?* You steal that from a museum or something?"

"It was my mom's." I tried not to sound defensive. "I thought the Hi8 would add some old-school grit. I have a *ton* of battery packs for it. Plus it's a semi-pro model. It's old, but it's built like a tank. And it can do things modern cams don't."

"Like shoot in standard def?" Larry quipped.

"It has night vision, for one. Infrared. A lot of newer cameras don't anymore. People figured out they could use it to see through clothes, so they stopped including it."

Larry sniffed in dry amusement. "It's not like we'll be on the island at night. What do we need night vision for?"

"To see through people's clothes," John muttered. "Aren't you listening?" He sat beside me in the back of the cab, frowning at his smartphone. "Damn it. I'm not getting any service."

Larry stretched out in his seat to fish his own phone from his pocket, checking. "Yeah, me neither."

"We're not on the local network." With my free hand, I reached in the backpack between my legs and tossed a new, unopened phone in John's lap. "I bought a prepaid."

John studied the packaging suspiciously. "This can't get online."

"Good," I said cheerfully. "That'll keep us focused."

They both groaned.

"So much for my fantasy football league," John growled.

Shaking his head, Larry sank into the passenger seat. "Man, I wish we'd just stayed local. We could've covered those girls that went missing from campus. The Middleton Three or whatever?"

I rolled my eyes. "Everyone and their mothers will be doing the Middleton Three. The *Muñecas* project will be *original.*"

Resting his chin on his fist, John scowled out the window at the brightly-colored street vendors of Mexico City. "I'm with Larry on this one, Carm."

At least that was one thing they agreed on.

It took an hour to reach the district of Xochimilco, on the southern outskirts of Mexico City. John and Larry sulked in silence. I watched the congested streets pass by, trying to record every palm tree, every bright storefront, every piece of graffiti and quaintly small car.

Soon, the multi-lane city streets turned into a narrow, unmarked road through rural marshes. I caught a glimpse of open water beyond the berm alongside the road—my first sight of the canals.

Shortly, we reached our destination: *El Hotel Trinidad,* a

small, cheap hotel overlooking the street vendors in the touristy downtown of Xochimilco. The square, brick row house was only two stories high, the white paint flaking off in patches. The windows were all barred.

I checked into *El Hotel* with the bored teenage boy manning the front desk, then helped John carry our bags up the dim, narrow staircase to our room on the upper floor.

As soon as all our bags were in and the thin, hollow door was closed, John flopped down on one of the twin beds, exhausted. Larry sat on the other bed, his back to us. I immediately turned my old, bulky camera back on.

"All right. We're here in our room at *El Hotel...*"

John groaned, sitting up. "Jesus, Carmen, can't you let us unpack before you shove that thing in our faces?"

"Sorry. I just want to get every detail of these luxury accommodations."

I panned the camera across the room. There were two beds, the plain backboards pressed to the wall. Above, a fan hung from the low, plaster ceiling, spinning slowly. On the opposite wall were a small dresser and the door to the tiny private bathroom.

"We can use this for behind the scenes features."

John lay back on the bed, which was far too short for him and left his sneakered feet dangling over the edge. "Ought to be fun trying to fit us both in a twin bed."

I said wearily, "I was trying to stay under budget. I thought it would just be me and Larry."

"Well, at least you reserved two beds," John muttered.

I shot him a poisonous glance, but he made a show of ignoring it.

Larry spoke up, smiling tightly. "If you don't like the bed," he told John, "you could always sleep on the floor."

His tone was light-hearted, but my heart sank, fearing John's reaction.

John said flatly, "With the cock-a-roaches? Nah. *You* could do it. Be a good sport and free up some bed space?"

Larry didn't look over. "Think I've been a good enough sport for one trip."

I could feel the tension building. I had to distract them before this got ugly. They'd be no help if they spent the whole trip fighting. Still recording, I moved to the small double windows and yanked the curtains open with my free hand. The streets below were jammed with low-lying buildings of red and white brick. I could see the thick, green swamp-land of the canals in the distance, all dark water and leaning trees hung with moss.

"Look!" I smiled. "You can see the canals from here."

I turned away from the window to record my sullen cast and crew, both of whom avoided making eye contact with each other or my camera.

"Come on, guys! We've only got this room for three nights," I reminded them. "We've got the rest of today to settle in, get some interviews with the locals. Then we head out to the island in the morning, make a day of it. On Sunday we can go back, get some reshoots if we need to. And on Monday we check out of here and head home."

"The best part," John muttered.

"Yeah, yeah." I forced a smile. "How about we get some food? Would that calm the rage?"

John eyed me warily. Then he rose from the creaking bed. "Fine. But first I gotta piss."

He lumbered to the bathroom and closed the door. When the fan came on, I lowered my camera and looked at Larry with a commiserating smile.

When I caught Larry's cool, intent gaze, my smile died.

"This should be fun," Larry whispered, now that we were alone. "Why on Earth would you *bring* him?"

I stepped closer. "We were fighting till the last minute.

I finally figured, if he wants to babysit me that badly..."

Larry looked away. "I thought you were breaking up."

"We did." I shrugged. "Then he kept calling. Promising me nothing happened. Promising he'd change. Take me seriously, take my *films* seriously, on and on."

"Promises in one hand. Shit in the other."

"Come on. He'll be useful to both of us. I can make him carry your stuff?" I tilted my head. "Are you mad?"

He was about to respond when the toilet flushed in the bathroom behind us. Larry blinked at the sound, and when his eyes opened again, the anger was gone, replaced by a sad kind of weariness. The smile that followed seemed a little forced, but I was still glad to see it.

"I just hope you know what you're doing," he said. "That's all. If you're happy, I guess, I'm happy."

John came out, wiping his hands on his cut-off shorts. Instinctively I stepped back from Larry. For some reason I felt absurdly guilty, even though we were only talking.

John looked back and forth between us, his eyes dim and guarded. For a moment, my heart lurched in my chest as I feared his reaction.

Finally he said, softly, "Ready for dinner. Think they got anything *American* down here?"

Larry and I exchanged glances.

"John hates Mexican food," I said, smiling anxiously.

Larry snorted. "You're dating a half-Mexican, you're *in* Mexico, and you hate Mexican food?"

"Yeah, yeah," said John, folding his arms. "They must have something familiar."

"We're kind of in the boonies, now. I think I saw a Starbucks?" I offered.

John took a long, slow breath, looking past my camera at me with doleful blue eyes.

"This is gonna be a *long* trip."

Chapter 3: Xochimilco

"Okay," I said. "Is the camera ready?"

Larry's small, high-end digital camcorder stood on a tripod in the corner of the parking lot. Larry leaned behind it, squinting one-eyed through the viewfinder.

"Camera's good, but the sun's behind you. I'm getting a glare." He waved me to one side. "Gotta remember your lighting. Most important part of composition."

"That's what I brought *you* for," I said sweetly. I stepped over until I stood in the shadow of the old, white-brick building behind me. "Better?"

He nodded. "And... action!"

I walked toward him, speaking my well-rehearsed lines.

"We're here on the streets of Xochimilco, a city with a history as old as Mexico itself. It was founded by Aztecs around the tenth century on the shore of what *was* Lake Xochimilco. This is what that lake looks like today."

I gestured at the flat, narrow street behind me. In the stark red light of late afternoon, the row of stout, blocky buildings cast a shadow over the road. A few yards down the block, school children laughed as they kicked a ball through the street. An old woman in a row house window watched our cameras warily.

"A thousand years ago," I said, "this would all have been underwater. The pre-Hispanic tribes of the time were forced to migrate here because of a drought. That's why they chose to live on the lake. They built their city on an island, *Tlilan,* and all around it they built these *chinampas,* or floating gardens. Man-made, agricultural islands built right on the lake."

I walked down the road. Larry quickly removed his camera from the tripod, holding it steady at his shoulder as he moved after me, leaving John to clumsily gather the tripod and bags.

"In between these floating gardens," I narrated, "the Aztecs left channels wide enough for boats to pass. These became the Xochimilco canals."

As I reached the end of the street and the row houses opened up, the swampy trees of the canal came into view in the distance. Beyond the line of mossy willows, birds circled in the open space above the water.

"Over the centuries, much of Lake Xochimilco and its canals have been filled in or drained. What's left is now a protected historic site. The floating gardens have merged to form larger islands or joined the mainland, and the few that remain are mostly abandoned."

Larry's lens whirred as he zoomed in for a close up. I turned to face the camera, trying to channel the impassive authority I'd seen my mom use in her old documentaries.

"But there is one floating garden that's still inhabited. In fact, it's said to have over a thousand inhabitants. But they aren't human. They're *Muñecas,*" I said. "Dolls."

"Spoiler alert!" John called. He was standing behind Larry, the tripod and bags at his feet, his arms crossed over his thick chest.

Despite myself, I giggled at his interruption. I was too excited to mind. "All right, cut! How was it?"

Adjusting his thin glasses, Larry pushed a button on his camera to review the footage. "I can work with it. I'll show you some editing techniques when we get back."

I grabbed his shoulders, peering over to see the Canon's LCD screen. "Should we do a reshoot? Just in case?"

John groaned. "I thought you said we'd get dinner?"

"We will, we will, I promise we will! But while we're out, we might as well get some footage, right? That *is* why we're here." I paused. "I think there's some food stands by the docks. We can get some shots of the canal and see if any locals will talk to us." I glanced at Larry. "You ready?"

Larry raised his sleek, handheld camera with a weary, sportsmanlike smile. "Ready."

Rolling his eyes, John hurried to fold the mobile tripod and shove it in its carrying case before following us.

We continued down the street, coming out in a broad parking lot, filled with cars. Across the lot was a row of vendors housed in squat, shed-like buildings. Many had seating space out front, under blue or black tarps supported by tent poles. People sat eating at picnic tables, and as we walked closer I smelled fresh meat grilling.

In the center of this row of buildings stood a large brick archway, labeled *Embarcadero Cuemanco*. Beyond this you could see the colorful little boats moored at the dock.

"You getting this?" I asked.

"We're rolling," said Larry.

"All right, we're here at the *Embarcadero Cuemanco*, the docks." I turned to speak to his camera as he followed me. "You can smell the fresh food cooking at the dockside food stands."

"No shit," John grumbled.

I smirked, waving them on, and we passed under the stone arches to the docks.

On the underside of the arches, a mural caught my eye. I couldn't tell whether it belonged there or if it was graffiti. I motioned to Larry. "Get this."

He waved the camera over it slowly. It was a painting of something resembling a woman. She was dressed all in black, with long black hair; but her face was blank and skeletal, mouthless, the eye sockets empty holes. Beside the mural was a single word, in red:

LLORONA.

"Weeping woman," I translated. "I think it's a local legend. Maybe they did it for Day of the Dead?"

"Day of the Dead?" Larry said.

I nodded. "Yeah. Also known as All Hallows' Eve?"

Larry smacked his head. "That's right. Only *you* would schedule a trip to a haunted island for Halloween."

I sniffed, amused. "It's not till Wednesday. We'll be long gone by then."

"Carmen, for real!" John raised his voice just enough to embarrass me in public. "I'm getting hungry enough to eat anything, even if it's Mexican. Or *a* Mexican. Can we *vámonos* already?"

Face reddening, I slunk through the archway to the docks on the other side, not meeting anyone's eyes.

Beyond the archway, a long boardwalk ran the length of the canal, lined with flower gardens. Brightly-colored rafts, called *trajineras*, anchored along the dock. The dark, opaque water of the canal stretched out behind them and in either direction. The water was perhaps fifty feet wide, fading into boggy marshes and trees on the far shore.

It was a Friday afternoon and the docks were crowded with people. A few were clearly foreign tourists, but there were natives, too—school-aged kids in backpacks; families milling the gardens; an old woman walking a little bulldog.

"I just want to get a few interviews first."

Before John or Larry could stop me, I approached the old woman with the dog. "Excuse me. *¿Habla Inglés?*"

The woman wore a hooded jacket, a scarf wrapped around her lower jaw, and loose sweatpants. She turned to me with a look of good-natured confusion.

"¿Habla Inglés?" I asked again.

She smiled and shook her head. *"No, no hablo."*

I smiled back and said, in Spanish, "That's okay. We are from the United States. Can I ask you a few questions?"

"Sí." She beamed into Larry's camera.

"And you don't mind if we film you, do you?"

Her smile was growing more and more wide-eyed with wonder. *"¿Es para una gran película de Hollywood?"*

"What she say?" John demanded, his hands on his hips.

I rubbed the back of my neck. "She asked if this will be in a big Hollywood movie."

Larry and John both laughed. Perhaps a little too fiercely, I said, "Well, who knows? Maybe it will be."

Turning back to the little old lady, I said in Spanish, "No, we're not from Hollywood. This is for a documentary. Can you tell us about the Island of the Dolls?"

As I spoke, the woman's affable smile puckered into a wide-eyed grimace. Shielding her face from the camera, she tugged her dog away, mumbling, "No, no, no."

Larry looked astonished. "The hell'd you say?"

I shrugged, bemused. "That we're not from Hollywood, and our film's about the Island of the Dolls?"

"Guess she really wanted to be in a Hollywood movie," said John.

"Or she really doesn't want to talk about the Island of the Dolls," Larry muttered.

No doubt he meant it lightly, but an awkward silence followed. With a frown, I watched the woman and her dog hurry off down the docks.

"I might have said something wrong," I suggested. "My Spanish may be rusty. Here, let's try these kids. Excuse me?"

I approached a young boy and girl—high school age, if

I had to guess. The boy held the girl's hand and they were smiling and laughing as I came by. The sight made me think of a time when John and I used to walk so close, when we first started dating, back in high school. Though I couldn't help but smile, it was a sad smile just the same.

"Hi. Do you speak English?" I asked. *"¿Hablan Inglés?"*

The two exchanged glances. *"Sí."* The boy gestured with thumb and forefinger. *"Un poco.* Ah, little bit."

"We're doing a documentary. Can you tell us anything about the Island of the Dolls? *Isla de las Muñecas?"*

The boy laughed. *"Mamá* says is bad to speak of it. We are not allowed to go."

The girl rolled her eyes. "Is a tourist trap," she said, almost angrily. "Is for tourists."

"Really?" I gestured Larry to bring the camera closer. "You don't believe in it?"

She shook her head, considering her words. "Is... no respect. Is a charmed place. Not a place for tourists, what they made it. They should have close it after Don Julio die, not turn it into a carnival funhouse."

"Don Julio?" John repeated, sounding bored.

"The hermit who lived on the island," Larry whispered. "The one who collected the dolls. *Try* and keep up."

"What can you tell us about Don Julio?" I asked.

Leading the boy away, the young girl waved us off. "Leave the dead in peace and They'll do the same for you."

I raised an eyebrow at John and Larry, who both shrugged. Then I offered Larry's camera a hesitant smile. "They all seem to *know* about the island," I said, "but no one wants to talk about it."

"Uh... Carmen?" Larry lifted his eye from the camera

to point over my shoulder.

I turned. Behind me stood a man, bent, bald, wizened. He wore a straw hat and faded blue overalls. The wrinkles in his old, brown face seemed to squeeze his eyes shut and pull his mouth into a permanent smile. The shaggy stubble on his cheeks and above his lips was flecked with white.

A little startled, I whispered, *"Hola, señor."*

"Hola, señorita." His dry lips peeled back to reveal a crooked brown grin. He spoke fast, in heavily accented English. "You ask about *Isla de las Muñecas?*"

John stepped closer, moving to my side protectively and staring the stranger down. I smiled. "Yes," I said, clearing my throat. "Yes, we're here to learn about it. We're doing a... *documental?* Can you tell us about it?"

His mischievous smile erupted into hearty laughter. "Oh, I can tell you about it. I know Don Julio's cousin. He found Julio on the day he died. Now he owns the island."

My eyes widened and I grinned. "Nuh-uh. Seriously? You know Fernando Santiago?"

He nodded. "He was a friend of my father's. He used to watch my brother and me when we were children."

"So, okay." I glanced at Larry's camera. "The story goes that Don Julio drowned a decade ago, and his cousin Fernando found his body in the same place where Don Julio had seen a little girl drown fifty years earlier."

"Sí," said the old man behind me, nodding.

I turned back to him. "So you know Fernando? Was all that true? About how he found Don Julio?"

"Sí," said the man. "Fernando was very close to his cousin. He was the only one who visited Don Julio on his island, trading crops in town and bringing back supplies and dolls."

I waved Larry closer. "You getting this?"

"On the day Don Julio died," said the old Mexican, "Fernando was helping Julio clear some land on the island for new crops. After this, they had lunch, and Don Julio told Fernando about a big fish he'd been trying to catch. It had escaped him twice before, but he was determined to catch it. He also told his cousin that the mermaids had been calling to him that day."

"Mermaids?" John repeated, sneering.

The old man nodded gravely. "Fernando said that Julio would talk of the mermaids sometimes. That he used to sing to them to keep them away. But that day Don Julio seemed upset. Almost frightened.

They are crying for me, he said. *Can't you hear the crying?*"

The Mexican man glanced out past the wooden railing of the dock to the bog-green waters of the canal. His smile was gone now, and his creased face looked sad.

"After lunch, Fernando went to feed the pigs and Don Julio went fishing. In the evening, Fernando came back to look for his cousin and found Julio floating in the canal. And Fernando swears he saw something else in the water, near the body. Something like a big fish."

"A big fish?" I hadn't heard that detail before in any of my research. I waved Larry and his camera closer, smiling eagerly at the Mexican. "Was it one of the mermaids?"

He shrugged. "Fernando say it had a long tail, like a snake. It swam away as soon as he appeared."

I nodded. "That's fascinating. Can you tell us anything else about Don Julio or the island?"

"Maybe." The Mexican man's sly smile returned. "But so much talking makes me hungry."

John rolled his eyes, but I was already reaching in my pocket for my money-clip. "Let's get supper! My treat."

"Finally," John grumbled.

"Si, gracias," said the beaming Mexican man.

We approached one of the food stands by the entrance to the docks—a taco place, figuring that would be the least offensive for John's white-as-a-ghost stomach. While we waited in line, I asked the old man more questions.

"What else can you tell us about Don Julio? What kind of man was he?"

He tilted his head. "Friendly. Always smiling. Always singing. Here in Xochimilco, we called him *Coquita,* after a little bird that lives on the canals. He was very devout in his faith, but—what's the word? *Charmed*, we would say."

"What do you mean?" I asked.

He shrugged, explaining with difficulty, "In touch with… a different world."

We ordered our food and the four of us went to sit at a table in front of the food stand. Larry set his camera on the edge of the picnic table to record us, then hunched over it protectively, eyeing anyone who came within ten feet. John nibbled his taco with increasing speed till he was devouring it, looking angry about it all the while.

"There are all kinds of legends about these canals." The old man surveyed the waterway. "Wars have been fought here. Tens of thousands killed. Long before the Conquest, the Aztec cities Tenochtitlan and Xochimilco battled over the fertile lake. And it's said that when Cortés and the *conquistadors* came, they dammed up the canals with the bodies of the conquered. They say skeletons still bob to the surface when it storms too hard. Folks around here lock their doors and stay away from the water after dark."

As we finished our meal, the sun was setting behind us, throwing long shadows over the dark canal. I watched a pair of unfamiliar birds flitter above the water, into a grove of dark green willows and weeds.

"What about Don Julio's cousin, Fernando?" I asked. "He runs the island now, right? Can you tell us about him?"

The man raised a bushy eyebrow. "Don't you know? Don Fernando is sick. He won't be with us much longer."

I frowned. "No, I didn't know. I'm sorry."

The man said, "That's why the island's closed."

I narrowed my eyes. "What do you mean?"

He shrugged. "It used to be open, for tourists, you know. Ever since they clear the canals back in the nineties, tourists been coming to the island. For a small fee, you could get one of the *trajineras* drivers to take you there."

He nodded toward the colorful flotillas lined up along the dock.

"Don Julio welcomed the visitors, and after he died, Fernando open the island in memorial to his cousin. Let the tourists walk the grounds and see the dolls. There was even a bathroom that cost five pesos."

"Yeah." I glanced at John and Larry, both of whom looked beyond impatient. "We thought it was open to the public. We thought we could get a boat to take us, for our film." I tried to hide the crushing panic from my voice.

The old man shook his head. "Not anymore. Fernando couldn't stand his cousin's island. He gave up maintaining it, believing it was cursed. He thinks his cousin's joined the other ghosts on the island. Now it's closed to the public, and that part of the canal is so overgrown, I don't think *anyone* takes that route anymore."

The weight of this news settled over me like a cold snow. I could feel my shoulders sinking.

"You're kidding," I whispered.

"No, *señorita*. Island of the Dolls is closed."

Chapter 4: Miguel and La Juanita

Later that night, we regrouped in our hotel room.

"What do you need that for?" John growled as I turned on my camera. "Don't you get it? This project's over."

"As bad as it looks," I said, "I'm not giving up, okay?"

I set my clunky camcorder on the dresser to record us, then returned to my bed. Larry sat on the other bed, plucking idly at his goatee. John stood at the window, holding the dingy curtain back to glare into the night.

"How do we know that guy knows anything?" said Larry. "Did you even get his name?"

I released a slow breath. "I didn't think to get it, no."

John whirled toward us, throwing his hands in the air. "Of course not! Too busy eating up all the crap he was feeding you. *Mermaids,*" he scoffed.

"It was good footage." I shrugged.

"For all we know," Larry went on, "that old guy was some hobo who'd say anything for a free taco. Maybe it was all crap."

"And if the island is closed?" John demanded. "If that part's true, what then?"

"Then going will be trespassing," I said quietly. "But I'm still going. There must be someone willing to take us."

John blinked. "Seriously? The girl who used to whine when I copied her homework is gonna break the law?"

"This is way more important than that," I insisted. "And think about it. I mean, who's going to catch us?"

As I spoke, I grew more convinced. I leaned back on the bed and smiled up at the low, plaster ceiling.

"This could be even better than we thought. It's the middle of nowhere, the owner doesn't visit. We'll have the whole island to ourselves. We can film anything."

Larry scowled. "But we can't use the footage if we're trespassing. Not commercially."

"It's *not* commercial," I said. "It's a student project for now. Look, I tried to get the permits, tried tracking down Fernando, but it's not easy, okay? I mean, studios have whole departments for this crap. Trust me, if we get picked up, they'll take care of the legal stuff. All we need to focus on is making the best film we can. And this is the perfect opportunity, when you think about it."

John laughed. "You're like a dog on a bone with this."

"You rather we go home with *nothing?* I put almost a thousand dollars into this. Equipment, hotel, airfare."

"She's right," Larry said. "We're here, we might as well put something together. Get some more interviews, if nothing else."

"No, I'm *going* to the island," I insisted. "Someone will take us, I'm sure of it. Money talks, right?"

Larry shrugged. "It *is* Mexico. Who cares about laws?"

"Hey, this is my dad's homeland you're talking about. Money talks no matter where you are. Just shut up and get some rest. We've got a big day tomorrow. We're going to the Island of the Dolls, one way or another."

I turned off the camera.

In the morning, after a hasty breakfast of cereal and bananas from a food stand out front, I turned my camera on again as the guys finished packing.

"John, can you carry some battery packs for me?" I asked. "My bag's running heavy."

"Uh, no." He gave me a sidelong glance. "My bag is full, too. With things like water, sunscreen, bug spray…"

"We don't need *everything*," I reminded him. "Just enough for a day trip."

"If we can even find someone to take us," said John, "I've got *exactly* what we need, and not a thing more."

"Whatever." I shut off my camera and eased it gently into my bulging backpack. Then I swatted one of the gnats buzzing around my neck. It left a red smear on my palm. I frowned at it unhappily. "Okay, bug spray, not a bad idea."

"See?" John patted his blue backpack. "Trust me."

Once everything was packed, we headed back to the docks, about a block from the hotel. I think we made it there around nine in the morning.

The rising sun beamed through the spindly trees across the canal. The shops and restaurants along the pier were hopping with customers.

I wore a simple red blouse with short sleeves, a pair of khakis, and sneakers. On my back I lugged my old high school book bag, bulging with my camera case and spare batteries. My dark, shoulder-length hair was still wet from the quick, lukewarm shower in the hotel. *Abuelita's* topaz earrings adorned my ears.

John held my hand in a tight grip. He wore a pair of blue jeans, his orange hoodie, and his camo baseball cap. Larry walked on my other side, dressed in a light-weight, black leather jacket over a red t-shirt, black jeans, and his usual Harley boots. He held his sleek digital camcorder at his shoulder, recording as we walked. Both Larry and John also carried backpacks with snacks and supplies for the day.

"So we're back at *Embarcadero Cuemanco*," I narrated as we came out on the docks. "We're going to see if we can get someone to take us to the forbidden island, against the warning of some of the locals. Yesterday we spoke to a family friend of the island's current owner, and he told us, uh, not to go, in short. He said it's cursed and most people stay away. But we're not most people, are we?"

"Some of us aren't," said John, squeezing my hand.

I filmed the colorful boats pulled up to the side of the pier. Called *trajineras*, the boats looked like rectangular rafts, shaded by pavilions or tarps painted in colorful murals of flowers, animals, or vegetables. The boatmen drove the boats using long poles to push along the shallow bottom.

"There are some strapping sailors." John pointed to a pair of old men talking in Spanish by the pier, their skin dried and cracked beneath fishing hats. They noticed John pointing and fell silent, glancing our direction.

I cleared my throat and approached with an awkward smile, asking in Spanish if they were *trajineras* drivers. The suspicion faded from their eyes as I spoke. With my fluent Spanish and dark skin, perhaps they mistook me for a local.

"Sí," they said. One added, smiling, *"Very* experienced."

"Would you take us to the Island of the Dolls?" I asked.

The man's crooked smile wavered. "What would such a pretty girl want with such an ugly place?"

"I know it's closed, but I can pay. Whatever it takes."

"Whatever it takes?" he repeated, smiling back at his stone-faced companion.

Something in the man's expression made John's hand tighten on mine. Staring him down, John growled, "What are they saying?"

The other boatman said in Spanish, "We won't take you, *señorita*. I would not have taken you when the island was open, and I will not take you now." He turned away.

His companion kept smiling at me and explained with a helpless shrug, "Those waters are haunted, *bonita*. Was haunted long before Don Julio and his dolls."

"Please. I can pay in American dollars."

I flashed a wad of bills. He looked down at it, but still shook his head regretfully. "I'm sorry, *chica*. If I could help you, I would. But no man in his right mind goes through that part of the canals. Not anymore. Those who have to won't stop on the island. Most won't even look at it. They say you can hear the dolls, calling to you as you pass."

"What is he saying?" John demanded again.

I turned away, frustrated. "He says they won't take us." I scanned the dock, looking for anyone else who looked like a sailor. My eyes alighted on another grizzly old-timer down the dock. "Let's try that guy."

But before I could get away, I heard someone call from behind me. "Yo! *Hola, señorita!*"

Looking back, I saw a young man in tattered khakis, sandals, and a tan fishing vest hurrying up the dock and waving at us. I lifted an eyebrow. "Are you talking to me?"

"*Sí!*" Stopping before us, the young man took off his straw hat and smiled. He was the same age as us, or a year or two younger. He stood a little taller than Larry, with short black hair, brown eyes, and full lips framed by a thin goatee. His vest exposed lean, muscular arms. In Spanish, he asked, "Did I hear you need a *trajinera* driver?"

"*Sí,*" I said. "But no one wants to take us."

"I'll take you wherever you need to go," he said, his brown eyes fixed on mine. "For the right price."

"What's he saying?" John demanded again at my side. "Do you speak English?"

"You're a *trajinera* driver?" I said, a little incredulous.

He smiled at John and responded in fluent English, "Yes. I said I can take you all where you need to go."

"For the right price," I added.

He nodded. "You say you have American dollars?"

"What's your name?" John asked impatiently.

"Miguel." His eyes drifted to my camera. "You making a movie or something?"

"That's right," I said. "About the Island of the Dolls."

For the first time, Miguel's smile dimmed. "That's a dangerous trip, *señorita*. The canals are very narrow. Easy to lose your way. This is where you want to go?"

"I thought you said you could take us anywhere?"

Miguel looked away. "It might take three, four hours to get there. And then I have to stick around to bring you back. It'll take my whole day. Besides, I heard the owner hates trespassers."

I couldn't tell if he was trying to negotiate or scare me off. Tugging my hand free of John's, I stepped closer. "How much would it take for you to bring us there?"

He considered a moment, then met my eyes with a flash of his confident smile. "Two hundred."

"Dollars?" I clarified, shocked. I'd brought only eighty and change, leaving the rest deep in my luggage back at the hotel. "Isn't that a little steep? *Muy caro?*"

"If you can find someone else..." He shrugged and made as if to turn away.

"Wait! Can't we negotiate? I could do, like, twenty..."

"One *hundred* twenty, maybe," Miguel said.

I swallowed, getting nervous. "Look, Miguel, we really need to get to this island today. I only brought so much cash. I could do fifty, I guess..."

His small, impassive smile wavered a little. "I didn't think Americans knew how to haggle," he said flatly. "Look, *señorita,* I make more doing fishing tours."

I couldn't believe this. Was he really trying to back out now that he knew where we wanted to go? Angrily, I took out my money clip, counting out the small wad of bills.

"Okay, one twenty? Fine. There's eighty here. You'll have the rest when we get back."

Miguel stared at the money, his eyebrows raised. "Eighty dollars?" he said, as if he couldn't believe I was really offering it.

John sucked in a breath beside me, then started to push me away, aiming a fake grin at Miguel. "Would you excuse us for *just* a second?"

Gripping my arm, John pulled me a few feet away.

"What?" I demanded. "We've gotta trust *someone.*"

"Yeah? But why *this* guy?" He glared over my head at Miguel. "You know why your dad made you schedule a taxi in advance? Because some of the cabs in Mexico City are fakes. You get in and they kidnap you and take all your money. You think these boats are any different?"

Chewing my lip, I looked over at Miguel. He stood with his straw hat against his chest, talking to Larry with an earnest smile. When Larry laughed at whatever Miguel was saying, I felt my own lips start to curl up in a grin.

John's frown only deepened. "Are you listening to me?"

"Yeah, I'm listening." I tugged my hand away, glaring at him. I tried to keep my voice down. "It's the same old control freak crap. I am *not* going back empty-handed."

"Carmen…"

"You said you'd prove I matter to you. You said you've prove you could change. So, prove it."

I turned away, storming back to Miguel. I seized his warm hand and pressed the wad of money to his palm.

"You'll have the rest when we get back, I promise."

Behind me, John gritted his teeth, but said nothing.

Miguel closed his hand reluctantly around the money. Then he met my eyes, his face serious.

"We leave by sunset," he said. "I don't want to be on that island when night falls."

"Sure," I said. "Not a problem."

"Good. Then we leave now?"

I hesitated, confused. "Which of these is yours?" I asked, looking at the boats up and down the dock.

Miguel nodded over the railing beside us. "You're looking at her."

Frowning, I looked over the edge of the pier at the empty space between two big, bright *trajineras*. Only when I took a step closer did I see the tiny boat in the empty space below. Unlike the others, this boat was smaller and lower lying. It also had no arch or canopy for protection from the sun. The long table at the center of the boat was held together by visible duct tape, and the rest of the boat looked in little better condition. The paint was faded, the boards warped and wadded with gobs of caulk.

"La Juanita," Miguel announced.

John laughed coldly. "I told you he'd rip you off."

I turned to Miguel, incredulous. "Is this thing even *safe?"*

Miguel looked crestfallen. *"Señor, señorita,* I promise, she'll get you there. Would I lie?" He flashed a roguish grin. His teeth were straight and white, but there was just a little too much space between a few in the front. He leaned back on the railing. "If you're scared of my little boat, you won't last ten minutes where we're going."

John wouldn't meet my eyes, glaring off at the muddy canal. I glanced at Larry for a cue, but he only shrugged, still holding his camera steady at his shoulder.

I looked back at Miguel. "We're not scared. You say it's safe, I'll take your word for it."

Miguel straightened. "Then are you ready to go?"

Slowly, my smile returned.

Chapter 5: Journey to the Island

Humming an unfamiliar tune, Miguel unraveled the rope that held his ramshackle *trajinera* to the dock. The three of us climbed on board, sitting on the cracked bench, John beside me and Larry across the table, stuffing his bag underneath.

I got out my camera and made one last check of my supplies, making sure I had all my batteries, cassettes, and other film equipment I'd need for the trip.

"Okay. From here on, we need every shot to count."

Getting my audio recorder out of my bag, I slid it over the tabletop to John.

"Here. Since you don't have a camera, maybe you should have this."

"What is it?" He frowned at it suspiciously.

"An MP3 recorder. You know, in case you want to record your experiences on the island."

John sniffed derisively, then hauled his own backpack up from between his legs to put the recorder away. His bag was a bulky knapsack, made of shiny blue fabric, sealed with Velcro and adjustable belts.

Larry eyed him across the table. "What's with that backpack, anyway? Looks like it's made of plastic."

"Polyurethane," John corrected. He shoved my MP3 recorder in the front pocket of the bag. "This's a fifty liter, waterproof, floating dry bag, for whitewater rafting. The whole world could sink and this baby'd still be floating, and dry as a bone inside."

Larry remained unimpressed. "Little overly elaborate for a field trip," he said.

John looked at him contemptuously. "See what you say when this shitty boat capsizes and all your camera bags are at the bottom of the river."

"Hey!" Bundling up his rope, Miguel hopped onto the boat. "*La Juanita* won't sink. Just watch. *Vámonos!*"

He shoved off from the dock with his foot. Then he stood at the stern of the raft and began to push us along with a long, flat-headed oar, out into the canal.

As I watched the dock drift away, excitement took root again. We were doing it. Despite the odds, we were making the *Muñecas* project happen.

I was actually naïve enough to think the worst was over; that from here on, it would be smooth sailing.

"If I drown," John muttered, "I *will* haunt you."

I kicked him under the table. "Be nice," I whispered. "He's doing us a favor."

Miguel stood at the back of the boat, using his oar like a pole to propel the vessel along the muddy riverbed. The muscles in his dark arms corded with each long, steady push, but he made it look easy, smiling all the while. The docks of *Embarcadero Cuemanco* slid away to the right, while to the left the canal stretched off into boggy swamp land and trees rising out of the water.

Raising my voice, I asked him, "Have you been to *Isla de las Muñecas* before, Miguel?"

Miguel's smile faded as he met my eyes. "I've brought tourists, *si*. Not recently, but before, years ago." His eyes wandered away again.

"What's it like?" I asked.

He shrugged. "About what you'd expect. You'll see."

I got the feeling he was avoiding the subject. I decided to try another approach. "How long have you been a *trajinera* driver? You seem younger than the others."

"I got the boat from my father," he said. "He died a few years ago, so I took over. I work most every day to bring money for my sister and *Mamá*."

"That's nice of you," John said, with light sarcasm.

"If I didn't need the money," Miguel added, "I wouldn't be taking you."

I tilted my head. "Why? Are you afraid of the island?"

He looked back at me with a tight smile. "What about you? Are you afraid?"

"That's not fair," I said. "I asked you first. But I told you, I'm not. I mean, it's just superstition, right?"

Miguel shrugged and said nothing. The pier drifted by on the right, spilling with tourists and locals. Larry was filming the algae-covered water of the canal as we floated past, and I realized I was missing footage. I raised my own camera.

"This your first time in *México?*" Miguel asked at last.

I loved the way he pronounced Mexico, with a hard *'h'* for the *'x'*. My dad said it that way, too. It put me at ease.

Looking up from my viewfinder, I nodded. "Yes, it's my first time. My dad was born here, stayed till he was ten. *Mis abuelos* brought him to America almost forty years ago. Far as I know, I'm the first in the family to come back."

Miguel smiled. "What do you think so far?"

I found myself returning his smile. His steady brown eyes had a way of holding your gaze. "It's growing on me."

John looked back and forth between us, his frown deepening. Perhaps to distract me, he poked my shoulder. "Hey, Carmen. What's that?"

Irritably, I turned my head to follow his gesture. We were approaching the end of the pier on our right. A crowd of people had gathered on the stage at the end of the pier. Many were dressed all in black, singing or chanting.

"Hell if I know." I aimed my camera. "Larry, get this."

"I see it." Larry laughed. "Some kinda witch's coven?"

"What are they saying?" asked John.

Tilting my head away from my camera, I listened. "It sounds like… *Llorona,*" I murmured. "*Weeping woman.*"

"Isn't that the word we saw on that mural, by the docks?" Larry asked.

I frowned as I remembered the odd mural, depicting the skull-faced woman in black.

"They're rehearsing," said Miguel. He rested for a moment with the pole lifted out of the water, allowing the boat to drift on momentum as we passed the stage. "For the play. Every year they put on a play for *Día de Muertos.*"

"Day of the Dead." I nodded. "What's the play about?"

"You don't know the legend of La Llorona?" he teased. "I thought you were part *Mexicana?*"

I turned my camera to Miguel. "It sounds familiar. Who is she?"

"Only another *superstition.*" Miguel smirked mockingly.

I smiled behind my camera. His playful manner also reminded me of my dad. "Come on, tell me."

Miguel put his oar back in the water and started poling us forward again. "Some say her real name was Maria. She was very beautiful. The most beautiful in her village, many centuries ago. Soft skin, bright eyes, full dark hair. Lips that yearned to be kissed."

Miguel's eyes found mine as he spoke, and for some reason I blushed, as if he were talking about me. John glared at me from the corner of his eye and I looked away.

"She was a—what you call it—a *widow,*" said Miguel. "A young widow, and a mother. The legend says she fell in love with a man of noble birth, very rich. But he didn't want her because of her children from her first husband.

He feared they'd contest with his own heirs for his wealth and title. So although Maria is very beautiful, the nobleman cannot wed her, and chooses another for his bride."

My eyes drifted back to Miguel. "So what does Maria do then?"

"She loses her mind," Miguel said, with a sad smile. "In madness and jealous rage, she drowns her children to prove her devotion for the man. And she brings him the lifeless bodies of her children and tells him, *look how much I love you! I've sacrificed my own children so we can be together.*"

I frowned, realizing I *had* heard this story before. "But the man still rejected her," I said.

Miguel nodded. "He was horrified, of course, by what she'd done. He cursed her, and sent her from the village, and ordered his men to bury the dead children in the lake.

"When Maria came to her senses and realized what she'd done, she raced back to the lakeside to look for her children. But they were already gone. She spent her last days in madness and exile, wandering the waterside, crying for her lost children and singing through her tears, desperate to lure them back to her. Some say, in the end, she ripped out her own eyes in despair.

"It's said she still wanders the waters of Mexico," said Miguel, "sometimes in the form of a terrible serpent, sometimes taking the form of a beautiful woman in black, forever weeping and searching for her children. She cries and sings to lure you in, charming all who see or hear her. She's irresistible, a seductress. She can make any man do her bidding. She can make you fall so madly in love you'll kill your own family for her, just as she did. And once she lures you to the water, she grabs you up and drags you down to join her in the depths."

His fingers flexed around his oar to demonstrate.

"It's said that if you hear her crying, it's already too late."

"What a charming story," John muttered, leaning on the table in a bored way with his chin on his fist.

I looked over at the crowd of actors on the platform as we floated past. "I think I have heard that legend," I muttered. "My dad must have told it to me, as a kid."

Larry frowned. "Let me get this straight," he said. "Those people are putting on a play about a woman who drowned her kids? And we're going to an island where a little girl drowned? Anyone else find that a little freaky?"

I laughed uneasily, looking at Miguel. "Nah," I said, teasing him. "It's just superstition. Right?"

Miguel smiled silently, paddling on down the canal.

"But it *is* a fascinating story," I added, watching the crowd of people on the stage. They fell behind us and out of sight, and their strange, low singing faded from hearing.

As the docks ended to the right, the banks of the canal became less defined—a swampy, muddy marsh overgrown with moss and reeds. The landscape hummed with insects and colorful songbirds. Buildings of brick, adobe, and wood overlooked the water from above the banks.

Slowly the banks fell away and the canal widened into a main thoroughfare, perhaps a hundred feet wide. The water was clearer and deeper. The brisk autumn air, chilly in the morning, was now pleasantly warm under the sun.

We passed other, fancier *trajineras* boats, stuffed full of tourists. One boat carried a full mariachi band, which, to my delight, started to perform as we floated past. Their festive music followed us down the canal long after they'd faded from view, echoing over the open water.

"Look," Miguel pointed. "Those are *chinampas.*"

"Huh?" said John.

"Chinampas," I repeated. "Floating gardens."

To the left, a series of wooden, rectangular boxes

floated on the surface, made of logs and plywood. Slender trees grew from the corners of each tiny man-made island, securing the raft in place. Squash, beans, and chili peppers were in bloom under the bright morning sun. Two swarthy men in sombreros stood on small, one-man boats, tending the garden beds and watching us pass with mute curiosity.

"You getting this?" I looked over at Larry to make sure he was filming. "This is how the Aztec tribes used to farm on the lake. See how well the stuff grows?"

Miguel added, "You'd never know we're in a drought."

I turned to Larry's camera. "What they'd do is build these wooden rafts to float on the water, then tie them to trees growing out of the lake, to secure them in place. Then they'd heap mud and sediment and fertilizer on top to make a literal floating garden. Over time, the rafts would deteriorate and sink, and the Aztecs would build a new raft on top of it, so eventually the *chinampas* expanded and anchored to the lake bed."

"So the Island of the Dolls looks like one of those?" John nodded skeptically at the little gardens as we passed.

"No. Those *chinampas* are new," said Miguel. "*Isla de las Muñecas* is much bigger, much older. You'll see."

Past the young *chinampas,* the canal narrowed and the music and activity faded, leaving only the chirping and buzzing of wildlife. Occasionally another boat or canoe passed, but these became fewer and fewer. On both sides the banks closed in and the trees formed a tight canopy, filtering the sun. It felt like floating through a warm, green tunnel.

"It's really beautiful here," I said, filming the vibrant scenery.

"Yeah," Larry admitted. "It really is." He was also filming, his back facing the table, his eye to his camera. I smiled, pleased to see him absorbed in the project.

Even John had no complaints, for once. He took his camo cap off and set it on the warped table at the center of the *trajinera,* then lifted his head toward the sun. "So much warmer than Colorado," he laughed, glancing at me.

For the first time since arriving, I felt no anxiety. The beauty of our surroundings and my success in finding a boat to take us had lightened everyone's mood.

If I hadn't been so eager to reach the island, I wouldn't have cared if the ride never ended.

Instead, the three-hour trip seemed to pass in the blink of an eye. The surreal sameness of the canals made it feel both endless and instantaneous, like a dream.

At some point Miguel turned the boat off the main thoroughfare, into narrower waters, clogged with green water lilies.

"Until the nineties," Miguel explained, "all this part of the canal, you couldn't go here because of the water lilies. They came and cleared them out. But now that tourists don't come this way, nature takes over again."

We passed more *chinampas,* the wooden edges frayed and sunken, many joined together. Most looked fallow, overgrown with gnarled, twisted trees hung with moss, obscuring our view inland beyond a few feet. Occasionally we saw some rangy cattle or goats, coming down to the reedy water for a drink. There were no more houses or buildings in sight on the banks, no sign of anyone else, only thick trees and boggy water.

I soon lost track of the turns Miguel took. The canals were labyrinthine, winding and looping between tiny, swampy islands and thickets of trees. Some of the small branches and waterways were visibly overgrown and clogged with debris, completely impassable. It would have been easy to lose your way; and with the sudden drops in water level, the unseen rocks and tangles of trees, one wrong turn could spell disaster.

Yet Miguel led us down the canal with slow, steady certainty. The boat became ensnared only once, down a particularly narrow passage, and he was able to push us out of the shallows with the pole. Otherwise there were no delays and no mistakes. A sheen of sweat shone on his brown forehead, and his face was set in grim effort.

I decided he was probably worth the money.

"Not much longer," he said. His full lips looked tight and pensive. He'd become distinctly less talkative as we proceeded. At first I figured that was because he was working so hard. Now I wondered again if he was afraid of the island. The idea troubled me. He seemed so smart, even wise, for his age. Why would he fear an old hermit's doll collection?

I reminded myself that these were a spiritual people; but I still found Miguel curious.

Or rather, I found myself curious about him.

Beside me, John started to grow impatient, swatting at bugs around him with his hat. "It better be soon," he said. "I'm getting hungry. And these bugs! The jackasses! It's like they're *attracted* to bug spray."

As I smirked and recorded him, something over John's shoulder caught my eye. Squinting, I zoomed the camera in. "Hey. What's that?"

John turned to look. His hand, still raised to swat bugs, froze in midair and sank slowly.

"Holy shit," I whispered, as the camera focused.

A hundred feet ahead, the canal widened into a much larger space. The noon sun flickered off the dark water. At the center of this space, an island rose from the shallow lakebed, enclosed in reeds and half-submerged trees.

And something gleamed white on one of the trees.

At a glance it looked like the severed head of an infant, a thing that might adorn the battlements of Hell. The one remaining eye stared blankly into space. Through the other empty eye socket, a stake had been driven to hold the doll's head to the tree. After years in the sun, the rubber flesh was faded white, like a bleached skull.

As Miguel poled us closer, I zoomed my camera out, for this was not the only grisly ornament among the trees.

Not by a long shot.

John whistled. Larry muttered, "Jesus."

The trees growing up from the water seemed to form a corridor, leading to the island. On each tree trunk, like a crucifixion, a doll had been pinned—or the remnants of one. There were heads, torsos, limbs, each staked into the marbled tree bark or wrapped up in old rusted wire. The dolls were in varying states of deterioration, some rotted and speckled black with mold, others nigh unrecognizable under layers of cobwebs.

I stood up from the bench on the boat, staring in amazement at the trees to either side as we poled slowly between them—slowly closer to the island.

"I guess we're here?"

I looked back at Miguel, but he was focused on poling, his head bowed, his eyes fixed on the floor of the boat, as if trying very hard not to look at anything else.

"I'll say," John answered, looking around at the dolls on the trees. His voice, for once, was quiet.

Larry smirked, amused by John's disquiet. "Hell yeah," he said. "You did it, Carm. We made it."

I smiled, realizing my heart was racing. Catching my breath, I pressed my eye to the viewfinder of my camera.

"Welcome to the Island of the Dolls," I whispered.

Chapter 6: La Isla de las Muñecas

Past the half-submerged trees, we drifted toward a small, crooked dock made of rough-hewn logs and thin tree stumps. Behind the pier, a set of shallow wooden stairs climbed the bank to a ramshackle, tin-roof pavilion.

All around were thick trees and vaguely tropical ferns. Dolls hung from these trees in thick bunches, like fruit. Severed heads impaled on tree branches watched with sightless eyes.

As Miguel poled up to the dock, the island felt eerily quiet, empty of the hum of insects and birdsong that had been so ever-present on the journey here.

For a moment, we all stood speechless on Miguel's *trajinera* in the silence of the island. I pulled my eye from my camera and exchanged glances with John and Larry, both of whom looked suitably awestruck.

"Well?" I prompted. I felt like I deserved some respect after the hell they'd put me through on the way.

Larry nodded. "It's definitely weird," he admitted. Holding his little camera in both hands, he put his eye back to the viewfinder. "Very, very weird."

Miguel poled the *trajinera* up to the little dock and grabbed a crooked piling at the corner of the pier, holding the boat steady with his wiry arms. Then he began to tie the boat to a mooring with an old, thick rope.

Larry hopped out and walked up the dock, turning in circles to film everything. I set my own camera down for a moment and reached for the prepaid cell phone in my bag. John glanced at me, swatting another bug at his neck.

"What are you doing?" John asked.

I grinned. "I'm gonna see if this phone can send a photo to my dad. It has a camera."

Yet as I turned on the phone, I frowned. "Huh."

John looked over my shoulder. "What?"

I looked up, frowning. "No reception."

"We're pretty far out," Miguel muttered. His eyes touched mine with a hint of his old smile; yet his voice was quieter than before, as if he feared someone might be listening.

"Yeah," I said, frowning. "Service was spotty even in Xochimilco. I guess I shouldn't be surprised."

I snapped a grainy photo, so I could send it later. Then I tucked the phone back in my backpack.

"Dad'll just have to wait till we get back to *México* City," I said, pronouncing *Mexico* in the native way. Then, shouldering my bag and hefting my camera, I stepped off the boat onto the dock. After the two-hour ride, my legs felt wobbly on solid ground.

Miguel crouched on the dock, securing the boat to a pinion with a thick, knotted rope. I looked back, chewing my lip. "You want to come with us?"

He met my eyes, his face solemn. "You paid for a ride, not a guide."

"You're not afraid, are you?" I looked around and laughed a little. "They're just dolls."

I could tell I'd stung his *machismo*, but he didn't argue, only folded his arms and glared off at the mossy water.

"What would it take for you to come with us?" I asked Miguel. "How about that two hundred you wanted?"

"Seriously?" John cried, grabbing my arm. "Haven't you paid him *enough*? We don't even need a guide. This island is like, five acres, max!"

But I didn't want to leave Miguel. I was still curious about him, and I couldn't shake the feeling he knew more than he was telling us about the island.

"Well?" I asked.

Miguel let out a long, slow sigh. "Two hundred?"

I nodded. "Not a bad deal, right? You've been here before, haven't you?"

"Yes," he said uneasily, then cleared his throat.

"Then you can show us around. Tell us what you know." I shook free of John's iron grip on my forearm. "It'll be good commentary for the film."

It was John's turn to sigh, shaking his head and joining Larry further up the dock.

Uncrossing his arms, Miguel stepped off the boat. "I can show you around," he said, his expression serious. He raised a finger. "But we leave when I say so. I don't want to be on the canals in the dark."

I beamed and extended my hand. "Deal."

He took my hand, shook it gently, and started to smile again. For a moment I wondered if John was right and I'd just been swindled. "Would you have done it for less?"

He beamed. "Maybe. You are a persuasive one, *bonita.*"

I blushed and looked over my shoulder. John was watching us intently from further up the dock, but even if he'd heard, I doubt he understood that Miguel had just called me pretty.

When I met his eyes, John made an exaggerated wave. "Any day now. The bugs are eating me alive."

Miguel checked the ropes on the boat one more time, then gestured me on. "After you, *señorita,*" he said quietly.

I smiled. "If we're in the middle of nowhere, why are you whispering? Afraid the dolls will hear you?"

He looked somber. "We're not supposed to be here. Besides, the dead have earned their peace."

Before I could respond, Larry suddenly shouted my name from further up the dock.

"Carmen!"

Alarmed, I sprang up the narrow, crooked stairs at the end of the dock. Above, the boardwalk ended at a little rusted pavilion, walled in on one side and heaped with boxes and crates. Dolls covered the plywood wall, rotting, draped in spider webs.

Larry stood at the center of the pavilion, taping.

"What?" I said, hushed. "You scared me."

"Just *look* at this shit." He grinned up from his camera.

Amused, I pointed my own camera at the wall of dolls.

Now, there's something you have to understand here. I don't know if I'm doing it justice.

I'm not exaggerating when I say *wall* of dolls.

The pavilion was perhaps twenty feet long, about eight feet high, and the wall at the back of it ran the full length. And the dolls were so thick on it you couldn't see the wall.

There were Barbie dolls and Ken dolls, baby dolls in all sizes and colors, even a few Teddy bears and Disney characters. Some were dressed in tattered, faded clothing. Others were naked, their rubber bodies ravaged by the elements for years—*decades,* in some cases. Some were bald; others still had long, dirty hair, tangled with leaves. Some had their eyes closed, some were staring lifelessly, and some had no eyes left at all.

Yet they *all* seemed to watch us.

"Yeah," I admitted, recording the wall of small, ruined bodies, "this *is* pretty weird."

Miguel came up behind us. "Don Julio used to send his cousin Fernando to trade crops in town, and Fernando would bring back dolls. They say Don Julio fished some out of the canal or dug them out of garbage heaps. Some were left by tourists while the island was open."

"What do those say?" John gestured at a pair of hand-painted signs across the pavilion, the white letters faded.

I tilted my head to read the Spanish. "Welcome to Don Julio's world-famous Island of the Dolls." Beside it was another sign, more recent. It read, "Trespassers will be decapitated and dismembered." I forced a laugh. "I guess that was a joke?"

John looked dubious. "The guy was obviously nuts."

Miguel shrugged. "That one may have been written by Don Julio's cousin. Don Fernando hates trespassers. Ever since he closed the island, he try to keep everyone away. I hear he's even sank boats that dock without permission." He looked around with a nervous smile. "Try not to disturb anything. We don't need him to know we were here. Come on. I'll show you Don Julio's favorite doll."

Adjusting his hat over his eyes, he led the way through the pavilion. We continued down the boarded path on the other side, into a thick grove. Dolls adorned every tree and hung like grizzly Christmas ornaments from ropes between the trunks. They were so thick in the trees that they seemed to form a second, unnatural canopy, rustling and moving in the breeze, their silhouettes blocking the sun.

"Wow," Larry said. "Never thought it'd be *this* creepy."

I had to agree. I never thought I'd be so affected. To me, the island's story was just superstition. Fascinating premise for a documentary, but superstition nonetheless.

Yet still, my heart was racing in a way I couldn't fully attribute to excitement anymore.

"No wonder the new caretaker couldn't take it," said John. "Only a real nut bar could live in a place like this."

Miguel frowned. "Bad luck to speak ill of the dead."

"To Don Julio, these weren't symbols of evil," I said, for John as much as for my camera. "It's creepy to us, but he had noble intentions, right? He wanted to honor the girl who drowned."

"Doesn't mean he wasn't bat shit insane," said John.

Miguel murmured, "It was not only to honor, but to *appease* her. To calm her spirit and the others that haunted him. Don Julio thought these dolls protected him."

I zoomed my camera on a ruined doll, its features turned black, as if it had once been burned.

"If he went to these lengths to protect himself," I whispered, "he must've been awfully scared of *something.*"

"Or, he was a frigging nut bar," John said again.

Miguel looked irritable, but his voice remained soft. "Come. The house is up ahead."

The doll-infested trees thinned and I saw a circle of ramshackle buildings. First was a small, flat-roof barn. Then an old outhouse, about the size of a tollbooth, the boards rotten and mildewed. An empty chicken coop, strung with steel wire. A half-collapsed shed. The curved, bone-like frame of a fallen greenhouse, the outer canvas torn into faded streamers.

At the back of the yard stood a small wooden shanty, half-buried in the foliage. Moss draped the gutters of the sunken tin roof, blending the shack with the landscape. A small set of crooked stairs led up to a tiny porch outside the front door, the railing hung with dolls. Above the door was another sign, the word *Museo* hand-painted in white.

"There," said Miguel. "The house of Don Julio."

I filmed the desolate scene. "Been abandoned a while, it seems like, but I don't see any graffiti or anything."

"Anyone who comes to vandalize never leaves again," said Larry, in a fake, movie announcer voice. "Man, can you imagine this place at night?"

"Right? It's scary enough in the daytime."

Miguel led the way across the clearing. The ground here was mostly hard-packed gravel and spits of tall weeds. In some places the earth itself had worn away to reveal the gray wooden framework underneath—the skeleton of the ancient floating garden.

I filmed the entrance of the cabin, zooming in on the word *Museo*. "So they turned Julio's shack into a museum for the tourists? What's inside?"

Miguel smiled a little. "What do you think?"

"I'm guessing... dolls?" John muttered.

Gingerly, probing each step for weak boards, I crept up the crooked stairs of the front porch. The one small window by the door was barred with crooked boards, the visible glass underneath opaque with dust and grime. The torn screen door swung in the breeze. Behind that, the front door was cracked open an inch, but when I pushed, it wouldn't budge. I peered at the gap, crawling with small spiders. I could see something glinting inside.

"It's locked with a chain." I turned to Miguel at the foot of the steps. "Can we get inside?"

Miguel looked uneasy. "If it's locked, we shouldn't."

"We're already trespassing," said Larry, moving up the stairs beside me. "Why not add a little B and E?"

"A little what?" said Miguel.

"Breaking and entering? Here." Larry put his camera in his backpack, then grabbed a chunk of firewood from a stack under the porch. With barely any force, he tapped the dark glass between the boards over the window. The pane shattered with a soft tinkle. Discarding the chunk of wood, he reached through the broken glass.

"Careful," I whispered beside him, vaguely surprised by his guts. The project must have finally inspired him. Larry, like me, was willing to do almost anything if he was passionate about it. A true artist.

He met my eyes with a mischievous smile as he fished around inside the house. "Hey, I'm black. I know all about breaking into things."

I rolled my eyes. "Please. You're from Castle Rock and you're barely darker than me."

"Don't record me doing this," he said.

Ignoring him, I kept recording. "Just be careful."

"I think I found the chain." His tongue pushed inside his cheek as he worked. "Yeah, I got it…"

Then his expression changed. His eyes bulged slowly and he screamed, wrenching his arm from the window. Shards of glass flew and his forearm opened in a long, deep gash as he raked past the jagged edges. I leapt away with a yelp as Larry backed into the crooked porch railing, clutching his bloody arm and staring.

"There's something in there!" he cried.

At the same time, the front door yawned open into darkness. I stared through my viewfinder, waiting for some skinless, half-burned doll to shamble out, grinning.

But nothing came.

"What was it?" I breathed.

"I don't know," Larry whispered, staring at me as he held his bleeding arm. "Something brushed my hand."

John swept up the stairs, holding a stainless steel flashlight. All swagger and bravado, he kicked open the front door like a SWAT guy, beaming his light inside.

Tiny faces looked back at us from the darkness.

Like the wall at the pavilion, the walls of the shack were covered in dolls. Scratched glass eyes gleamed in the flashlight like animal eyes at night.

John took a cautious step over the threshold, aiming the light around the interior. The wooden floor was blanketed in dust, the floorboards warped and uneven.

"Be careful," I whispered. I took a step closer to film over his shoulder.

Wherever John's flashlight roved, it revealed some new horror. Body parts in piles under a workbench. Stumpy, curved infant legs dangling from the ceiling where dolls hung from the rafters, some still in shoes, socks, even roller skates. Dolls with clown paint, dolls in hats, dolls with guitars. Dolls missing eyes, dolls without limbs, dolls with mold growing from placid, open mouths.

"You see anything?" I asked breathlessly.

"Uh, yeah," said John. "Some goddamn crazy shit."

"Nothing *moving?*" I clarified.

"Only spiders." He shone the light on the wall next to the door, where a rotted baby doll hung by the window. The rot around her empty eye sockets looked like deep mascara. "There are dolls here by the window. Maybe your hand brushed one of them?" He glanced back at Larry, only just concealing his contempt.

"Or a spider touched you," I suggested, feeling a little queasy. In the beam of John's light, I could see the tiny spiders moving through the layers of cobwebs on the doll.

Larry snorted angrily, his jaw clenched as he worked it over in his mind. "I guess it could have been," he decided. "Maybe I'm freaking myself out."

"You sure freaked *me* out." I turned to film Larry. He stood on the corner of the tiny porch, examining his arm, where he'd slashed it on the broken window in his panic. "You screwed yourself up, too. Great."

"It's not bad," he said, as blood dribbled through his fingers. "Just a scratch. Anyone bring any Band-Aids?"

Still looking around inside the shack, John slid out of his bright blue backpack and handed it out the door to Larry. "Check the front pocket."

"When was the last time you had a tetanus shot?" I demanded. As my fear dissipated, I grew more and more upset—at Larry, of course, but also at myself, for getting scared so easily. "Now we'll have to find a doctor down here. And who knows how long that'll take, how much filming time we'll lose?"

"I got us in the house, didn't I?" Larry fished out a zippered first-aid kit from John's bag, marked with a red cross. "Geez. You sure planned ahead."

"Always be prepared," John replied smugly.

"What's that?" Larry jeered. "Boy Scout motto?"

"Nah," said John. "The *prepper* motto." From the doorway of the shack, he grinned at Larry's blank look. "My dad's real into that whole survivalist, guns and gold, prepare-for-Armageddon crap. Let's just say he taught me a thing or two about what to put in a bug-out bag."

Larry looked impressed, which pleased me. I *told* him John had his uses.

At last, Miguel slinked up the porch stairs, standing behind Larry. "What did it feel like?" Miguel asked quietly. "The thing that touched you?"

"Huh?" Larry looked at him, surprised. "I don't know. Hairy, maybe." He looked at his hand. "It could've been a doll's hair, I guess. My hand must have brushed it."

"Did your hand brush a doll," Miguel asked, "or did the doll brush your hand?"

I smirked at Miguel. "Don't tease him. Come on! I'm paying you to guide me, so get up here and guide."

Miguel shifted his weight from foot to foot, gazing up at the dark shack with a look of dismay. I followed his eyes, looking into the darkness of the yawning doorway.

"Show us the house of Don Julio."

Chapter 7: The House of Don Julio

Miguel stepped lightly past John into the shack, as though he feared an ambush or trap. The old, warped floorboards groaned under his sandals. The dolls watched him silently from the walls, from the rough-cut shelves, from the floor.

I came in behind him, looking around through my camcorder. The inside of the house was all one room, crammed with dolls. The rafters were low enough that John and Miguel had to duck. At the back, the room dropped down to a dirt floor, two feet lower, which made the space tall enough for them to stand upright. Sunlight beamed through the cracks in the shoddy plywood walls. As my eyes adjusted, the darkness seemed to clear from the room, like smoke.

"This shit is seriously grungy," John remarked, waving his flashlight over the cobweb-covered dolls, hanging from the walls and rafters.

I could see only a few objects in the whole shack that *weren't* dolls. At the back stood a workbench, so rickety it appeared to be supported mostly by the stacks of wooden crates and crumbling boxes beneath it. The workbench held a tool box, a rusted bow saw, and a few other yard tools. A walking stick and a shovel leaned on the wall.

My eyes lit on a framed portrait, hanging near the work bench. The frame was ornately carved and hung with crosses and rosaries. The portrait showed an old man in a straw hat, with wrinkled skin and a big, gap-toothed smile.

I zoomed in on the photo. "Is this Don Julio?"

Miguel cleared his throat. *"Sí,"* he replied. "The Lord

of the Dolls. They say he was a kind man, but his passions drove him to exile. In his youth, he studied to become a priest, learned to read and write. But he spoke blasphemy. Claimed he could speak to God. They threw him out, so he took to preaching in the streets of Xochimilco. At that time, in Mexico, this strictly was not done. Only the clergy could speak about God, and no one could speak *for* God. His stubborn faith got him into fights, even trouble with the law. Finally Don Julio left the city, and came here."

Larry peered in through the door, wrapping the cut on his forearm with gauze from John's first-aid kit. Then he lifted his little camcorder from between his legs and joined us at the back of the cabin. He kept panning his camera in a circle, as if afraid to leave his back to the dolls.

"What's this?" I asked.

On the floor under the portrait of Don Julio stood an old, almost life-sized doll, perhaps three feet tall. She wore a full pink skirt and frilly blouse, faded nearly white. Her blonde hair was braided with dead flowers. A wire arch surrounded the doll, also woven with flowers, the petals long rotted to brown, puckered cinders. At the doll's feet was a round, empty donation tray, covered in spider webs.

Miguel stepped closer, "That is Rosita. The first doll Don Julio found, and his favorite. He claimed it washed up the day after he saw the little girl drown. He believed it belonged to her, that her spirit lived on inside it."

I squatted before the strange little shrine to get a close up. The doll's eyes stared back at me, the blue paint so faded they appeared almost colorless. Fissures ran through her plastic face, and the wooden body beneath her tattered dress looked gray with age, like old clay. Black, long-legged spiders crawled sluggishly on the wall behind her.

"So this was the drowned girl's doll."

"Si." Miguel crouched close beside me, whispering, "Visitors used to leave tokens to this doll, asking for luck or making wishes. Don Julio believed that keeping the doll and making offerings to it would appease the spirits and they would protect him."

John moved up behind us, glaring down at Miguel mistrustfully. "Protect him from what?"

Miguel shrugged. "Other spirits. *Vengeful* spirits. A ghost is only an echo, an emotion too strong for death to silence. Sometimes that emotion is sadness or regret, for a wrong done in life or some business left unsettled. Other times, the emotion is only anger. Madness. Vengeance." He swallowed. "Don Julio believed both kinds of spirits haunted this island."

"What do *you* believe?" I asked, with genuine interest.

Instead of answering, he reached into his pocket and fished out the wad of dollars I'd given him to ferry us here. Taking one of the tens, he laid the bill carefully in the empty platter before the doll, Rosita.

Bowing his head, he murmured in Spanish, "Please, *bonita nina,* accept this humble token. Give us sanctuary from the restless dead. In respect I ask for mercy under *Dios. Gracias,* amen."

I held back my smile as Miguel rose. "Is that how the local people honor her?"

He rubbed the back of his neck, as if embarrassed. "Did you want to see the rest of the grounds?" he asked. "We only have so many hours of daylight."

"Yeah." I stood. "I think we got enough footage. Right, Larry?"

Larry stood by the door. He looked up with a shaky, humorless laugh. "I'm done whenever you are."

Outside, we climbed down the porch steps to the

overgrown yard. I took a deep breath, relieved to be in the sun again.

Yet the feeling of being watched did not diminish. There were just as many dolls outside, hanging from the buildings and staked to the trees. Everywhere I looked, some silent visage looked back.

The afternoon had deepened. Shadows fell at new angles through the fern-like leaves. From the sound of it, the wildlife of the island had accepted our presence. Insects were humming again, and a bird cried shrilly in the distance, strange and foreign. It was comforting, after the silence.

"This way," said Miguel.

He led us through the clearing—what might have been considered Don Julio's backyard. We passed dilapidated animal stalls and broken sheds covered in tarps, sticks, and years of fallen leaves. These, too, housed broken dolls and heaps of plastic body parts.

The dolls outside were even more decayed than the ones in the houses. Many were almost unrecognizable, the faces melted, streaked with dirt, covered in spider webs thick as cotton candy. Some even looked scorched, as if at some point they'd been burned.

Through the trees, I glimpsed shimmering water up ahead. We'd reached the far side of the island. The ground was muddy. Trees grew from the shallow water, hung with moss. In the distance, the canal faded into a reedy bog. The landscape felt very isolated.

"So this is the end," I said, standing above the bank. "This island really isn't that big, is it?"

"No," said Miguel.

Frowning, I videotaped the dark, still waters. "But it's relatively shallow, right? Could someone swim through there, if they had to?"

Miguel shrugged. "Sure. I don't know if I'd go very far from the island, though."

"Why not?"

"Snakes. Alligators." His eyes darted over mine, not meeting them. "Things in the water. This way."

He led us along the shoreline. Here, especially, the wooden beams and piers that formed the framework of the floating garden were visible in places, where the earth heaped on top had sloughed away, like the flesh from an aging skeleton. The island was low on the water, almost submerged, buzzing with gnats and dragonflies.

"Gross," Larry groaned as thick mud sucked at his Harley boots. "This shit's messing up my boots!"

"Why'd you wear that out here anyway?" John sneered.

"I didn't bring anything else," Larry snapped. "I didn't know I'd be trekking through a swamp."

We looped back through the trees, till Miguel stopped us in a small clearing. I could see Don Julio's buildings in the distance. At the center of the clearing, a tall, twisted juniper grew up from a rotted tree well.

"This is the center of the island," said Miguel. "The floating gardens were built around trees, to hold them up. This tree was the first, when this island was first built. They call it *el árbol del corazón*, the heart tree."

Curious, I stepped closer with my camera, recording the rough bark. As I moved on top of the wood platform surrounding the tree, the boards creaked and groaned.

"This tree feels very old," I said. "I wonder how—?"

With a sharp crack, the rotten boards just beneath the soil gave under my feet. Next thing I knew I was falling, dropping my camera as my fingers scrabbled against the tree bark, searching for a hand-hold, in vain.

Then a strong hand seized my arm, yanking me back

from the crumbling tree well. I toppled backward, pulling my rescuer down with me into the tall grass beside the tree. I expected to look up and find John.

Instead, Miguel's soft brown eyes met mine.

"You okay, *señorita?*" he asked.

John stormed up, yanking me rudely to my feet and glaring at Miguel. "What are you doing?" he growled— either at me or Miguel, I couldn't tell.

I ignored them both in a surge of panic. "My camera!" Shoving away, I lunged back for the tree. The old gray boards of the platform that surrounded the tree had cracked and two of the boards had fallen through, down into some dark cavity at the heart of the island.

My camera's strap was snagged on a jagged splinter of wood; the camera swung a foot below in the gloom, by the trunk of the tree.

I threw myself at the edge of the opening, grabbing my camera before it fell completely.

"Careful!" Larry said, filming a few feet away.

"Shit, shit, shit!" I muttered, furious at myself. Fishing my camera cautiously out of the hole, I sat up, inspecting it and breathing hard. Yet the camera was still recording, and as I inspected the lens and exterior, I saw no signs of damage. I kept inspecting it, not trusting my luck, or the early-nineties craftsmanship.

"Everything okay?" Larry asked.

"Did you hurt yourself?" asked John.

"No, I think everything's okay. Yeah. It looks like it's still recording. I don't see any damage."

Through the camera, I looked down into the opening under the heart tree. Several feet below, a long, wooden platform nestled amidst the huge, gnarled roots of the tree, half-submerged in muddy water.

I was looking *through* the island, I realized, through its wooden framework to its ancient foundations.

"There's, like, a big void here by the tree roots," I said. "You can see right through to the canal. This old *chinampa* is falling apart."

"Gotta be careful," Larry teased. "Don't want to have to find a doctor, right?"

"Yeah." I frowned. I thought I saw something through the mud—some icon carved or painted on the wooden platform down there. I switched on the camera's night vision for a better view, but when I looked for the emblem again, I'd lost sight of it altogether.

"John, hand me that flashlight," I muttered.

Looking unhappy, John offered me his heavy, stainless steel flashlight. I took it with my free hand and aimed it down through the fissured floorboards.

Still, I didn't see anything on the wooden slab at the bottom of the pit—either the little emblem I'd seen there was hidden again by mud, or it had only been a trick of the lighting after all. As I scanned the flashlight higher up the tree trunk, though, I gasped.

"Hey, there's something carved in the tree!"

Toward the base of the thick tree trunk, a foot above the white roots and muddy wood foundations, someone had carved two words and a number into the bark:

DOÑA MARINA

1526

"*Doña Marina,*" I read. "1526? Is that a *date?*"

Miguel looked over my shoulder at the carving, dumbfounded. "*Doña Marina?*" he repeated. "It can't be."

Then he whispered another word, one I didn't know. "*Malintzin.*"

"Huh?" I frowned, turning my camera back to Miguel. "*Malintzin?* Is that Spanish?"

He looked at me solemnly. "No. It's a *Nahuatl* word."

"A Nah-*what*-el word?" said John.

"The Nahua," said Miguel, "were the Aztec tribe that lived in Xochimilco, before the Spaniards came."

"What does *Malintzin* mean?" I asked.

"It's a name for a woman," said Miguel. "A famous woman in Mexican history. Without her, the Mexican people of today would not have been born. She was a very beautiful Nahua woman, given to Hernán Cortés and the Spaniards as a slave. Cortés called her by a Christian name, Doña Marina. It's said she used her knowledge of local languages and politics, as well as her considerable charms, to worm her way into the inner circle of Cortés.

"At his side, *Malintzin* sowed the destruction of her own people. Some call her the real conqueror of Mexico. They say that Don Cortés could never have conquered the natives without his Doña Marina. Many see *Malintzin* as a traitor to her own people. This is why in Mexico we say *malinchista,* to mean a disloyal person."

"When did she live?" I asked.

"In the time of the Conquistadors. 1520, 1521. She was not seen much after the fall of Tenochtitlan."

Gesturing down toward the tree carving, I whispered, "Then she would have been alive around 1526?"

Miguel rubbed the scruff on his chin. "It's said that in her later years, Doña Marina lived on an island south of Mexico City. It could have been this very floating garden."

"Wow." I glanced at Larry and his camera excitedly. "That's so weird. What a cool find!"

John smirked. "Anyone could've carved that."

Miguel nodded. "Anyone could have. Even *Malintzin.*"

I smiled at him. "It's been fascinating having you as a guide. I'm learning a lot about my culture."

Miguel returned my smile.

John cleared his throat deliberately and looked at his watch. "Gonna get dark soon. Shouldn't we head back?"

His smile vanishing, Miguel looked away. "That's right. I think I've shown you everything. We should go."

I made a disappointed sound. "Aw! If you insist. I wouldn't want to be here after dark," I added with a laugh.

The four of us started back toward the docks, passing the derelict house of Don Julio. The day had passed in a blink. Now afternoon was ripening into dusk, lighting the island in disturbing shades of red. Dolls sat patiently around the tree trunks, strung from wires hung between trees like gruesome wind chimes. Severed, child-like heads topped branches, the plastic mottled and rotten, paint chipped away, eyes fallen from empty sockets.

Somehow, especially at this hour, the scenery reminded me of some eerie, abandoned carnival. As if somewhere there were a switch waiting to be thrown that would bring all the silent dolls back to life with a motorized whir.

I could almost hear the calliope music. Could almost see the dolls dancing to it, and hear their mechanized laughter. Batteries not included. Batteries not required.

I shivered.

As we walked, I stretched my arm, my shoulder sore from supporting my heavy camera. Beside me, Larry looked through footage on his camcorder's LCD screen.

"So what'd you think?" I asked him.

He smiled wearily and admitted, "You were right. It turned out good. Unique."

It meant a lot to me. I grinned.

"But I for sure would not want to live here," he added,

smirking. "No wonder Don Julio went crazy."

Before anyone could reply, a sudden *bang* interrupted us from the right, over by Don Julio's buildings.

I froze, glancing at Larry. "Did you hear that?"

His wide-eyed expression answered for me; he stood still as a deer in headlights. John frowned. Miguel gaped. We listened for a long, breathless moment in the silence.

"Yeah," John muttered finally. "What was that?"

Taking a deep breath, I turned to Larry. "Put your camera back on." It was for the film, of course. But also, for some reason, I always felt more secure having a camera running—as if recording whatever happened to me could somehow protect me from harm.

"Carmen," Larry said reluctantly.

"Just put your camera on!" Taking a step toward the buildings, I called timidly, "Hello? Is someone out there?"

Silence answered. The insects had stopped buzzing. The only sound was the distant, raucous cry of a foreign, unfamiliar bird. It sounded almost like a child's screaming.

I got out my own camera, as well. Coming around the corner of the empty, half-fallen barn, I swung my camera around the clearing, looking for any movement in the buildings or the woods beyond.

"Hello?" I called, louder and more confident. "Anyone there? You guys heard it, too, right?"

John hovered close behind me, but the other two hung back. "I heard it," Larry said softly, filming.

"Hey," said John. "Who was the last one out of the dead guy's house?"

I frowned. "Why?"

"I thought it was me." He pointed. "But I don't think I closed the door."

I followed his gesture with my camera. Sure enough, the crooked front door of the house was closed. Only the outer screen door remained open, creaking in the wind.

"Is that what we heard?" I whispered. "The door slamming? You sure you didn't close it?"

"Maybe I did," he shrugged. "I don't remember."

"Hello?" I called, one last time. "Is anybody here?"

A gust of wind rustled the treetops, and the dolls swayed in the branches, seeming to dance and move in the gathering gloom. Nothing else answered, and slowly the rhythmic buzz of insects rose again out on the bog.

"Maybe it was the wind," John suggested softly.

"But the door closes from the inside," Larry muttered.

John only shrugged, a rare uncertainty in his eyes.

"Creepy," I muttered finally, my heart still pounding.

Larry lowered his camcorder, still staring at the silent cabin of Don Julio and its closed door. "Can we go *now?*"

"Yeah," John said. "I'm down for that."

"Me, too." I forced a small, fake laugh. "Come on."

I stepped back, filming the old gray cabin for as long as I could before turning away. Somehow I resisted the urge to look over my shoulder, to watch my back.

The thicket of trees and foliage between Don Julio's house and the dock looked more sinister in the low light of late afternoon. The deepening shadows made the pale ruined dolls skeletal and monstrous.

I wouldn't have admitted it, had anyone asked, but I was relieved to be leaving. Even a skeptic like me.

"Okay," I said, hoping to brighten the mood and end the day on a positive note. "So day one is complete. I think we got some real great footage."

"I'll say," John said. His voice remained much quieter

than usual, his bombast finally diminished. "I definitely think you guys are getting an *A* on your project."

"Yeah?" I brightened. "You think it'll be good enough to pitch to studios?"

John shrugged indulgently, putting a hand on my shoulder. "I don't see why not."

It was enough to make me smile.

We were walking down the crooked steps of the dock, toward the place where Miguel had tied up the boat. I set my camera to night vision to get some final shots, then lowered it with a wince. With the extra-large battery, the bulky old camera weighed almost ten pounds, and my shoulder ached from carrying it.

"Man, I'm tired," I said. "How about I treat you all to dinner once we're back? Miguel, you want to join us?"

John was about to protest; I knew him well enough to expect it.

Then something caught his eye up ahead, and his face changed. His glare loosened and his mouth hung open.

I followed John's gaze, and my own eyes widened. For a moment I wasn't sure if I understood what I was seeing. Slowly, I raised my camera again to record it.

"What the hell?" Larry cried, coming up behind us.

Up ahead, the crooked pier extended a few feet into the dark waters of the canal, the rough-hewn log pilings stacked with doll heads.

But the dock was empty. There was no rope around the piling, no *trajinera* moored at the dock.

Miguel's boat was gone.

Chapter 8: Stranded

"What?" I whispered. "Where the hell is it?"

Miguel pushed past us, rushing down the dock. *"Mi barco!"* Clutching his head, he fell to his knees by the piling where he'd tied the *trajinera*. *"¿Dónde está mi barco?"*

John turned and glared at me. "What's he saying?" When I didn't answer, John stormed down the deck to tower over Miguel. "Where's the boat?"

"I don't know!" Miguel cried in English, shrinking a little under John's imposing shadow. His brown eyes were wide with increasing panic. "I tied it here! I tied it up!"

"Then where the hell is it?" John cried.

"I don't know!"

Stunned, I stood videotaping at the top of the crooked steps. I kept comparing what I saw through the viewfinder to what I saw with my eyes, wanting to believe that one or both was deceiving me.

"So," I narrated, in a shaky voice, "we just returned from touring the island. Now we're coming back in the afternoon, and our boat is nowhere to be found."

John glared back at me. "Would you stop worrying about your film for two seconds?" He thrust a finger at Miguel. "This idiot just got us stranded here and you're still worried about your little *documentary?*"

Miguel stumbled to his feet, cornered by John at the end of the tiny dock. "I tied it up," he said again. He turned to me desperately. "I tied it up—you saw me!"

I didn't look up from my camera. "That's right," I said, my voice croaking. "I saw him tie it up."

"The hell do you know about knots?" John growled, glaring at me. "He obviously screwed something up or the boat would still be here!"

"Unless someone *untied* it," Larry murmured softly.

A pause followed—and suddenly Miguel bolted.

"Hey!" John lunged for him, but Miguel evaded him, climbing the stairs toward me. His wide eyes barely saw me. I stepped aside, filming as he passed.

"Miguel," I croaked, moving after him. "Miguel!"

He ran along the edge of the island, looking out at the water, searching for his boat. I heard him muttering to himself in Spanish, but I couldn't make out the words.

"Stop him!" John shouted.

"He didn't do anything wrong," I said, exasperated.

Miguel stopped on the shore, clutching his hair and sweating bullets. *"Cristo,"* he whispered, sounding on the verge of tears. *"¡Metí la pata! Me equivoque al venir aquí."*

I said, "Let's stay calm, okay? Let's think about this…"

John nodded at Miguel. "What's he saying?"

I sighed. "He says he was wrong to come here."

"What's that supposed to mean?" John said.

Miguel whirled on us, his face contorted in fear. "It's the island!" he shouted. "Don't you see? It's the island!"

He waved his hand. Eerily, as if on cue, the trees above moved in a passing breeze, and the dolls seemed to dance amid the branches.

For the first time, I felt genuinely afraid. But I had to remain the voice of reason. This was my project, after all. I'd brought them here. I felt a responsibility for them. And besides, if we didn't hold together, the project fell apart.

If *I* lost my cool, who would hold them together?

"Look. It's just the wind. Okay?" Catching my breath,

I gestured at the trees. "See? It moves the dolls. I bet it's what slammed the door closed at the shack."

"And the wind untied the boat, too?" John demanded.

I swallowed, confronted with the unlikeliness of it. "Maybe the tides changed and sucked it out?"

"There are no tides in a goddamn lake," John snapped.

"You don't have to shout at me!"

"Then stop filming and take this shit seriously! Your Mexican hero just fucked us all over."

Lowering my camera, I glared up at John. "It's not his fault! He tied the boat up, what more do you want?"

"Exactly, *he* tied it up! So if it came loose, it's *his* fault!" He jabbed at Miguel. "How well do we even know this guy? How do we know he didn't set this up?"

"Set *what* up?" I cried. "Why would he do that?"

"Oh, I don't know. Let me paint you a picture. Talk tourists into going with you to a deserted island. Strand them where no one can help them. Steal their credit cards? Kill them? Fill in the rest, I don't know."

Miguel stepped up to John, puffing up his chest and glaring. "Yeah? Suppose I did want to kill you, *esse?* How would I pull that off by myself?"

"Because you're *not* by yourself," said John. "You were with us all day, so someone else had to fuck up the boat. Maybe whoever Larry heard back at the shack?"

"*Is* there someone else on the island?" Larry asked.

Miguel shrugged his hands in exasperation. "If there is, they're no friend of mine."

"Guys," I said, "you said it yourselves. Miguel never left our sight. We have no reason not to trust him."

"And no reason *to* trust him, either," John muttered.

"It was the island," Miguel insisted.

"Oh, horse shit!" John cut him off.

"Guys!" I shouted. "Maybe Miguel made a mistake. Maybe he didn't tie the knot right."

"But I did!" Miguel said. "It was double-knotted."

"Maybe the wind loosened it. I don't know. My point is, there's no reason to blame Miguel, and definitely no reason to blame anything supernatural. All right? Just look at the bright side. At least it's more good footage."

I was only trying to lighten the mood, but I instantly regretted my words. John groaned out loud. Even Larry growled, "What do you mean by that?"

"Nothing," I stammered, "just, you know. It's a twist. A hook. It'll make the film that much more compelling. I mean, I'm just saying!"

Larry's eyes were locked on mine angrily. *"You* didn't do this, did you?"

"What? No!"

"You sure?" Larry said. "You and Miguel, you're not in on it together? That's why you're defending him now? Oh my God." He rolled his eyes and made a small laugh. "I mean, has the joke been on us the whole time?"

"No!" I was truly insulted. "Who do you think I am?"

"I don't know, but I know you're obsessed with this stupid film. I don't know what lengths you'd go for it. Is this all some sick reality TV shit with us as your lab rats?"

Stammering, I looked to John for support, but his face was flat. His eyes seemed to consider me, what I could do.

"I had *nothing* to do with this!" I said. "I can't believe you'd even think that. Look, we're all scared right now, but let's not blame each other."

"Then who *should* we blame?" John asked softly. I didn't like the clinical way he was studying me.

I tried to think. "Don Julio's cousin Fernando hates trespassers, right? Someone told us he's messed with boats before."

"Yeah," John said dryly. "*Miguel* told us that. Very convenient."

"It's true," Miguel insisted. "Everything I said is true."

Larry shook his head, disgusted. "Sure. Whatever."

"Stop it!" I shouted. "Can we focus on the problem here? Why don't we look around, for a start? Maybe the boat didn't drift far."

We walked in silence, making another loop around the edge of the island. The trees were now black shadows, and darkness lay beneath them. The sky had grown overcast, and the wind in the trees threatened a storm.

John got out his flashlight. It was the only flashlight between us; Larry and I hadn't thought to bring one. After all, this was supposed to be a day trip. What use were flashlights on a day trip, right?

I held my camera in one hand, filming as I walked. In the other I held my little burner phone, hoping for a signal somewhere—but the signal icon's red X never wavered.

With every minute, the sun sank lower behind the trees across the canal, and my hopes of finding the boat sank with it.

The full weight of the situation was still settling over me. Things had changed so suddenly. What was supposed to be a fun day trip had now become something much more serious.

"I don't see any boat," Larry said. "Can't we just make a swim for it?" I couldn't tell if he was joking. His face looked forlorn as he clutched his bandaged forearm.

Miguel shook his head. "You can try," he said sullenly. "But the canals are treacherous, even in good weather.

And I told you. There are things in the water."

As we returned to the empty dock, Miguel sighed and came to a stop, and I knew the search was over.

"I could maybe build a raft," he said. "But it will take time." He looked at me with baleful brown eyes. "I don't think we're getting off the island, *señorita.*"

"Oh, Jesus," Larry said faintly. "So we're stranded?"

I raised a hand, hoping to stem the rising panic—theirs and mine. "Only for tonight. Some boat will pass in the morning and we can get help."

Larry looked at me like a mistrustful animal, his glasses glinting from John's flashlight. "You sure about that?"

I nodded, reassured by my own words. "The canals are a tourist attraction, right? We're not *that* far from the city. Someone has to come."

At that moment, thunder crackled in the distance, loud and sharp as a whip. Through the trees overhead, I could just make out the dark clouds moving in from the north.

"Well, we can't stand out here all night." I could barely see John's face behind his flashlight beam, but his voice sounded grim and reckless. It was his bar-fighting voice, used whenever he was about to start trouble. "And there's still one place on the island we didn't check."

I saw Larry wilt beside me. "The cabin."

"You said something touched you when you reached in the window," John said. "And we all heard that door slam on our way back. What if there *is* someone else on the island?"

The thought chilled me. I'd had the vague feeling I was being watched all day long. And who wouldn't, with a thousand dolls staring at you, right?

But what if someone really was watching?

Someone—or some *thing?*

"If there was someone here, we would've seen them." I wanted to sound confident, but my voice was almost pleading. "Come on, guys. You're freaking yourselves out over—what? Some wind and a bad knot?"

"Maybe." John eyed Miguel. "Maybe not. Anyway, we can't just stand out here if a storm's coming."

Another sharp peal of thunder punctuated his words, followed by a long, low rumble.

I took a deep breath, then nodded slowly.

"Yeah," I agreed. "He's right. We should go back and check out the cabin."

I felt a quiet chill pass through my companions at the prospect, and for a moment no one spoke. At our backs, the last purple glow of daylight faded on the canal.

Larry hefted his camera again with a miserable sigh. "All right. If you say so."

"John?" I prompted. "You got the light. You want to lead the way?"

He hesitated, aiming his flashlight down the corridor of dark trees at the center of the isle. Pale, sightless faces swam up out of the gloom wherever the light passed.

Slowly, John started to walk. The rest of us followed close behind him and the light. Dead leaves rustled under our shoes, loud in the preternatural silence. The flashlight threw strange, moving shadows in the trees as we passed.

"Jesus," Larry whispered, barely a breath. "I thought this place was bad in the daytime."

Despite myself, I kept filming everything. I barely even realized I was doing it. It was just a self-soothing habit, as unconscious as a child sucking her thumb.

"Yeah." In night vision mode, my camera cast a small infrared light ahead of it to light its surroundings, turning the image pale, grainy, and black and white. I could see several feet in each direction. Dolls gazed back from every tree. "Bet you wish your fancy newfangled camera had night vision now. It's super creepy."

Thunder rumbled again and a wind brought the dolls to life. The movement was disturbingly lifelike, especially in the disorienting black and white of my viewfinder.

As I scanned my camera across the sea of plastic faces, I saw a pair of tiny lights, like reflective animal eyes.

I swept the camera through the foliage toward the eyes, and my breath caught in my throat.

Through the trees I saw a figure, dressed all in white and standing amidst the ferns and brush. Long, brown hair fell over her face in a wet, dripping curtain. In her arms she clutched a baby doll to her chest.

Even as she came into frame, the girl lifted her head with a chilling slowness.

A scream caught in my throat and I looked up from my camera, squinting into the dark.

There was nothing there. I looked back through the viewfinder at the infrared image. Nothing there, either. No dripping wet girl, no set of glowing eyes. Only baby dolls amid the trees. One had long, ratty brown hair hanging in its eyes.

"Carmen?" Larry whispered. "What is it?"

I sighed shakily. "Nothing. Just seeing things. These dolls are really terrible at night."

Up ahead, John stopped, lowering his flashlight to the ground and getting low himself. "Hey." He motioned us to the ground. "We're here."

I turned my camera toward John, and what lay beyond.

In the dim, starless light of the clearing, the cabin of Don Julio awaited.

Chapter 9: Nightfall

Ducking into a crouch, I joined John at the edge of the clearing, aiming my camera at the silent buildings.

"You see anything?" I whispered. I was shivering, but I told myself it was only the cold. It had been warm during the day, for late October; now, in the sun's absence, the air was sharp and chilly, especially with the wind.

John frowned, holding his big hand over the flashlight beam to conceal it and squinting in the darkness. "I don't think so," he whispered back. "Looks pretty deserted."

Raising his flashlight, John rose and stepped into the clearing. The rest of us followed him, slipping past the half-collapsed barn, the eaves strung with swaying dolls.

Lightning flashed in the distance, briefly illuminating the scene. Thunder rumbled in the darkness that followed. John bounced his flashlight from building to building. The light picked white faces and tiny bodies out of the gloom.

"There's no one here," I said, perhaps for my own benefit. I disliked the desperate tone of my voice.

Not satisfied, John turned back to the decrepit cabin at the back of the clearing, holding it in his flashlight's beam. "What about there?" he demanded. "Maybe that's where Miguel's keeping his accomplice."

I looked at the little one-room building with dismay. The shack seemed to squint back through its boarded, broken window.

I wanted nothing more than to be indoors *somewhere*, with a door between me and the whispering trees of the night. But of all the places in the world to stay…

John went first, climbing the stairs slowly. The old wood squealed in protest beneath even his softest steps. He held his flashlight with the beam pointed downward, the long, steel handle held upright like a cudgel, ready to swing at anything that moved.

I stood at the foot of the steps, videotaping him. "Careful," I whispered. Miguel and Larry clustered behind me, looking around in the darkness.

Moving to the door, John kicked it open, then swept inside, clearing the interior with his light in a quick, jerky way. He seemed to shrink as the tension eased out of him.

"Nothing here, either." Somehow he sounded both disappointed and relieved. "If there's someone else on the island, they must be good at hiding."

Climbing the porch steps, I leaned into the musty shack, recording. John's light passed over the silent dolls on the walls, glinted off the portrait of Don Julio, gleamed on silky spider webs in the rafters. The room looked just as we'd left it earlier, only even darker now at night.

Behind me, Larry peered in suspiciously, aiming his camera around. "We really gonna spend the night *here?*"

"Unless you packed a tent?" John snapped. "You want to sleep out there, be my guest."

Muttering something, Larry turned away to record the dolls at the back of the room. John sat heavily on the wooden step to the sunken, lower portion of the room, where the floor turned to bare earth. He put his flashlight on the floor, pointing at the ceiling to light the tiny room.

Meanwhile, Miguel slunk into the cabin at last. He looked around, his lips pressed into a tight line. Saying nothing, he moved to the back and sank to his knees in front of the shrine that housed the drowned girl's doll.

"Let's see," John said, fishing through his backpack.

"Here we go." He took out a red box of matches and went to a glass lamp on the wall by the portrait of Don Julio. Striking the match, John carefully lit the old candle in the lamp, bringing a soft, muted glow to the tiny shack.

"That should save us some batteries," he said, turning off his flashlight. The candlelight was much dimmer, and darkness lingered around the corners of the room.

"Speaking of batteries," I muttered. "Mine are running low." I opened my bag and removed one of the extra-large battery packs, swapping out the one in my camera. Then I set the camera down on top of the workbench, to record us. "There we go."

"Man," Larry whined, looking up from his viewfinder at the dolls. "Can this get any worse?"

Looking at Larry, I noticed fresh blood darkening the gauze on his arm. I sighed impatiently. "Larry, you're bleeding."

He held up his arm, frowning at it. "Must've broke the scab."

I moved closer to inspect it, but I had no idea what I was doing. Just the sight of the red blood soaking through the white gauze made me a little queasy. "God, we need to get you to a doctor. John, a little help?"

With a rumbling sigh, John came over. Seizing Larry's arm, he peeled the gauze away from the sticky, half-clotted wound. The cut was about three inches long, thin, ragged. I winced at the sight. Larry recorded it with his good arm.

John held up the bloody gauze, sniffed it, and shrugged. "Seems like it's healing clean. Put a fresh wrap on it, you'll be fine. You could use a few scars."

Larry glared at him, but said nothing.

In the momentary silence, I heard Miguel muttering something at the doll's shrine.

He was on his knees, bowing his head before Rosita the doll. "Give us mercy, please," he whispered in Spanish. "Forgive us our trespass and give us sanctuary from the restless dead."

By now, we were all watching him. John grumbled, "What's he saying?"

My voice broke a little as I answered. "A prayer."

"Hey, enough with the creepy shit!" John said. "Stop trying to freak us out."

Miguel scowled back at John. "I'm *trying* to protect us."

"What are you so afraid of?" I asked him. "You've been scared since we got here."

Miguel's face softened and he looked back at the doll. Despite John's warning look, I moved closer, kneeling by Miguel's side.

"You said you've been here before," I said. "Did something happen? Something you're not telling us?"

He sighed. "You would not believe me if I told you, *señorita*. You say you won't believe until you've seen. But you don't even believe what you *have* seen."

That took me aback. I thought about the phantom girl I'd seen—or *thought* I'd seen—in the woods on the way here. Then I said, "Sometimes even our eyes can't be trusted, when we're afraid, or we're not thinking clearly. We can see things that aren't really there."

He sniffed. "See? I haven't even told you and already you dismiss."

"A good documentary is about building evidence," I said. "Whether or not I believe it, I still want to know."

"At this point," Larry muttered, "I'd say we *deserve* to know."

Miguel looked from me to John and Larry, listening at the back of the room. Then he lowered his eyes.

"I was giving a tour of the island, years ago," he began. "I was only sixteen. One of the first tours I gave after I got the *trajinera* from my papa. Back when Don Fernando was running the island for tourists to visit. There was hardly anyone that day. I was with a family of Americans, very wealthy, and we had the place almost to ourselves.

"The family was laughing," he said. "Taking pictures, making jokes. Making fun of it, you know. No respect. They thought it was... what's the word? *Kitsch?*"

He lowered his voice. I had to lean closer to hear.

"I remember I had a bad feeling in my stomach from the moment we stepped off the boat. They say the island either accepts you or it rejects you. And those people, the island rejected. Something didn't want us here."

Thunder rumbled in the distance and skeletal branches tapped the tin roof, moved on the wind. I looked around, uneasy. The dolls seemed to listen with rapt attention.

"We were making our way around the island," Miguel continued. "My English was not so good back then, and most tourists were not so nice as you, *señorita*. So I was hanging back, letting them look around, not saying much. Then I saw something."

His soft brown eyes started to look more distant as he fell deeper into the memory. He stared off through the dirt floor at the foot of the doll's shrine.

"It was just from the corner of my eye," he said. "But I saw something moving in the woods." He gestured vaguely through the walls of the house. "I turned and saw this one doll, mounted on a tree. Its hair was all burned away. Its eyes were melted, black holes, staring at the ground. The face was blank, you know, no expression, the mouth sort of open, like a baby.

"As I looked at it, I felt this *fear*, like I'd never felt. I couldn't move. I couldn't breathe.

"Then the doll's head *moved*. Stiffly, like a corpse, it raised its empty eyes to look at me. And then it smiled."

Miguel turned to me, his gaze still distant, unfocused.

"I cried out, and blinked in surprise," he said, "and when I opened my eyes, the head was down again. The smile was gone. I didn't know if I'd seen it at all. But the *fear* was still there, gnawing at my insides. I waited for the family back at the dock, and from that day on, I'd bring people to the island, but I never set foot on it myself."

I forced a smile. "But you did for me."

His eyes focused on mine a little, but he didn't smile back. "Yes. You're a very persuasive *chica.*"

I realized how close I was leaning to Miguel and got to my feet. "That's quite a story," I said.

Miguel looked away. "I knew you wouldn't believe me."

I studied Miguel, trying to read him. John seemed to think Miguel was some kind of conman; that he, alone or with help, had made the boat disappear on purpose. And couldn't that be possible? How well did we know Miguel, these people, this land? Was I letting Miguel's charming smile and flirty comments get the better of me?

I almost *wanted* to believe John was right, that Miguel was behind everything. In a way, that would be so much simpler. But I simply couldn't convince myself. Miguel's fear seemed too genuine, and I saw nothing for him to gain in lying to us.

"I believe you," I said finally. "I believe you *saw* it. But like I said, sometimes our eyes can't be trusted." When Miguel looked unencouraged, I added, "Look, nothing's going to happen, okay? We're all together."

At length, Miguel stood and turned from the doll, meeting my eyes with a thin smile. "I hope you're right, *señorita.*" He moved past me, into the room.

"I *know* I'm right. Just think of it like a sleep-over."

"Minus the sleep," Larry quipped. He'd wrapped his cut in new gauze and sat cross-legged, looking uneasily at the dolls. "I don't think I'll get a wink in here tonight."

I joined John, sitting on the step to the dropped floor on the other half of the room. Miguel sat warily a few feet from the rest of us. "I wonder what my family is doing," he muttered. "I hope my mother is not too worried."

"You really care about them," I said.

He glanced at me. "Won't *your* mother worry, too?"

My smile thinned. "I don't think so. She's not with us. She died giving birth to me."

"Oh." Miguel looked down. "Sorry to hear that."

"My mom was Abigail Warren-Benitez. *The* Abigail Warren? She was a filmmaker? *Eden Lost?*" Miguel smiled and nodded without recognition. I shrugged. "That was her big film. About poor families in rural Colorado. She met my dad filming it. Around when they got married, *Eden Lost* was sweeping all the indie festivals. A studio was offering big bucks for her next film. It was the start of a bright new career. And then *I* happened.

"My dad says it wasn't my fault. There were just… *complications*. Whatever that means. But I guess I've always felt kind of guilty over it, you know? Maybe that's why this *Muñecas* project is so important. Like, if *I* can pull off my film, then her dream will live on through me."

Larry said seriously, "For what it's worth, I'm a huge fan of your mom, Carmen."

I laughed, teasing him. "I'm a huge fan of *your* mom. No, seriously! All those cookies she's always mailing to campus?" I shook my head wistfully, imagining the taste.

Larry rubbed his stomach. "Ugh, don't tease me. I'm really missing dinner about now."

John leaned over, opening his big blue dry bag. "Let's see. I've got some protein bars, some bags of trail mix and raisins. Some iodine tablets and filters for water..."

"Wow," Larry said. "You really take this survivalist shit seriously. You said your dad taught you all this?"

"My dad taught me everything," John said, not looking up. "*My* mom was never around. Left us when I was little. So yeah. Dad taught me how to survive. Whether I wanted to listen or not." He chuckled. "That was lesson number one: do what he says, or else. If you didn't, you took your medicine. The dose was forty whacks with his belt."

He took out a bag of trail mix, emptied a handful into his palm, and passed the bag on to me. I ate from it greedily, then passed it on to Larry.

"One time," John continued, "he brought me out into the middle of a national forest and left me there for the weekend. Even took my bag. Had to find my way to a gas station and call him to pick me up. He was so proud."

"Sounds like a great guy," Larry said, barely hiding his look of horror.

"I remember that," I told John. "That was, what, sophomore year in high school?"

He nodded. "Right before I asked you out."

"Where did your mother go?" Miguel asked, confused.

John fixed him in a cool stare. "Kind of a rude thing to ask, bud. Like I said, in my dad's house, it was either his way or the highway. I guess she chose the highway."

I'd never gotten much more out of John than that, but I'd often wondered what his dad had done to the former Mrs. Cavill to make her leave. John still lived with his dad while studying business at the community college, but they'd never been close. All I knew was I always felt a little weird at John's house. Something about the way his dad looked at me gave me the creeps.

"Wish I'd brought some beers," John said, perhaps to change the subject. "A nice cold Shiner."

Larry laughed. "Or some weed." He was still holding John's trail mix, digging toward the bottom of the bag.

"Nah," said John. "Wouldn't want the paranoia."

"Yeah, you're paranoid enough," I agreed.

He smirked, looking away.

Miguel swallowed, eyeing the near-depleted bag of trail mix in Larry's hands. I noticed his gaze and cleared my throat. "Larry? You mind passing the food along?"

"I only brought enough for three," John said quickly.

Larry hesitated only a moment before leaning over and handing Miguel the rest of the bag. John glared at him.

"What difference does it make?" Larry muttered. "It's just trail-mix. We'll all be hungry again in an hour."

"At least I brought something," John growled. "Aside from heavy-ass camera shit I have to carry for you."

Before Larry could respond, lightning flashed and crackled outside, loud enough to make us all jump. The thunder followed almost instantly, rumbling on and on.

"Damn," said John, as it died. "That's close."

"Still no rain," Miguel lamented. "After such a long drought, even the *chinampas* are dry."

Outside, the wind wailed. It came in through the thin plywood boards, through gaps as wide as my fingers. The cobwebs in the rafters waved like tattered flags and the candle in the glass lamp flickered, throwing shadows over the dolls, who watched on every wall.

It was cold, too—much colder than I'd expected. I felt the chill even when I donned my hooded sweater over my blouse.

We sat there on the dusty floor, looking up at the tin roof as it rattled. Slowly, the dry thunder moved off.

But the wind remained.

"Man," John said, "that wind really wails out here. No wonder Don Julio had to *sing* to the mermaids. How else could they have heard him over the noise?"

"We should rest, if we can," I said reluctantly, pulling my sweater closer. "The sooner we're up in the morning, the sooner we're off this island, hopefully."

I retrieved my camera from the work bench and turned it off.

John opened his pack and took out a small bundle. When he pulled a rubber band away, it expanded into two big beach towels. "I didn't bring a blanket or anything," he admitted sheepishly. "But we can use these."

He handed one to Larry and spread the other out for the two of us. Miguel looked on from across the room, his face forlorn. "Sorry," I said. "We only packed for three."

John sprawled out on the towel, his hands behind his head. I lay beside him, pressing to him for warmth. After a moment, he put his arm around me.

Larry lay down on his towel as well. After a moment, Miguel leaned back on the dusty floor, using his bag as a pillow, his straw hat on his chest. The candle in the glass lamp burned low.

Even after our early rise and long, strenuous day, I found it impossible to sleep in this gloomy shack. As if the sightless gaze of a hundred grungy dolls wasn't disturbing enough, the island outside was alive with strange sounds—the groaning of trees, the tapping of branches on the roof, the eerily human whine of the wind.

Just as I drifted off, I thought I heard something else altogether—not a branch on the rooftop, not a sound from outside, but something much closer. In here, with us.

For a moment I wasn't sure if my mind was playing tricks on me again. I lay on the towel on the cold floorboards, staring at the dusty cobwebs in the rafters, afraid to move, afraid to breathe, my ears straining to listen.

John lay beside me, his camo hat over his face to keep the gnats away. He seemed undisturbed. No doubt it had just been something outside, I told myself. Just the wind.

John was right. The wind was really terrible here.

I willed myself to close my eyes, let my tense muscles relax. Slowly,

Then the sound came again: a subtle scratching, like small, soft feet pawing and scraping at the wood.

"The fuck!" Larry cried, leaping to his feet.

I sat bolt upright. John pulled his hat away and sat up beside me, blinking toward the sound. "What? What is it?"

"John!" I screamed, pointing.

Something was moving on the other side of the room, in the darkness of the dirt floor section.

"There's something in here!"

Chapter 10: Bumps in the Night

John grabbed his flashlight and turned it on, waving it into the darkness beyond the candlelight. Shadows moved behind the dolls, creating the eerie illusion that the dolls themselves were moving, their heads turning in the light, just like Miguel had described.

Near the portrait of Don Julio and Rosita's shrine stood a work bench, and under the bench was a stack of decrepit crates, dirt-filled clay pots, and other refuse.

As John's flashlight moved over the bench, I saw the gleam of two yellow eyes, looking out at us from amidst the junk piled underneath—just like the eyes I'd seen in the woods outside the cabin. The eyes were low to the ground, about the height of a doll. My heart stopped cold.

They blinked once in the light, then were gone.

"Oh my God," I said. "There's something under there."

For a moment, John's flashlight lingered over the work bench, trembling. But nothing happened. Nothing moved.

"You saw it, didn't you?" I spun toward John, wide-eyed. "You saw those eyes?"

Jesus, was I losing my mind?

But John nodded very tightly, his eyes never leaving the dark space under the work bench. Slowly, he rose to his feet, and inched toward the bench.

"Don't!" My voice was practically a squeak.

"Carmen," John whispered, not looking back. "Get out of here. Now."

Larry immediately grabbed his bag and made for the door, whispering under his breath, "Oh shit, oh shit…"

Miguel beat Larry there, throwing open the door to the roaring night.

Instead of running, I reached for my camera. I sat where I was on the towel, recording John and trembling.

Very slowly, John crept over to the bench where we'd seen the eyes. He leaned closer, aiming the flashlight at the darkness underneath, the beam shaking.

All at once, the crates stacked under the bench toppled over with a crash, and some dark, imperceptible shape lunged out with a wail. John leapt back, swinging his flashlight wildly and falling on his ass in the dirt.

The flashlight fell across a yellow eye, and in the clarity of adrenaline and the graininess of night vision I discerned the rest of the creature.

It was a cat—desperately underfed, its upraised fur patched in gray, coiled amid the fallen boxes and swinging its tail in agitation.

The cat pounced with a hiss. John fell back, shielding his head with a cry; but the animal only leapt past him. Too fast to track with my camera, it skittered over the crooked floorboards, past Larry and out the open door, leaving the loose screen door swinging in its wake.

"Jesus!" John got to his feet. He brushed away dirt and a spider on his shoulder with a disgusted look. Then he tried to laugh it off. "I should've brought clean underwear."

The rest of us laughed as well—even Miguel. It was an awkward, grateful laughter, both embarrassed and relieved.

"Yeah," Larry said, coming back inside. "This place is gonna give me a damn heart attack."

"You okay?" I asked John.

He nodded, trying to appear nonchalant.

Narrating to my camera, I said, "Okay. Well, that was an interesting little bump in the night. Courtesy of—what, was that Don Julio's old cat or something?"

"Could've been feral," said John, shrugging. "About scared the shit out of me."

"Yeah." My heart rate was only just returning to normal.

Miguel came back into the house reluctantly, and Larry closed the door, smiling. "Should've seen your face," Larry told John. "What'd you think it was, a doll come to life?"

"Shut up!" John snapped, without humor. "You're the one who ran away."

I returned to my yellow beach towel, brushing away a thin spider crawling over it before I sat. As the fear and panic wore off, I was left with only rationality, and it was such a relief. All the pieces fit into place and the greatest fear—the fear of the unknown—began to recede.

"Larry," I said, "that cat is probably what touched you earlier, when you reached in the window. Don't you think?"

He chuckled softly. "Now that you mention it, I guess it felt kind of like a cat nuzzling my hand."

And it explained the eyes I'd seen in the darkness, right before we reached the shack. If there was one stray cat, there was probably a whole colony living on the island.

John sank back onto the towel beside me, grumbling, "Let's hope that's the last disturbance for the night."

Slowly, the tension leaked out of the tiny shack, like steam through the gaps in the wood slat walls. The cat's presence satisfied me more with each moment. It seemed to lend credence to my insistence that there was a rational explanation for everything. How many of the noises and incidents we'd witnessed on the island could be explained by a few feral cats? Probably a great deal, I told myself.

Hell, a determined cat could've even chewed through the rope on the boat. Unlikely, sure, but cats *were* assholes.

John wrapped his arm around me on the towel. It was

the first time we'd been this close in weeks.

At length, he asked, "You sorry you came here yet?"

I considered it a moment, yawning. "No," I scoffed. "What's to be sorry about? In the end, this is all just more footage. Poets gotta suffer for their art, you know?"

Those words would return to haunt me.

John said nothing. His thumb moved in slow circles on my shoulder through my sweater. Snuggling up to him, I let my head rest on his chest.

I lay awake a while, staring into the gloom of the ever-shrinking candlelight. The winds had died and silence reigned, broken here and there by a shrill animal call or the buzz of an insect.

I must have started to doze at last, for suddenly I found myself startled awake, lifting my head from John's chest and blinking in the gloom.

Something had disturbed my sleep.

It came again—a soft tapping on the screen door.

Sitting up, I glanced at my companions. Larry and John were asleep on their towels. Miguel was slumped against the wall in the corner, his eyes closed.

"Miguel?" I whispered. "You awake?"

He didn't respond.

The sound came again, rapping gently at the door. It sounded low to the ground. I figured it was the cat again, scratching to get in.

Slowly I rose to my feet, disoriented, still half-asleep. As I crept to the door, the pawing outside fell silent, as if waiting. I held the old brass handle for a moment, then wrenched the door open all at once, hoping to scare the cat off so it would leave us alone.

But when I opened the door, the cat wasn't there.

There was nothing outside at all.

The storm was over and the clouds had cleared out. The moon shone in the night sky, illuminating the little porch and Don Julio's buildings in the clearing. Beyond, darkness ruled under the trees. I could just make out the still, infantile silhouettes hanging high in the branches.

I looked around, frowning. Had I imagined the sound, after all?

Then I noticed something on the porch—a dark circle, just in front of the door.

A puddle.

I crouched to touch it, confirming it was water. The surrounding boards were white and dry as bones in the moonlight. I looked up at the cloudless sky and wondered where this moisture could have come from.

Then I saw another, smaller stain of water, a few feet away on the deck, followed by another, and another.

Footprints, I realized. Wet footprints. I could see them leading down the crooked stairs of the deck, through the muddy yard toward the center of the island. The tracks looked human, barefooted—and very small.

Swallowing, I stepped back and closed the door.

But when I turned, the walls of the cabin were gone.

I looked around, bewildered. Suddenly I was standing outside, in the woods at the center of the island. The thick juniper tree stood up ahead. The heart tree, Miguel had called it: the tree that had anchored the original floating garden that grew over centuries into *La Isla de las Muñecas*.

Someone stood at the foot of the tree.

It was a shapely young woman, dressed in sheer, flowing white. Her back was turned to me. Her long black hair was all around her, snapping in a wind I didn't feel.

Someone tugged my sleeve, and I looked down. At my

side stood a young Mexican girl. She was soaking wet, her brown hair hanging in her face, dripping into the grass. Her bare feet were half-buried in mud, though all the ground around her was dry. She wore blue jean overalls, and in her hands she held a doll that was almost as tall as she was. The girl's eyes were the same pale, faded blue as her doll's. I recognized it as the doll Rosita from the shrine in the cabin.

"Rosita," I murmured.

As I turned to look at her, the little girl stared through me, expressionless. But the doll in her arms craned its head to look up at me.

"She never sleeps…"

The voice seemed to come from inside my own head, like someone else's thought fully formed.

"Nothing heals in death… her madness only grows…"

Faintly, as if from underwater, I heard a female voice. As the sound came into focus, I realized it was weeping.

Slowly, as if with great effort, the woman under the tree began to turn. As she did, her dress darkened from white, to gray, to black, the lacey fabric turning torn and ragged.

Beside me, the dripping drowned girl tugged at my arm, staring straight ahead. The doll in her arms studied me with an appraising look.

"It may already be too late."

When I looked back, the woman under the tree was gone—but the soft weeping continued in the darkness.

I looked for the drowned little girl, but she, too, was gone. Only the coolness of her touch remained on my wet sleeve. I looked all around, searching the dark trees for her, breathing in shallow gasps. Silent dolls looked back at me, frozen in perpetual innocence.

The weeping voice surrounded me, more beautiful and powerful and haunting than any song I'd ever heard. I could hear other sounds inside the weeping—the same voice laughing, the same voice *singing*.

"John!" I screamed in panic, turning to run. "Larry!"

I turned to flee into the woods, but the way back to the shack seemed unfamiliar. As I spun in circles, I found myself facing the shore, near the dock. The place where Miguel said the girl and Don Julio had drowned.

The water was bubbling out there, dark and deep. Something was coming to the surface.

I turned—but when I tried to run, I couldn't lift my foot. My shoes were stuck in the thick gray mud of the lake bank, holding me in place.

Then a pale, skeletal hand reached up from the canal behind me, seizing my ankle in a deathly cold grip.

I screamed, kicking and tugging at the cold hand, but the bony fingers were impossibly strong. As I struggled, another hand reached out of the mud and seized my wrist, pulling me off balance, down into the marsh.

The last things I saw were the cold green surface of the water, rising up as I submerged with a final splash—and the pale, hollow smile of something waiting underneath.

Then cold darkness took me in her arms.

Chapter 11: Uninvited Guests

"Carmen!"

I awoke to Larry shaking me and hissing my name, and I sat up so fast he had to leap back to avoid being head-butted. Drenched in sweat, I gasped for breath and tried to regain my bearings.

We were still in the old shack. Thin, gray light filtered through the thick gaps in the walls.

That meant we'd made it through the night.

Larry crouched beside me, touching my shoulder. His big curly hair looked messy from sleep. "You all right?" he asked. "I can't believe you're sleeping through this."

"I was having a nightmare." I rubbed my eyes. Already I was starting to forget parts of the dream; but I felt wet with sweat all over, wet enough to make my sweater damp. As panic receded and I returned to my senses, I became aware of a commotion outside. "What's going on?"

Larry's full lips pursed in a frown. "Oh, nothing. Just your boyfriend and his usual, uh, diplomacy." Then he added, "Your nightmare's about to get a whole lot worse. We have some uninvited guests."

I swallowed, frowning. "What's that supposed to mean?"

Then I heard John raise his voice outside: *"I swear to God, if you're lying to me—!"*

And I realized Larry and I were alone in the cabin.

Miguel.

Pushing past Larry, I stood—and my shoes squished beneath me. I looked down to find the soles of my shoes caked with dark mud. Even the laces were smeared with it.

I didn't notice my shoes being so filthy when I went to sleep last night, and the mud seemed strangely wet. Fresh.

Was this mud from exploring the island yesterday—or from visiting the heart tree and the canal last night? Could my dream have been more real than I thought?

Before I could give it much thought, more shouting outside distracted me from my muddy shoes, and I rushed through the open door.

Outside, it was cold enough to make my breath frost. A thin, dewy fog lay over the island, obscuring the golden sun peeking through the trees on the eastern horizon.

John and Miguel were both in the yard out front. I stumbled out to the rickety porch railing in time to see John throw a punch, striking Miguel square in the jaw and knocking him flat. Miguel's straw hat flew in the air.

"No more lies!" John shouted, stooping over Miguel and aiming a finger at him. "Tell me what you're up to, *now!*"

Miguel cringed on the ground, raising a feeble hand in self-defense. Blood dripped from his forehead.

"John!" I shrieked, rushing down the stairs. With all my weight, I threw myself at him, hitting and pushing him; but with my size against his, it was like hitting a wall.

"What the hell are you *doing?*" I demanded.

Larry came out of the shack behind us, filming with his sleek handheld camcorder at his shoulder.

Glaring at me, John thrust an angry finger at Miguel. "This asshole's still fucking with us!"

On the ground at John's feet, Miguel looked dazed. In a sloppy, drunken way, he recovered his sombrero, pawing at the bloody gash on his forehead.

"Leave him alone!" I cried. "The hell is *wrong* with you?"

Larry came down the porch steps behind us, clearing his throat. "Uh, Carmen?"

I whirled toward Larry, bewildered and angry. He stood under the porch, recording something there. As I realized what it was, my jaw unclenched and hung open.

All at once I understood why they were fighting—and what Larry had meant by *uninvited guests*.

Four dolls sat in a row in the weeds at the foot of the porch, staring sightlessly into the distance.

One was a brown Mexican ragdoll in a straw hat.

One was a dark-skinned boy with a large black afro.

One was a bleached-white, bald baby boy with one blue eye.

The last was a little girl, her brown hair pulled back in a ponytail.

Exactly one doll for each of us, I realized. Even the clothes seemed to bear a vague resemblance to our own.

"What the hell?" I whispered, dumbfounded. "Were these here last night?"

"Hell no!" John fumed. "I didn't see them. Did you? No, this is *someone's* idea of a joke!" He glared at Miguel.

Miguel was getting to his feet, wobbling a little. "I had nothing to do with it."

"Yeah?" John said. "Then who left the dolls, huh?"

"I never even left the cabin!" Miguel jerked a hand at Larry. "He found them! Ask *him!*"

John turned to Larry. "Good point, Larry. You're the only one that left the cabin this morning."

Larry raised his hands, his camera still strapped to his palm. "I just came out to take a leak, and there they were."

John threw his hands in the air in frustration. "Well, *I* didn't go anywhere last night, and *you* didn't go anywhere till this morning. Did *you* leave the cabin?"

He spun, casting his accusing glare in my direction. I

swallowed, surprised. For a moment I wasn't sure what to say, because I'd *dreamed* of leaving the shack, dreamed of standing by the heart tree with the ghost of the drowned girl and... something else.

She never sleeps. Her madness only grows.

And there was mud on my shoes this morning.

Before I could respond, Miguel spoke for me angrily. "Did you *see* her leave? Did you see any one of us leave?"

"No," I scoffed at last, perhaps too forcefully. "I didn't go anywhere. I slept like a log. Your fighting didn't even wake me this morning."

"I barely slept at all!" Miguel shouted. The gash on his forehead was swelling into an angry knot the shape of John's knuckles, trickling blood. "Every noise, every tap of the trees, I heard it. I don't know if I slept more than ten minutes all night. And I tell you, *nobody* left that shack!"

"Then who put this shit here?" John demanded. "If you didn't do it, and there's no one else here, then who?"

Miguel looked back at him, unspeaking.

With a bitter laugh, John put his hands on his hips. "What, you think this is supernatural? I mean, is that what you expect us to believe? A *ghost* did it?"

Miguel avoided John's eyes, his expression one of cool, controlled rage. No one answered John, but his suggestion alone, voiced so nakedly, disturbed me. It seemed to echo in the silence, along with the voice of the girl in my dream:

It may already be too late.

"Guys," I said finally. "Listen. They must have been there all along, okay? It's the only explanation."

Same with the mud on my shoes. We'd traipsed all over the island yesterday. The mud on my shoes must have been there ever since, and I'd only just noticed this morning, when I looked.

But John rolled his eyes. "Oh, please. Did *you* see the dolls there last night?"

"No," I snapped. "But that doesn't mean they weren't there. I mean, look around. There are dolls *everywhere*. There must be a doll for every person on Earth. Can you honestly say you'd notice any particular dolls out of the bunch?"

"Uh, four dolls that look just like us?" John said. "Set up outside the building where we're sleeping—yeah, I think I'd have fucking noticed that, Carmen!"

While we argued, Miguel slinked past us. From the corner of my eye, I saw him approach the four dolls slumped in front of the sagging porch. Larry stepped back, still filming.

Miguel dropped to his knees before the row of dolls, and began to pray.

"Please, spirits," he mumbled in Spanish. "Have mercy on us. Forgive us our trespass and give us sanctuary from the restless dead."

John noticed my attention drifting over his shoulder. He followed my gaze to Miguel, and before I could stop him he stomped toward him.

"John, wait!"

"Enough of this!" John cried. He stormed past Miguel, swung his foot, and kicked the nearest doll—the one that looked like me—sending it flying into the brush.

"No!" Miguel cried, standing and backing off. "Stop!"

Grunting in rage, John kept kicking and stomping on the dolls. "Fuck this shit!" he shouted at the top of his lungs. His eyes roved through the trees, as if seeking a challenger there, some punching bag to absorb his fury. "I've had enough, you hear me?"

"Stop it!" Miguel tried to grab him—but John flung him down with a roar, looming over him while Miguel raised a hand from the ground.

"Please," he gasped. "Don't anger the spirits…"

By instinct, I wedged myself between them, breaking them up. It wasn't the first time I'd held John back from a fight. Grabbing his arm, I tugged him away from Miguel.

"Come on," I pleaded. "Don't mess shit up!"

John turned to glare at me, shrugging out of my grip with surprising force. "Why not?" he said, with a rough laugh. "You think I might *anger the spirits?*"

Blushing, I snapped, "You're the one being irrational!"

"Me?" John screamed, starting to turn red in the face. "Me, *I'm* irrational? You're talking about *dolls* protecting us from *angry spirits,* and *I'm* the irrational one?"

I shrank back, surprised. I'd seen John angry before, but not like this; not this wild, cornered-animal desperation.

Dumbfounded, I watched as he whirled on his heels and stooped to grab the nearest doll—the one wearing a straw hat, like Miguel's. The little, baby-sized hat fell off as John stormed past us, holding the doll by one leg.

Miguel's eyes widened in horror and dismay. Clutching his bloody forehead, he cried, "No, please!"

Miguel moved to stop John, but John was too fast, striding into the woods. Larry and I hurried after them, moving through the dawn dimness under the trees.

"You want protection?" John yelled. "How's *this* for protection?"

He reached the old pavilion above the canals and turned to us with an awful grin. Then he raised the doll in both hands, dropped and kicked it, punting it out over the water. It landed with a splash, several yards off shore, and sank slowly into the green algae.

"Protect *this!*" John shouted, flipping off Miguel, then the dolls in the trees. "Anyone who fucks with me, you'll end up just like that!" He pointed at the sinking doll.

Miguel lunged for John, grabbing his sweater by the collar. "Idiot! If you anger the spirits, we are all forsaken!"

With a look of pure disgust, John planted both hands on Miguel's chest and shoved him back easily. "Fuck you, fuck the *spirits*, and fuck these dolls. I'm—"

I walked up to John and slapped him, hard enough to turn his head.

Instantly I regretted it. He turned to stare at me, his blue eyes locking on mine with enough ice to set my heart racing at an even faster tempo.

"John," I said. "You need to stop. Take a breath."

Slowly, his hand went to his reddened cheek. "Did you just hit me?" he said, his voice low and incredulous. "Tell me you didn't just hit me."

Larry came to my side, lowering his camera. "What, you gonna hit her back, bro? Make her *take her medicine?*"

John's eyes never left mine. They were angry, but it was the hurt in them that made me look away.

"Sorry," I said. "I'm just... we're *all* stressed out, okay? Can we all just calm down for one minute? Okay? Both of you, just back up a step."

Still glaring up at John, Larry took one step back to appease me. John scowled at me a moment longer, then turned, waving a hand. "Do what you want. I'm done."

He went up the crooked stairs to the pavilion above the pier and leaned against a post with his arms crossed, staring into the foliage. Larry shook his head, glowering at me and raising his camera again. "Sorry you brought that asshole yet?" Larry muttered.

I avoided Larry's accusatory gaze, looking over my shoulder at Miguel. Miguel stood on the pier, still looking despondently at the canal, where the doll had gone under.

"Look," I said, gathering my thoughts. "We're all tired, we're all hungry, we're all a little spooked, right? So isn't it possible that maybe we're not thinking clearly? Letting our imaginations run away with us a bit?"

"Damn it, Carmen," John muttered, "if those dolls had been there before, we would've seen them. You're a goddamn filmmaker. Aren't you supposed to have an eye for detail? How could you have missed that?"

The comment stung, but I refused to rise to it. "I don't know where those dolls came from," I admitted. "I don't care. All I know is we have enough to worry about without fighting. Can we just focus on getting out of here?"

Larry moved closer, still filming. "Definitely," he said. "What'd you have in mind?"

I looked around, considering it. "Now that it's day, we should move camp down here on the dock, so if a boat passes in the canal, we can flag them down. Right?"

"Yeah," Larry said. "Makes sense to me."

John said nothing, still leaning sullenly on a post at the top of the stairs and staring at the canal.

Miguel sat on the pier, gingerly touching his bloody scalp and looking at the doll heads fixed on the pilings of the dock. *"Desamparado,"* he mumbled, shaking his head. He sounded close to tears. *"Desamparado."*

Forsaken.

The word chilled me. "Come on, Miguel," I said. "It's all right. Let's go bring our stuff down here. We're gonna get off this damned island, okay?"

But in my mind, the voice of the ghost in my dream still echoed:

It may already be too late.

Chapter 12: Forsaken

In sullen silence, the four of us returned to the shack. John led the way, stomping through the foliage. Larry and I followed, Larry still filming. Last came Miguel, hanging back, his bruised face twisted in a scowl.

Dawn struggled to penetrate the thick canopy of fern leaves and ruined dolls. The pre-dawn fog burned away with every minute, and the sky looked clear and dry. Birds began to sing over the canals and the insects buzzed.

As we approached the house, I saw the three remaining dolls, scattered about around the porch where John had kicked them in his tantrum. John spat at the ground as he passed, hurrying up the stairs and shoving through the door of the shack.

For the first time in what seemed like ages, I had time to gather my thoughts. I stood in the yard for a moment, looking at the dolls. The one that looked like me was lying at the edge of the trees where John had kicked her, her rose red lips parted slightly in perpetual baby innocence, her soft brown eyes staring through me.

John had a point. How could I have missed these dolls here the night before? And if they weren't here already, then how had they gotten here?

Miguel came into the yard, avoiding everyone's eyes and holding a handkerchief to his bloodied scalp. Once again I wondered—could John be right? Could Miguel be messing with us?

But even if he could be blamed for the lost boat and the overnight appearance of these dolls, what about the mud on my shoes? Had *that* been there before last night?

I tried to push these thoughts away. If I thought about it too long, I'd only scare myself into more irrational thinking. A strong person, a strong *director,* wouldn't think this way. I had to stay focused. Whatever was happening on the island didn't matter; all that mattered now was escaping with our lives and our footage.

After a moment, I went back inside the shack. While John and Larry gathered our things in sulky silence, I went to the other side of the one-room shanty, to inspect the shrine of the drowned girl's doll. The layers of dust and cobwebs said the doll hadn't been moved in some time.

This calmed me a little. Of course it hadn't moved. When I'd seen it last night, in the arms of the drowned girl, that had only been a dream.

Focus.

I slung my backpack over my shoulder and left the shack of Don Julio, hoping it would be the last time.

With our supplies in tow, we made our way back to the dry-rotted pavilion overlooking the dock. The sun was shining, but last night's thunder had brought a change in temperature, and it was much colder than the other day. Autumn had arrived, even here in Mexico.

Back at the dock, I stood above the pier, filming the silent green waters. "Today is Sunday," I said, turning to Miguel. "Isn't that a big day for the canals? Locals and tourists all come out on Sundays."

He met my eyes sullenly. *"Sí."*

"Someone has *got* to come through here," I said, as brightly as I could. "All we have to do is wait."

Standing under the pavilion, John slapped his neck loudly, rubbing away a smear of blood that was formerly a mosquito. "And what do we do in the meantime?" He glared at Miguel. "Just stand here and wait for whatever your buddy's got in store for us next?"

"How about breakfast?" I suggested. "Would that calm you down?"

John laughed unpleasantly. "Maybe if we had any. We ate all the trail mix last night." Crouching, he opened his backpack and rooted through it. "I got two protein bars. Peanut butter and chocolate chip. Who wants what?"

Larry looked up from his camera to scowl at John, no longer making the effort to hide his distaste. "They call this a floating *garden*. Surely there's food somewhere?"

Down on the pier, Miguel leaned on one of the pilings. Through a reluctant sigh, he said, "He's right. Don Julio grew food on this island. Maybe food still grows."

Adjusting his straw hat, he climbed the stairs of the dock, passed through the pavilion and into the woods.

Lowering my camera slightly, I said, "John, don't you know about edible plants?"

John rolled his eyes and stomped after Miguel, leaving the pavilion. "Here," he said, pointing at a thicket of bushes near the bank. "These blackberries are nice and overripe. Probably not the tastiest, but hey."

Miguel moved cautiously closer, reached into the thicket, and plucked out a small, soft berry. He put it in his mouth, chewed slowly. His eyebrows rose. "Not bad."

"Yeah," John muttered. "You're welcome."

I turned off my camera and joined them at the bush, taking care of the sharp thorns as I picked a few berries. The fruit was soft and mushy, dying on the vine, with a bitter, earthy sweetness, but I didn't care. I was ravenous.

Miguel picked berries beside me. I watched him from the corner of my eye, still wondering if he could be trusted.

He caught me looking and I forced a smile. "Sorry," I said, gesturing at the ugly scab on his forehead. "He shouldn't have hit you."

Miguel's eyes skittered away from mine. "He shouldn't have kicked the doll," he muttered.

I frowned. Was his superstition real? Or all play-acting?

Clearing my throat, I said, "John has some first-aid stuff in his pack. I can take a look at that cut for you."

His small smile returned, but it didn't touch his eyes. *"Gracias, señorita."*

Larry set his camera up on the tripod and joined us, picking berries. John sat under the pavilion, staring out at the canal.

Suddenly John leaped to his feet, crying out. "Whoa—hey!" He turned to us with wide-eyed surprise, waving with one hand and pointing at the canal with the other.

I swallowed the last handful of mushy berries, leaving dark juice on my palm, and bolted back to the pavilion. As the canal came into view, I saw what John had seen.

A boat was coming down the waterway.

Beyond the open span of water in front of the dock, the canal narrowed in the distance, where it intersected with a larger thoroughfare. Out there, past the reedy marshland, a colorful *trajinera* passed slowly through the intersection. As it drew closer, I could even hear the faint trumpeting of *mariachi* music.

"Oh," I said, starting to grin. "Oh, thank God."

"What is it?" Larry cried, running after me.

"It's a boat!" I shouted.

John was already out on the dock, waving his arms in the air and shouting. "Hey!" he cried. "Hey, over here!" His voice bellowed over the open space.

I sprang down the steps to join him, crying in Spanish: "Help us! Help us, please!"

Even as we started to shout, a cold wind moved over the island, swallowing our voices. Miguel joined us on the dock, then Larry, both shouting. But the wind only grew louder, shaking the trees. The groaning of the trunks sounded almost human.

Despite our cries, the *trajinera* kept drifting down the canal. As it came into the open, crossing the intersection, I could see the tiny shapes of the people on the boat.

"Can you hear us?" I shouted in Spanish. "Please! We're stranded! We need help!"

I couldn't hear their music anymore, over all the wind and shouting. Had they stopped playing because they'd heard us, I wondered? Would the boat turn down into the little cove, to save us?

"Please!" I shouted. "They *have* to hear us."

But the boat didn't turn down our tributary. It kept going through the intersection, passing us by. The tiny people under the boat's roof didn't even look our way.

"Where are they going?" Larry cried.

"No!" John roared. "God damn you Mexicans, are you fucking deaf?"

Miguel took a step back, supporting himself on one of the dock pilings, as if he were about to swoon. "It's no use," he muttered. "They can't hear us."

"Hey!" I screamed, my voice breaking. *"Hola! Hola!"*

Larry put a hand on my shoulder. "Don't hurt yourself."

The boat was almost out of sight now, drifting through the reeds. As it faded from view, the wind seemed to quiet again and the trees grew still around us.

"God damn it!" John roared. He found the head of a doll, mounted on one of the pilings, and hurled it into the water, sending it skipping over the dark surface.

Miguel advanced on John, his gapped teeth bared in a snarl. "Stop! Don't you get it, *baboso?* It's *your* fault they can't hear us! Your fault we're forsaken!"

John didn't give an inch, shouting in Miguel's face, "You're the one that lost the boat!"

"You've angered the spirits," Miguel said, lowering his voice. "Now we may never leave."

John scoffed. "What's that supposed to mean?"

Finally, I snapped. Spinning toward them, I screamed, "Shut up! Shut up! *Shut up!* Do you think all your fighting helps a damn thing?"

"I don't understand," Larry said. "How did they not hear us? We could hear their music and everything."

Leaning on one of the pilings, I stared out at the water, rippling slightly in the last whispers of wind.

"It was like they didn't even *want* to look at us." I frowned. "Remember back in Xochimilco? Some of the boatmen we asked to take us here said they wouldn't even *look* at the island if they passed it, for fear of being cursed."

Larry smirked humorlessly. "They probably thought they were hearing spirits, calling to them. Probably scared the shit out of them."

"Maybe," Miguel muttered, behind us. "Or maybe the island doesn't want us to be heard."

John turned toward him, raising a finger. "One more word like that and I'll mess you up for real. You hear? I ain't fucking playing this game! No more bullshit, son!"

His words were angry, but the look on his face was one I'd never seen on John—a look of desperate fear.

"John," I said, with compassion as much as appeal. "For the last time. Leave him alone."

He glared at me. "Or what?"

Larry moved up to join us, on Miguel's other side. His voice was low, deep, and quiet. "Or you might find yourself getting voted off the island, bro."

John turned to look at Larry, and his expression faded

into contempt. Without a word, he spun on his heel, stalking away to the other side of the dock and pacing there like a caged animal.

When John backed off, Miguel sighed and sagged down to sit on one of the pilings. He held his face in his hands.

"Desamparado," he whispered again under his breath.

Forsaken.

I swallowed, frowning. "There must be some way to get a boat's attention."

Across the small dock, John snorted in derision. I raised an eyebrow his direction. "What's so funny?"

"You want to vote me off the island." His voice was light with a sort of unhinged amusement. "But you'd all be helpless without me, and you know it."

"If you have something to add—"

"A signal fire," he growled. "What we need is a signal fire. If we do it right, that'll get their attention, maybe for miles around. But since when did we ever do things right?"

I blinked at him, surprised. A smile bloomed on my face. "Yes," I whispered. "A fire. That's exactly what we need."

"Yeah," Larry laughed softly. He was looking at the head of a baby doll, pinned on one of the pilings. "A fire big enough to burn the whole thing to the ground."

"That, *bro*, is one thing we'd agree on," John said grimly.

I smiled, my hope restored. "Yes. A fire sounds like a start. Good thinking, John."

He nodded, looking somewhat suspicious of the praise.

Then, from the corner of my eye, I noticed Miguel. He was still slumped atop one of the pilings, like some old gargoyle in a tattered straw hat. His hands hung limp in his lap, and his eyes stared over the pier, a million miles away.

My smile faded. "Miguel?" I asked. "Did you hear? We're going to make a signal fire."

He nodded. "Yes," he said, his voice dry.

My chest tightened. Why was he not cheered by the prospect of the fire?

Forsaken. I heard his word in my head, like a curse.

"They'll see a fire, won't they?" I don't know why I needed his approval so badly—but I did. "They'll come if they see a fire?"

Miguel smiled, uncertain. He glanced past me to John, who stood at the end of the dock with his hands on his hips, glaring at us. Miguel said, "Maybe, *señorita.* Maybe."

Gently, he stepped past me, going wide around John on his way back to the pavilion above the pier. I watched him go. I was certain he'd wanted to say something more before he'd seen John watching and thought better of it.

I thought I knew what he was thinking, because the thought had also occurred to me.

Supposing that there *was* some force, as Miguel believed, that had kept those people on the boats from hearing us— if that force, whatever it was, could keep those people from hearing us, could it also keep them from seeing a fire?

And against that kind of power, what could anyone do?

It may already be too late.

Was it even possible for us to be saved? Or was it true, what Miguel had said?

Were we already forsaken?

Chapter 13: Fuel

It was already almost noon by the time we got to work building a fire. Watching the *trajinera* sail past had been another hard blow to morale, but I refused to give in to despair or irrational thinking.

We regrouped at the pavilion. John found a large rake amidst the stacks of junk and cleared a space beside the pavilion overlooking the canal. He squatted, inspecting the ground.

"I brought matches," he said. "But we're gonna need some fuel. There was firewood by the old man's shack. With any luck, it's dry."

"Right." I nodded. "I'll go back for wood, then. Larry? You want to come with me?"

Larry shrugged. "Sure."

"Whoa," John said, "you're not going anywhere."

I was getting sick of his overprotective routine. "Then how are we supposed to get the firewood, honey?" I asked, with cloying sweetness.

John rose to his feet. "Let Miguel get it. Prove he's worth something other than losing boats."

"Unlike you, Miguel actually speaks Spanish," I said, with as much patience as I could muster. "I thought he could stay with you, in case a boat comes?"

"You speak Spanish, too," said John.

In a low voice, I added, "I thought you'd want to keep an eye on him."

"Really?" John said. "That's why you want to go off in the woods with Larry?"

"Would you rather I go alone?" I couldn't believe he was letting his petty insecurities cloud his judgment—now, of all times.

"I don't want you out of my sight," John growled. "I don't trust Larry. I don't trust Miguel. I don't even know if I should trust you anymore."

I narrowed my eyes. "What's that supposed to mean?"

From the pavilion, Larry interrupted. "Guys, all I know is I am *not* spending another night on this island. Which means we need a signal fire. Which means we need wood. So…"

He unslung his backpack, turning off his camera.

"I'll go get some wood. You guys figure out the rest."

"Wait," John said. *"I'll* go. I want to look around again anyway, see if there's anything else we can use." He turned to me. "You're coming with me. Larry, Miguel, you can stay and watch for boats. Got it?"

"Who put you in charge?" I asked softly.

He glared. "This isn't about your little documentary anymore, Carmen. This is about survival."

I sighed, waving him to lead on. "Have it your way."

Larry and Miguel exchanged wary glances. Then Larry rolled his eyes and took off his backpack. "Whatever."

John glanced over his shoulder as he left the pavilion. "Don't turn your back on him," he advised.

The two of us set off into the woods, under the eerie, constant vigil of the dolls. John moved brashly, traipsing through the dead leaves and branches.

I scowled at his back. "You know, you don't have to be such an asshole all the time."

"Me?" he growled, still keeping his voice low.

"Oh, you want to go off in the woods with Larry? Really? I'm

just trying to get us off this island. I mean, I agree. This is a serious situation, okay? A *life or death* situation. This is *not* the time to air our dirty laundry."

John stopped, looking back at me. "Then when is the time, Carmen? You said we'd talk about you and me and instead all I'm getting is the world's worst beach party!"

"I said we *might* talk about it, when I got back."

"Well, we're talking about it now," he said.

"And *you're* the one that insisted on coming on this trip—for what? To make sure I don't sleep with Larry? You know how ridiculous and insecure that is?"

"Oh, please. I've seen how Larry looks at you."

"Yeah, you're one to talk," I snapped. "Drooling over every piece of ass at the airport. And let's not forget who started all this."

I didn't want to get into this now, not with so much else to worry about. I'd hoped to put off this conversation till after the trip—or maybe forever—but John was right. It seemed we were talking about it now.

"I mean, you think *you* feel paranoid?" Suddenly all the force had left my voice. "You think *you* feel insecure?"

"Yeah, but Carmen, I apologized! I know I made a mistake, going to that party to begin with, and baby, if I could go back in time—"

"Don't *baby* me. And sorry doesn't fix it, John."

"I know that, but look—I'm *trying*. I'm trying to make it work. I'm trying to move forward. And what are you doing? Going off on a romantic trip to Mexico?"

"Oh, it's been *so* romantic, hasn't it?"

"That guy has wanted to bang you since the day he met you."

"Larry is my friend. Nothing more."

"God, you're so naïve."

"And you're such a Neanderthal asshole! All I wanted was to make a film."

"Yeah, your precious *film*. You still put your little project with Larry over everything else. Including us." Glaring at me, he asked point-blank, *"Are* you the one fucking with us? Losing the boat, all that shit?"

It upset me that he'd even ask; maybe that was the point. "Of course not!"

"You sure? You didn't, like, pay Miguel to bring us out here and then sabotage the trip? You keep saying how it's going to be such *good footage.*"

It was the final straw. All I could do was stare at him, feeling the tears well in my eyes. His face softened slightly and I hated him for it, hated him for his pity. But that *was* his cycle, wasn't it? Brashness, then regret. Destruction, then sorrow for what's lost.

I turned away so he wouldn't see me start to cry.

"Sorry I'm so *obsessed,*" I muttered petulantly, fighting back tears. "I'm sorry for having a dream."

He rolled his eyes. "Carmen, I understand that," John said, "but you need to understand how *I* feel."

"How *you* feel? For God's sake, John, you cheated on me! Or are you forgetting?"

"Because I *needed* someone, Carmen! It was just a kiss, some drunk girl at a party that *you* were too busy to attend. Why? Because you were studying movies with *Larry.*"

"From what Linda told me, it was more than a kiss."

"Linda doesn't know shit."

"Oh? And the girl at the gym that day, telling you to call her? She was just *drunk*, too, right?"

"Carmen, I know you were hurt. I get it, okay? Some

drunk girl kissed me who I don't even know and I'll never see again. So you invited Larry to Mexico."

I started to argue his version of the facts, but he raised a hand to stop me, and frankly I was out of breath anyway.

"I get it," John continued. "I understand why you did it. But now we have to move forward. *That's* why I came on this trip. Because I thought we agreed I was gonna support your hobbies and you were gonna make more time for us. Right? That's why I came. To support you. And to be together."

He took a step closer, taking my hand in his. I looked up into his blue eyes uncertainly.

"That's the honest truth." His voice was much calmer now. He smiled. "And I need you to start being honest with me."

I felt my face tighten. "I've always been honest with you, John. I've always been there for you. Don't try to make what you did into my fault."

"I'm not talking about the past. I don't care about that. I don't care about Larry. I just want the truth."

Tugging my hand out of his grip, I stared at him coolly for a moment. "John, I'm *telling* you the truth. Whatever's happening on this island, I have nothing to do with it."

That seemed to satisfy him. With a thoughtful nod, he frowned at the canal, beyond the tiny dock. I wondered what he was thinking.

Was that fear in his eyes?

Finally he straightened, reaching a decision. "It must be Miguel, then, like I thought. Let's hope Larry keeps an eye on him. Come on, I think it's just up here."

The trees parted and we entered the overgrown yard of Don Julio. Even in the high noon sun, it looked dismal. The air seemed thicker here, harder to breathe.

I followed John into the clearing, feeling the eyes of the dolls all around me. Unable to help myself, I removed my backpack and took out my camera.

"Here's the firewood," John said quietly. He squatted by the knee-high stack of knotted wood, covered in a blue tarp at the foot of the shack porch. He slid out a log, raised it, and kissed it lightly. "Feels dry. But there's not much for a signal fire." He looked around, his heavy brow knotting. "I wonder if there's any more."

He started wandering around the side of the house, cautiously. I followed him, filming. "Careful," I said.

At the back of the house, a torn awning spanned out from the rooftop, covering a cluttered patio area. Empty milk cartons and other piles of debris, half-covered in tarps, were stacked against a back wall strewn with dolls and fishing nets.

As John prodded around in the clutter with his foot, I turned my camera toward the ramshackle barn, a few yards away. The double doors were open, sagging from their rusted hinges. Filtered sunlight fell on the interior through the fallen back wall.

Curiosity got the better of me, and I figured John was right behind me. I moved closer to the barn, filming.

Inside, more rusted farming gear leaned against the walls, including a wheelbarrow missing one handle. Bales of hay stood in columns, like snowmen, spaced irregularly throughout the barn. As I frowned at one, I noticed a small, feathered rod, jutting out of the thick hay.

"Carmen?"

Startled, I whirled, but of course it was only John. He stood a few feet behind me, in the doorway of the half-fallen barn. He was grinning and waving impatiently.

"The hell are you doing now? Come here!"

I followed him out as he returned to the awning at the back of the shack. There was something big there, hidden under a tarp amidst the clutter. John pulled the tarp away to reveal what looked like a car engine in a rusted square frame. Empty red gasoline cans fell over beside it with a hollow clatter.

"What is it?" I asked doubtfully.

"Pretty sure it's a vintage, Mexican gas generator. Look, these are some kind of weird old electrical sockets."

"Won't fit anything we have," I said.

"No," John conceded, "but, look at this." He opened a cap on the side and took a whiff, recoiling a bit. "Oh, yeah. There's gas in here, baby. I bet I can siphon it out if we can find a bit of hose."

I gestured back at the barn. "There's some more farm equipment in there."

We returned to the barn, John moving purposefully, me hanging back and recording. Again I noticed the hay-stacks, the feathered bolt jutting from one of them.

"What do you think these haystacks are for?" I asked.

John paid me no mind. "Hey, this is perfect." He grabbed a loop of garden hose. "Carmen, think you can get that wheelbarrow? We can haul the wood and gas."

"I'll try," I said irritably, putting my camera in my bag.

The wheelbarrow was brown with rust and missing one handle, shoved up against a cobweb-covered shelf. I tugged it gingerly, trying not to grip it too tightly, as if full contact might infect me with something. It didn't budge until I gave it a mighty jerk, ripping it away from the wall.

A wooden case fell from the shelf, spilling open on the dirt floor with a metallic clamor. More iron bolts rolled out, like the one in the haystack, along with a cross-shaped apparatus of splintered wood and steel. As I frowned down at it, I realized what it was.

I stood. "I'll be damned."

John looked back in the doorway. "Everything okay?"

I turned to him. "Is this... a crossbow?"

The wooden stock was dry-rotted and the steel bow at the end looked crooked, as if the weapon had seen many years of abuse. I ran my thumb over the curious emblem painted on the stock, so faded and peeled it was almost unrecognizable. It looked almost like an old coat of arms.

I felt like I'd seen the emblem somewhere before, but I couldn't place it. I figured it was just déjà vu.

John came closer. "Whoa! Where'd *that* come from?"

"It was at the back of this shelf. You think it belonged to Don Julio?" I gestured at the straw bales. "Looks like someone was doing target practice, doesn't it?"

John's brow furrowed again. "I thought Don Julio was a religious man. What would he want with a crossbow?"

"Especially since a weapon like this would be illegal in Mexico," I muttered. "He must've thought he needed to protect himself. But from what?"

Gently, John took it from my hands, looking vaguely impressed as he inspected it. "My dad has a composite crossbow. Bought it from Outdoor Pro. But *this* looks like it was made by a blacksmith a thousand years ago."

"Maybe it was just a souvenir," I said uneasily.

John shrugged. "Well, that's about all it's good for at the moment. It's broken. See?" He pulled the wire down toward the notch in the shaft, but it didn't catch. "Might be fixable, but..."

He placed the crossbow in the wheelbarrow.

"First thing's first, let's get our fuel."

Chapter 14: The Cross and the Coquita

We piled our supplies on the broken wheelbarrow. Then John pushed it on its crooked wheel through the woods back to the dock.

As the pavilion came into sight through the trees, I saw Miguel and Larry standing under it, facing the water, their backs turned to us. Larry was filming the water. Over the creaking wheel of the wheelbarrow, I heard Miguel talking in a low voice, but didn't catch the words.

John set the wheelbarrow down with a clank at the edge of the pavilion, and they both turned. "Interrupting something, boys?" John asked.

Larry came over. "Miguel was talking more legends," he said, in a bored way. Before I asked, he held up his little camera, strapped to his palm. "Don't worry, I got it."

"Here's what *we* got," John said. He started taking out the red gas cans he'd siphoned from the generator, setting them in the grass.

"Whoa," said Larry. His eyes trailed from the gas cans to the firewood and other gear piled on the wheelbarrow.

"Yeah." John grinned. "Won't have to worry about getting a fire started. If anything we'll have to worry about keeping it under control."

Gathering firewood under his arm, John went to the space he'd cleared earlier in the grass beside the pavilion and started to stack the wood in a neat pyramid. "Guys, look around for some sticks for kindling. Get some wetter stuff, too. Keeps the smoke nice and thick."

Larry set his camera on a crate under the pavilion. "See any boats?" I asked.

He shook his head. "None yet."

I drew a breath. "Well, good. Now when one *does* come, we'll have a fire, so they can't miss us."

John continued emptying the firewood and tools we'd scavenged off the cart, while Larry and I gathered up dry kindling. It felt good to turn my mind off for a moment.

Miguel lingered by the shore, staring out forlornly at the canal, waiting for a boat with the single-mindedness of a dog waiting for a man to come home.

When we'd built a small campfire, John used Don Julio's rusted shovel to dig a trench and turn over the dry grass around it, just in case it spread. Then he spritzed gasoline on the wood, lit a match, and dropped it.

The fire roared to life, consuming the dry leaves and kindling in a blaze. As it spread over the wood, it settled into a bright, even flame. Smoke rose from it in a thick, curling tendril, reaching up through the tree canopy.

"Awesome!" I cried. John and Larry smiled wearily.

"What now?" asked Larry.

John put his hands on his hips, catching his breath. "Now we see if the next boat manages to miss us."

"So just wait?" Larry said doubtfully. He rubbed his stomach with a dark sigh. "Guess it's more blackberries."

"Actually," John said. "How'd you like some fish?" He went back to the wheelbarrow.

Larry scowled. "Like you found *fish* back there?"

"Better." John grinned as he pulled out two slender fishing rods. "I'll teach *you* to find fish."

Larry groaned. I smiled. "At least it'll pass the time."

John brought me, Larry, and the rods down to the dock. John held up one rod, letting out some of the line. Miguel watched us from the steps, content to be ignored.

"These are fly rods," John explained. "You ever do any fishing, Larry?"

Larry shrugged sheepishly. "Not really. You know, played a few video games about it."

John's eyebrows rose slowly. "Yeah. Well, it's not that hard. Fly fishing is a little different from using regular bait. There's no weight or tackle, so you're using the weight of the line itself to cast. You want to swing it in an arc, like a whip, almost. Watch."

He took a step forward, swinging the old fishing rod. The heavy line looped over his head and unraveled over the marshes, out into the canal. John frowned.

"Not much length to the line, anyway. I like to let it drift a minute or two, reel it in slow, and try again. Here." He handed the long rod to me and grabbed the other, holding it between his thighs as he tied another hairy fake fly to the line. "You try it."

Larry took the rod reluctantly, and gave an awkward swing over his head. The fly sagged limply in front of him.

"Pull it back smooth," said John. "Don't snap it, you'll lose the fly. Just let the line unravel behind you, then flick it forward. It's all in your wrist."

I trolled the line through the marshes for a moment, then brought it in and recast it. Don Julio's old bamboo rod was less supple than the ones I'd used before, but I put the fly more or less where I intended.

Larry gaped at my cast. I shrugged, smiling. "Let's just say this isn't the first time John's taken me fishing. That used to be his idea of a romantic date."

"What girl doesn't love a picnic?" John grumbled. He climbed the dock stairs, shooting Miguel a cold glance as he passed him where he sat on the steps. Then John stood on the ridge above the pier, by the fire.

"I didn't mind the fishing picnics," I admitted. "Better than the *no* dates we have now."

"You know, talking scares the fish away?" John said.

"Except for *that,*" I growled. "I hated hearing that."

Nestling my rod against the railing, I lowered my backpack and got out my camera. Then I turned it on and set it on the dock behind me to record us.

"Other than that, fishing's not so bad. Kinda relaxing. Gives us something to do while we wait for a boat."

Eventually, Larry managed to cast his line out into the canal. He leaned against the railing of the pier, scowling at the dolls adorning the pilings. "Nothing relaxing about any of this," he muttered.

Larry let his fly drift, probably scared to cast it again. I reeled and recast mine, again and again, in different parts of the canal, but the only thing biting was the mosquitoes.

In the silence, I noticed an odd clicking sound behind me. When I turned, I saw a fat little bird with marbled gray feathers, about the size and shape of a dove, perched in a tree branch a little further down the bank. It fluttered its wings and I saw a flash of crimson red underneath.

"What kind of bird is that?" I asked Miguel.

Stirring from his sullen trance, Miguel said softly, "We call it a *coquita*. Very common on the canals."

I smiled, delighted. "That was Don Julio's nickname in Xochimilco!" Propping up my rod again, I grabbed my camera to zoom in on the bird. "Handsome little guy."

Behind me, Larry was much less enthused. The wind had finally pushed his line back in. As he reeled it in, he said, "Is this really the only way we're going to eat today?"

John answered, "Maybe not the only way."

I looked up. John stood by the fire, on the bank above the dock, holding the broken crossbow.

Miguel looked over, unfolding his arms slowly. "What is that?" he asked. "Don Julio had that?"

"I know, right?" John said. "Not the kinda cross you'd expect a good Christian to carry. But the guy's got a whole target range in a barn back there. My dad would love it."

Coming closer, Miguel crouched by the wooden box that held the crossbow bolts. John took a step back, eyeing Miguel mistrustfully. "What are you doing?"

Miguel picked up the box, turning it over. The same little emblem I'd seen on the crossbow was also painted on the case, faded and scratched to almost nothing. Miguel ran his finger over it.

"This seal," he said. "I know this seal."

Leaving my fishing rod propped at the pier, I grabbed my camera and climbed the stairs to join them by John's fire. I leaned closer, looking over Miguel's shoulder with my camera as he studied the faded seal.

The emblem was in the shape of a shield, split into four quadrants, with another striped shield in the middle. The four quadrants bore a two-headed bird, a set of three crowns, a lion, and a kingdom on a blue shore.

"The same seal is on the crossbow," I said. "I feel like I've seen it somewhere else, too, but I'm not sure where."

John sat on the edge of the pavilion, a few feet away. He glanced briefly at the emblem on the stock of the bow, then continued to jigger at the trigger mechanism with his pocket knife.

I turned to Miguel. "What is it?"

In a hushed voice, Miguel said. "It's a coat of arms, given to Hernán Cortés when he conquered Mexico."

"No," I said. "For real?"

Miguel nodded, running his fingertips over the ancient crossbow case. "I'm certain," he said, in a hushed voice—

almost afraid. "This is the mark of Cortés. How did Don Julio come by such a thing?"

As if in answer, the *coquita* bird clucked on its branch above us, tilting its head.

Suddenly Larry cried out on the dock behind us. I spun, expecting a boat—God, let it be a boat!

Instead, Larry was tugging on the fishing rod, which was bent near in half in his hands. I saw a ripple, cascading out on the surface by his fly.

"Whoa!" he shouted. "Think I got something!"

Even as he spoke, the rod bent further and Larry stumbled, saved from falling in only by the railing. I rushed back to the dock, but it was too late. Larry tugged back—and the line snapped with a loud *pop*, sending Larry sprawling on the dock. The broken fishing line draped the railing, clinging with moss.

"Damn it, Larry," John groaned. "There are only so many flies. You gotta pull it in *gently!*"

Larry stood up, looking at me helplessly. "That thing felt huge! There was no way I could've reeled that in."

I giggled a little. "These rods are small. You'll feel it, for sure." Setting down my camera, I took another of the fake flies from the tackle box John had found. The flies looked hand-strung, woven with gray strands of human hair—Don Julio's, I imagined. "Here, I'll tie your line. If I remember how…"

"Don't bother," Larry sighed. "It's hopeless. We're never gonna eat anything."

Something *thrummed* behind us, followed by a soft, high-pitched squawk. I gasped and looked back, my eyes tracking a soft flutter of red wings as the *coquita* fell from its branch, its fat breast nearly split in half by an iron rod.

John held the bow, grinning. "Guess I fixed it. Maybe

you won't be eating, Larry, but I'll be having pigeon."

"Seriously?" Larry cried, annoyed.

Squatting, John picked up the bolt, examining the fat little bird skewered on it with a laugh. "Just messing with you. Won't be much, but there's pigeon for all."

Returning to the fire, he set about plucking out the bloody feathers. I grabbed my camera and came back to the pavilion, followed by Larry.

"I need some Y-shaped sticks," said John.

"You're really gonna eat that?" Larry said doubtfully. "What if there's, like, diseases or something?"

John rolled his eyes. "If you'd rather go hungry, that's fine. More for me."

Larry's eyes drew down. "Yeah, right."

I was a little horrified for the bird, but that faded as John started to roast it, using the crossbow bolt as a spit and turning it slowly. The savory, chicken-like smell made my mouth water, and my stomach reminded me in a long, low grumble that I hadn't eaten a real meal in a day now.

The *coquita* wasn't a real meal, either, especially split four ways; but as I ate my greasy, half-charred morsels with greedy abandon, I didn't think I'd ever felt more grateful.

Afterward, we sat together around the fire, wiping our bloody fingers in the grass, for the moment content.

"Thanks, John," I said afterward. "That hit the spot."

Smiling, he reached out and held my hand.

"Yeah." Larry patted his belly. "Gotta hand it to you, man. I was afraid what we'd do if we were stuck here much longer."

"Don't worry," I said, my optimism refueled by the warm fire and a full belly. "A boat will come any minute now."

John took a belt from his blue dry bag and fashioned a strap for the crossbow, shoving bolts through the holes in the belt. He fastened the belt across his shoulder like a bandolier, the crossbow on his back. When he caught me eyeing him, he shrugged. "What? I might as well keep it. Might be useful."

I rolled my eyes. "Just put it back when we leave."

Miguel said nothing. He sat a little away from the rest of us on a rickety stool under the pavilion, still looking out at the water. He kept startling at every animal sound, every rustle of the wind in the trees.

As the rest of us lounged by the fire, the afternoon reached its golden peak and began to wane. Shadows lengthened under the trees, crawled sluggishly out from under the dolls. With the shadows returned my doubts.

"Any minute now," I said again, my voice hollow. The optimism of lunch had turned to fear and indigestion. The combination of stress, half-cooked meat, and ripe berries had twisted my guts into knots.

"Anybody know what time it is?" John asked at last. "I left my phone at the hotel."

I checked the timestamp on my camcorder. "About four thirty," I said, with surprise and dismay.

John chewed on that with gritted teeth, then turned to glare at Miguel. "I thought Sunday was a big day for the canals? How have we not seen a single soul?"

Because, I found myself thinking, *we're forsaken.* That's what Miguel had said, when John kicked his doppelganger doll in the canal.

Now Miguel sat very still on his stool, his face pale, his eyes looking off through the darkening horizon.

"Is like I say," he muttered. "No one takes this part of the canals anymore."

"There's still plenty of daylight left," I said, chewing my lip. "Get more smoke going. There must be someone out there who can see us."

John fanned the fire with a big, flat fern leaf, then tossed the leaf into the flames. It curled slowly, sending up a thick plume of smoke.

Larry sat across the fire, his camera in his lap. His deep, powerful voice seemed strangled and subdued. "And if no one comes before nightfall?"

No one answered. The answer was obvious. If no one came, it meant another night here.

Afternoon dwindled in the west, darkening the woods at our backs. I kept staring out at the canal as the light grew dimmer and dimmer, until I could no longer see much of anything.

Finally I realized—

It's already too late.

—that no one was going to find us. Not before dark.

Someone had to say it.

"Okay," I narrated for my camera, with a reluctant sigh. "It's getting dark. Too dark to see out there."

"Shit." Larry groaned. "You gotta be kidding."

Next to the fire, John straightened with a stretch and a bear-like groan. "So much for your fire idea. What next?"

For a moment, I could only look back at them mutely. My stomach hurt, my heart seemed unable to slow down, and I could no longer even pretend to have any answers. All I wanted, more than I'd ever wanted anything, was to be safe back home, two thousand miles away.

But it seemed that wasn't in the cards. Not today.

I took a deep breath. "There's only one thing we *can* do. We'll have to get ready for another night here."

Chapter 15: Dark Waters

As stars began to glitter in the night sky, we sat around the fire at the dockside pavilion, drained and dirty. John prodded the flames sullenly with a stick, his orange hoodie crumpled and smeared with soot. I sat to his right, cross-legged, my camera on the ground beside me. Larry sat to my right, his leather jacket draped over his shoulders against the wind. Miguel stood by the pavilion, leaning on the post, his muddy straw hat in his hands.

For a long moment, the only sound was the crackle of fire, the soft hum of insects, and the rhythmic buzz of frogs. None of us spoke, each of us struggling to process the fact that we were stranded for another night.

"We can't give up," Larry said at last. "Now that it's night, they'll see the fire even better, right?"

Miguel shook his head. "No one is stupid enough to be on the canals at night. Most stay away from the water past nightfall." He lowered his voice, looking doubtfully at the still waters. "Maybe we should stay away, too."

"What are you suggesting?" I asked him.

He hesitated. "I-I'm not suggesting anything, *señorita.*"

His reticence annoyed me. "I'm *paying* you to guide us," I reminded him. "What do you think we should do?"

He looked down, then murmured in Spanish, "I don't want to stay by the shore, *señorita.* I think we should go back to the house. Perhaps if I pray to the doll—"

"English!" John yelled. "English, motherfucker!"

I turned away from Miguel with a tired sigh. "He says we should go back to the shack for the night."

John scoffed. "What's he got planned for us there?"

Miguel looked out at the water uneasily. "I just have a bad feeling about the water at night."

"And that haunted old spider-shack is better?" Larry asked. "I only stayed last night because we had no time for anything else. Now we've got a fire, clear skies, a little shelter." He nodded at the dilapidated roof of the pavilion.

John frowned, nodding. "We're *barely* more exposed here than in that shack, and the weather's fine. I already lugged our shit out here. Main thing is, I can't keep a fire going from the cabin." He glanced at me. "Right?"

All three of them were looking at me, waiting for the director's cue.

Reluctantly, I said, "It does seem logical to stay here, by the fire. Just in case someone *does* pass on the canal."

Miguel sighed, looking out at the water. I saw his fear and doubt, and I wondered if I'd made the right choice. It seemed like the *logical* choice, but maybe logic wasn't the best framework—not here, not anymore.

But that was only fear talking. Fear and desperation. Nothing had happened yet that I'd been unable to explain with some good old fashioned logic. Right?

I pushed my doubts away.

Once again, we prepared to make camp. John shook out the towels we'd used at the shack and spread them under the pavilion, close to the fire. Miguel changed the Band-Aid on his head, wincing as it peeled away. Larry checked the bandage on the cut on his arm. The gouge was scabbed over and seemed to be healing, from what I could tell, but I was no doctor. One more reason the sooner we were off this island, the better.

The wall of dolls loomed at the back of the pavilion. Their soft, child-like faces glowed in the firelight. There were more of them in the trees outside the pavilion, watching silently. At times they seemed to rustle and dance, and I had to remind myself it was only the wind. It had to be just the wind.

We sat on the edge of the pavilion floor in the glow of the fire. It couldn't have been past eight, yet it was already pitch black and I felt exhausted, ready to sleep. Despite that, I had a feeling it would be another restless night.

"If we had a few s'mores," Larry said. "it'd be almost like camping." He was trying to be funny, though his voice sounded a little strained.

I gripped my stomach, still cramping with a curious mix of hunger and indigestion. "Man," I muttered, "don't tease me. I'd kill for a s'more right now."

"We could tell ghost stories," John said dryly. "Miguel seems to know a few."

He shot a dark glance at Miguel, who was keeping his distance from the rest of us, pacing on the pavilion and staring pensively at the canal.

Larry sat with his knee bent, hugging it loosely and glaring into the dark trees beyond the firelight. "Tonight's the last night we had the room reserved. What do you think'll happen to our stuff if we're not back tomorrow?"

"The hotel'll probably throw it out," John said darkly.

"Don't worry about it," I said. "We'll be back in time."

John cleared his throat, and said quietly, "We should set up watches. Keep an eye on the fire, and everything else." He glanced at Miguel, who was out of earshot.

I nodded. "Good idea. In case a boat passes."

"I'll take the first watch," said John.

Larry and I spread out our beach towels beneath the pavilion. I lay down with my head on my backpack, my camera at the ready beside me.

There, I remained wide awake, despite my exhaustion. Through a hole in the pavilion roof, I looked up at the stars above the island. It was dark here, and the sky looked very clear. There were so many stars up there that the sky looked almost alien, like the view from another world.

Instead of joining us, Miguel sat on the steps of the dock, looking out at the water with his back turned to us.

Again I wondered if I'd made a mistake in staying on the dock instead of returning to the cabin, like Miguel wanted. The cabin had been creepy, but being exposed out here somehow felt even worse. The feeling of being watched, pervasive since I arrived, was only growing.

I had never felt more far from home.

The wind picked up, and the dolls danced eerily in the trees. I could hear Miguel praying softly in Spanish, a few feet away on the dock steps, as well as the buzz of frogs and the distant splash and lap of the canals.

Slowly, my eyelids closed at last.

And then Miguel started screaming.

I shot upright on the towel in time to see Miguel come bolting up from the dock, his face contorted in terror.

"What?" I cried, alarmed. "What is it?"

He stood before me at the top of the stairs, pointing frantically at the canal. "There's something out there!"

As I got to my feet, I followed Miguel's gesture and saw circular ripples on the canal, as if something big had splashed the water. Tiny waves broke against the dock.

"There's something there!" Miguel looked from me to the other two in panic. "There's something in the water!"

John stormed closer, followed by Larry, who hung back, holding his camera.

"What is it?" John demanded. "I don't see anything."

"Right there!" Miguel pointed. He lowered his voice, looking anxiously at the water. "It was there, I swear it!"

John turned to me accusingly. "Did *you* see anything?"

I shook my head. "I mean, there were ripples. Maybe a fish?"

"If this was a fish," Miguel said softly, "it was a *big* fish."

I frowned. The way he said that reminded me of something, but groggy, exhausted, and frightened as I was, I didn't make the connection at first.

"We should not be here," Miguel whispered. His eyes were wide and white. "You think the house is bad, but the canals… the canals are the source…"

I hurried back to my bag, turning on my camera. It came alive with a slow whir. "Come on," I urged.

By the time I could look through the night vision, I saw only dark water, choppy from the wind. I lowered my camera with a sigh. "I don't see anything, either."

With a snort of disgust, John shook his head and turned away. "Fuck this guy. Go back to sleep."

Miguel started to protest, and I pinched the bridge of my nose between thumb and forefinger. "Can't you give it a rest, Miguel? Give it a rest and get some sleep?"

His eyes widened in surprise as I spoke, and he closed his mouth slowly. I could see him sag as he realized even I was no longer on his side—not in this. I had to nip this in the bud before I let myself get carried away in irrational silliness, too.

"Señorita," he said at last, "I am not making this up. There's something out there!"

"Please," I said. "I just want to get some sleep."

But Miguel raised a finger, his face strained with fresh fear in the dim firelight. "Listen!" He stared for a moment into space, then his eyes focused on mine. "Do you hear it?"

I strained to listen, but I heard no sound over the bog but the whine of the wind and the crackle of the fire. The insects and frogs had fallen silent.

"Do you hear it?" Miguel demanded, looking at me, wide-eyed. He grabbed me by the shoulders and started to shake me. "Please, *señorita! Do you hear it?*"

Still holding the camera, Larry lunged in to protect me, shoving Miguel back with his free hand. "Get off her!"

But Miguel clung to me, his eyes startlingly wide, his lips peeled back in a grimace that revealed his clenched, gapped teeth. Terrified, I tried to push him away, holding my camera up away from him.

"Please!" he cried. "Can't you hear the crying?"

I froze, my breath catching in my throat.

Then John came out of nowhere, slamming Miguel and sending him sprawling. I almost tumbled with him— but John reached out to catch me, holding me up.

"The hell are you doing?" John glared suspiciously at both Miguel and Larry. "Don't touch her!"

Larry raised his free hand in innocence, still filming. Miguel lifted himself up from the dock, glaring at John. "I'm trying to *save* her, before you get us all killed!"

John loomed over Miguel, his huge fists clenched, veins bulging in his thick arms.

I could only stare at them, speechless, unable to even lift my camera and keep filming.

Can't you hear the crying?

Now it all came back. When Miguel mentioned a 'big fish' a moment ago, I hadn't remembered where I'd heard that before, but now I did.

The old Mexican man we'd spoken to in Xochimilco had told us that, on the day Don Julio drowned, his cousin saw a 'big fish' in the water near Julio's body.

And I remembered something else that old man had told us: on the day he died, Don Julio had mentioned hearing mermaids in the water, calling to him.

They are crying for me. Can't you hear the crying?

Those had been the last known words of Don Julio.

"Please," Miguel said, rising to his knees. "We have to get away—"

John kicked him down, pinning him to the warped dock under his sneaker. "Shut *up!* Do I have to gag you?"

Finally I stirred from my trance and lunged at John, trying to push him away. "Damn it, John! Let him be!"

He looked down at me with contempt, then stepped aside. Miguel rose to his feet, looking at me desperately.

"Please," he said. "We have to get away."

Narrowing my eyes, I whispered, "Did you really see something? A *big fish* out there?"

"Carmen…" John began, impatiently.

I raised a hand, waiting for Miguel to answer.

He breathed heavily, his eyes wide and unfocused, as if he barely knew where he was. I slapped him lightly out of his shock. "Hey! Miguel! Can you hear me?"

His head rolled toward me, and his dark, baleful eyes met mine. "We have to leave," he whispered. "We have to go. Whatever it takes. We can swim if we have to."

I frowned. "We'd drown," I told him. "You said so yourself, yesterday."

But Miguel was beyond reasoning. He moved past me, heading toward the dock. "We can swim," he declared. "It's our only chance. Into the water. Yes!"

To my vague horror, he approached the dock's edge and slid out of his sandals, setting them neatly aside. Then he sank down, dangling his feet over the side of the dock.

I turned to John, who looked as dumbfounded as I did. "Stop him!" I screamed.

Larry was already rushing down the dock. Sliding on the crooked boards, he wrapped his arm around Miguel, pulling him back from the edge. In his other hand, Larry held his camera away to protect it from harm.

Miguel tugged against him wildly, and Larry struggled to hold him down. The camera fell from his hands and I gasped as it clattered on the dock.

Then John rushed to join Larry, holding Miguel down from the other side.

"Let me go!" Miguel screamed in Spanish. "Let me go!"

I swept down the stairs. "Miguel, you'd never make it. You'd drown!"

Still struggling against the others, Miguel tilted his head to leer back at me, tears streaming from his eyes. "It's her," he cried, laughing. "It's *her!*"

Holding Miguel down, John glared up at me. "Can't we throw the asshole overboard? He wants to go, let him!"

"Miguel!" I said. "You have to calm down!"

He stopped fighting and began to sob. "But don't you hear it? Don't you hear the crying?"

I leaned closer, studying him. "What is it you hear?"

His eyes rolled up to look at mine. They were bloodshot, red from crying, and yet he smiled.

"It's *her...* " he whispered. "She wants vengeance. But she'll never be satisfied."

"Who?" I asked. "The little girl? The drowned girl?"

He said nothing more, closing his eyes. Slowly Larry and John released him, remaining close to him in case he made any sudden moves, but he didn't move at all.

He simply lay on the dock, and wept.

Chapter 16: Vanished

We waited out Miguel's hysteria.

His weeping turned to hyperventilating, then a quiet catatonic state. John practically dragged him back up to the pavilion, throwing him on a beach towel. There Miguel lay, staring up at the rafters in the low, guttering firelight.

Still breathing hard, I looked around at the dolls in the dark trees, their features as blank and unseeing as Miguel's.

In all the panic, a few moments ago, I thought I'd seen the dolls turning their heads, turning to look at the canal. Of course that was only an illusion, a combination of the wind moving the dolls and my mind playing tricks on me. Just the wind, and nothing more, I told myself.

It was becoming a tired refrain.

Larry and I lay down again. John resumed his sullen watch, glowering into the fire at the edge of the pavilion.

The evening drew deeper, the stars twinkling through the holes in the roof. It was getting cold, much colder than I'd expected for Mexico; if not for the fire, it might have been *too* cold. I hugged my knees to my chest for warmth under my hooded sweater.

In the silence of the night, I kept replaying everything Miguel had said. Even now, I saw no logical reason to suspect he was faking it or messing with us. Indeed, his fear seemed all too real. And I had to admit, it was very creepy out here by the water. I could see how the lap of the wind and waves could be mistaken for persuasive voices, whispering in the night.

Can't you hear the crying?

But *someone* was messing with us. If it wasn't Miguel, then who—or what?

I kept thinking of the drowned girl, too, and the dream I'd had the night before—if it *had* been a dream.

It may already be too late.

I lay awake, surrounded by the strange sounds of the island. The dolls seemed to whisper, the sound just audible under the wind. The dark waters of the canal slurped and splashed. Just fish, I told myself.

The big fish.

Before, my disbelief had been adamant, like armor, protecting me from the power of this place. Now, as that disbelief began to chip away, the island seemed more powerful than ever.

John and Larry switched places at the watch, midway through the night. John lay beside me, unslinging his crossbow and setting it within reach. Miguel lay on his towel, very still, facing the canal.

At last my eyes could hold themselves open no longer, and I drifted into dark and dreamless sleep.

When I opened my eyes, it was morning.

I sat upright with the immediate sense that something was wrong. John was no longer beside me. The air had grown bitterly cold. The fire by the pavilion had run down to embers, glowing in the soft, pre-dawn light.

And Miguel's towel was empty.

Larry and John were speaking in agitated voices, down on the dock.

"I told you, I was standing right here the whole time," Larry was saying.

"And you didn't think to, I don't know, pay attention to the fucking camp site? Do you understand the meaning of *keeping watch?*"

I sprang to my feet. "What's going on?"

They ignored me. "I was watching for *boats,*" Larry cried.

"Oh yeah? Or were you sleeping at your post?"

"No!" Larry said defensively. Then he clutched his head. "I-I don't remember the whole night. But I know I didn't hear anyone come or go from the camp. I don't know where the hell he went, God damn it!"

A cold pit formed in my gut as I looked around the camp and pieced together what they were arguing about.

"Where's Miguel?" I asked.

Standing face to face on the dock, the two guys turned to look my way at last. John had his teeth bared in a snarl. Larry's eyebrows were pinched together in worry.

"He's gone," Larry said.

I blinked at him. "What do you mean, *gone?*"

"Gone!" John shouted. "Disappeared. Vanished!"

"But... *how?*" I could feel my jaw sagging open.

John shrugged in exasperation. "I get up to take a piss this morning and Larry and Miguel are both gone. Larry's down here on the docks, spacing out at the canal, and the Mexican? The one guy we needed to keep an eye on? God only knows!" He glared at Larry.

"Look," Larry spread his hands in an appealing shrug, "I was standing right here. He couldn't have gone far, all right? Maybe he went to the bathroom."

I looked around, bewildered. Panic bled through my grogginess. "Miguel?" I called. "Miguel!"

As I spun around, I saw something across the pavilion that made a chill run down my spine.

In the soft pre-dawn light, three child-like silhouettes sat at the end of the pavilion, their little feet dangling over the edge.

Hardly believing my eyes, I moved closer, stepped out in front of the pavilion to see their faces.

Of course, somehow, it was *them*.

There they sat—the afro-haired black doll, the blond blue-eyed doll, and the mocha-skinned baby girl. From the edge of the pavilion, the dolls stared vacantly into the woods, as if on a watch duty of their own.

Three dolls; one for each of us again, with Miguel gone.

"Oh, Jesus," I whispered. "Oh, Jesus Christ."

John and Larry came over, their mouths falling open.

"Don't touch anything," I said quickly, moving past them. "I want to film this."

Behind me, John uttered a high, humorless laugh. "You're fucking kidding me. He did it again!"

Going to my bag, I removed my old camcorder and started it up, filming Miguel's empty towel.

"So," I said, shakily, "we woke up today, the morning of Monday, October twenty ninth, and our guide is gone."

John and Larry stood at the end of the pavilion, looking at the dolls. Neither seemed to want to get too close.

"Miguel has vanished," I said, "and the dolls are back."

As I stepped out from under the pavilion's roof, the row of dolls came into focus. Their grungy, ruined faces stared through me in a mockery of innocence.

"What do you think, Carmen?" John asked sarcastically. "Were they here last night and we just didn't notice?"

"No," I whispered. "These were *not* here last night. And they're definitely the same dolls that were at the shack."

"So someone moved them here," Larry said.

"Someone," John growled, "named Miguel." He stepped closer to the dolls. "I should've thrown all *four* of these in the water and been done with it!"

"Don't!" I cried, with more force than I intended. John stopped, blinking back at me. "Please," I whispered, "leave them be. Just forget them, okay? Don't touch them. Don't *look* at them."

John's surprise only increased as I spoke. "What, are you afraid of them?"

The question gave me pause. I evaded it. "Don't you think we have more important things to worry about? Like what happened to Miguel?"

Larry studied the grassy ground, chewing his lip. "She's right. We have to find Miguel. It's the only way we'll know what's really happening."

Grinding his teeth, John muttered, "Good. I'll make him tell us what's going on if I have to *beat* it out of him."

Larry said nothing, but his stern expression said that, for once, he didn't disagree with John. I had to admit, I was also desperate for the truth. It felt like I was losing my mind. I had to know what was happening here.

"The island's not very big," I said softly. "He can't have gotten far." I lowered the camera, chewing my lip. "Come on. We find Miguel, we find the truth."

Chapter 17: The Heart Tree

Still holding my camera, I set off toward the center of the island. John and Larry scrambled to follow, grabbing their backpacks.

After two nights of no sleep and little food, I'd begun to feel strung out and edgy. My eyes were red-rimmed and dry. The whole world had taken on a disorienting, fuzzy unreality, as though the waking and dreaming worlds had started to blend together.

Even now, a part of me kept hoping this was a dream. That I'd open my eyes and find myself back at home, safe in bed, my dad cooking downstairs and the dog lounging at my feet.

I kept hoping I'd wake up, but I never did.

The rising sun barely touched the ground through the thick canopy of dolls overhead. Their soft rustling sounds seemed almost like laughter.

Partly to drown out the sound, I shouted, "Miguel! Can you hear me?" Then I repeated the same thing in Spanish. *"¿Puedes escúchame?"*

Can't you hear the crying?

After a moment, Larry joined me, adding his smooth, deep baritone to my voice. "Miguel!" His shout sounded almost angry. "Miguel! Come on out!"

"Are you hurt?" I called. "Please, answer me."

"This island is tiny," John muttered. "If he was still here, he'd *have* to hear you."

"Not if he's *unconscious,*" I snapped. "What if he fell? What if he's hurt or something, John?"

John shook his head dismissively. "I bet he's long gone. Think about it. Last night he realized we weren't going for whatever con he was pulling, so he makes a scene, acts like he hears *something in the water*, then slips off and abandons us. This is just one last mind-fuck for good measure."

My doubts lingered as we approached the cabin of Don Julio. The buildings looked just as we'd left them the other day. "Miguel?" I called. I had to make myself yell; my unconscious instinct was to keep my voice low here, like in a museum or a church.

At the cabin of Don Julio, I fell silent. Everything seemed as we'd left it; yet I couldn't shake the feeling that something was off. Different, somehow. I was sure some of the dolls had changed position in the trees, and ones I'd seen the day before were no longer here—as if they'd picked themselves up and moved in the night.

"Miguel?" I called softly at the dark, foreboding cabin. "Are you in there?"

Nothing answered.

I hesitated a moment, then started up the creaking stairs. John stepped after me. "What are you doing?"

"I have to be sure," I replied.

I reached out and pushed open the door, letting it creak open into darkness. Inside, the doll heads looked back, their pale rubber skin reflecting the dim light of dawn from outside. I moved very slowly, holding my breath, so I could hear if anything moved inside.

Nothing moved.

I sighed and stepped back, frowning. "Check the other buildings," I said.

Splitting up briefly, we each went to separate corners of the yard. John checked the outhouse, holding his nose. Larry poked his camera into the dilapidated barn. I looked around the old chicken coop, surrounded in wire fence.

Cupping my hands by my mouth, I shouted, *"Miguel!"*

Only eerie silence answered. Even the birds and insects were quiet.

"Carmen," John said quietly, "we need to go back and get the fire going."

I chewed my lip, at a loss. "No," I said, desperately. "He must be here somewhere."

"I really don't think he is," John said. "Look, I want to find this guy, too, but if we don't keep that fire going and get off this island, we're *all* toast."

Larry mumbled, "He's right about that."

I sighed. "All right. We'll go back. But when the fire's set up, we're looking again. I'm not giving up."

As dawn brought color back to the trees, we returned to the pavilion by the waterside. The three dolls were there to greet us. I walked wide around them, and to my relief, John and Larry both ignored them.

We ate a cheerless breakfast of more blackberries at the shore. They were getting harder to pluck; the freshest and easiest to reach were already gone, so we were fishing through the brambles for the last rotting blobs. The fruit squished between my fingers into black jelly, sweet enough to set my teeth on edge.

As we ate, John fixed the fire, muttering, "Should've never let this go out in the first place."

Larry wiped blackberry juice on a handkerchief, then handed it to me. I cleaned my fingers.

"I don't know what happened," Larry mumbled. "I don't remember falling asleep. All I remember is being by the fire one minute, and the next minute I'm down on the dock, it's morning, and John's shouting at me."

"You were spaced the fuck out," John said. "Like I

said, I woke up and Miguel was gone, and you were just standing there on the dock, staring into space."

I looked at Larry from the corner of my eye. He met my gaze with a worried expression, and I looked away.

"The stress is getting to us all," I said. "I wouldn't worry about it. You might have been sleepwalking. I used to do it when I was younger."

I remembered my dream of the drowned girl, and the mud on my shoes in the morning.

"Maybe I still do," I added quietly.

John drizzled gasoline over the fire pit and rekindled it with a match. He leaned forward, blowing the flames to urge them higher. Quickly the sticks and leaves lit up and the fire bloomed across the logs.

"All right," I said. "Now we have to look for Miguel."

John shook his head. "Fuck Miguel. I'm staying right here. Someone has to watch for boats."

I laughed impatiently. "No, we're not doing this again. I'm going, John."

John turned back to the fire. "Whatever. Go, then." His coldness matched my own. "What do I care anymore?"

I blinked at him, surprised he was actually willing to give up an argument. Surprise quickly turned to suspicion. "So you don't care about me anymore?"

John rolled his eyes. "That's not what I said. Jesus, you want me to go with you, I'll go. But I swear to God if any boats pass and we're not here…"

"They'll see the fire," I said. "It'll be okay for another hour or so. We'll hear them if anyone lands."

Adjusting my backpack, I took out my camera and started filming. Then I set out, narrating as I went.

"Okay, so it's around ten o'clock. We're going out to

look for Miguel again. The sun is out. It's a clear day. Not bad weather."

It was just empty chatter, something to fill the silence as we walked. My throat was too dry to keep shouting, and besides, John was right; if Miguel was anywhere on the island, he would've heard us shouting by now.

That meant he was either no longer here, or no longer in a condition to hear or answer.

We made a circle around the shore, retracing the steps Miguel had taken us on the first day. Slogging through the marshy lowlands at the back of the island, John swatted at flies and complained. Larry had his camera out, as well, filming everything around us.

None of us saw anything—no sign of any human soul.

"It's like he vanished into thin air," Larry muttered.

"Larry," I said, "the other day, when John and I went to get fuel and you and Miguel watched the camp, did he say anything to you?"

Larry paused, frowning. "Nah. He didn't say much of anything. Pretty pissed about, you know, John beating the shit out of him and everything." Then he hesitated. "Well, he did get a little talkative at one point. Talking about some old legend or other, I don't know."

I cocked my head in genuine interest. "What legend?"

But Larry only shrugged behind his camera. "I don't know. I mean, I have the footage if you want to find it."

"Do you remember what he said?"

Larry raised an eyebrow. "Actually, yeah, now that I think of it." He waved a hand for me to follow and turned, plunging into the woods.

I followed him uncertainly. As we passed through the woods, I saw the tall juniper tree up ahead—the one Miguel claimed was the oldest tree, the center of the island. *El*

Arbor Corazon, he'd called it: the heart tree.

My mouth became even drier. The ghost had taken me here, too, in my dream. But why?

"He was talking about the lady who carved this."

Larry nodded at the carving on the tree, barely visible, down below the wooden frame of the artificial land.

Doña Marina, 1526.

"The crying lady," said Larry. "He didn't want to stay by the canal because she lives down there under the water. He said that once you hear her cry, it's already too late."

I froze up at those words, remembering the words of the ghost in my dream.

It may already be too late.

"No," I squeaked, my voice breaking. Then I cleared my throat. "No, that's not right. You're talking about *La Llorona.* The weeping woman, who killed her own kids. The woman who carved in the tree was *Malintzin,* an Aztec girl who helped Cortés. They're separate legends."

Larry shook his head. "I'm sure he was talking about La Llorona. The one they were doing the play about, back at the dock? Miguel said they were one in the same."

I frowned. "Doña Marina—*Malintzin*—is the same person as the woman in the La Llorona legend?"

"In some versions of the stories," Larry nodded. "That's what Miguel said."

Despite the circumstances, I found myself fascinated by this new aspect of the island's history. I was glad I was recording it. "Wow," I muttered. "So the person behind the La Llorona legend might have lived on this very island, back in the time of the Conquistadors."

"Come to think of it," Larry muttered, "Didn't Miguel act like he heard something last night? What was it he said? *Don't you hear the crying?*"

I nodded, my breathing coming very shallowly. Once again I felt the sense of unreality, the blurring between waking and dreaming.

"That's what he said," I agreed. Swallowing, I turned to look at them. "And according to the old Mexican man we met back in Xochimilco, those were also the last words of Don Julio. His exact last words."

I saw something change in Larry's brown eyes behind his glasses.

John blurted, "Oh, what horse shit!" He stood a few feet behind us, his thick arms crossed. "All this proves is Miguel knows how to spin a story. What's new?"

I let John's interjection go unanswered. At this point, I didn't have the energy to engage with him. He was like a noisy dog you get tired of shushing; you just learn to live with the barking.

As we trekked back across the empty island, I found myself hoping that Miguel would be waiting for us at our camp site. I'd walk up and find him sitting by the fire, wearing his confident, roguish smile. It felt like if only he was back, somehow everything would make sense again. There'd be no ghosts. No crying. No things in the water.

But as we returned to the camp site, now in the early afternoon, we found no sign of anybody. Only our fire, guttering low once again—and the row of three dolls, tiny simulacra of ourselves, slumped and sightless on the edge of the pavilion.

John squatted by the fire, stoking it with fresh wood. Larry stood around, holding his camera but no longer filming. "What are we supposed to do now?" Larry asked.

I didn't know. Increasingly I found myself at a loss. I didn't understand what was happening to us, and I had no idea what to do about it.

"We've got the fire going." I shrugged at the smoke.

John shook his head, standing. "This fire's not cutting it. No one is gonna save us. We gotta try something else."

I lifted my eyebrows. "If you have an idea, I'm all ears."

"Oh, it's not *my* idea," he said, turning to smirk at me. "Your buddy Miguel thought of it, that first night. But like he said, it'll take time. So we'd best start now."

He turned to the canal, and his smirk faded into a look of grim determination.

"We're gonna take matters in our own hands," he said. "We're gonna build a raft."

Chapter 18: First Watch

We spent the afternoon scouting for supplies. John found a bundle of old, worn rope in the pavilion, as well as some planks from the fallen barn. Larry and I dragged some logs and fallen trees back to the camp site.

I kept an eye out for Miguel, but saw no sign of him.

At one point, Larry stumbled over the three dolls, still sitting on the far end of the pavilion. "Oh—for fuck's sake! Carmen, I'm moving these things."

I rushed over, holding a hand to my chest. "Don't!" I cried. "Come on, just leave them alone!"

But Larry insisted, shaking his head. "Sorry, I am *not* having these creepy things staring at me all day. John, you want to give me a hand?"

"Gladly."

Larry grabbed the doll that looked like him daintily by its hand and carried it toward the tree line. John picked up the doll that looked like me and hurled it unceremoniously into the foliage.

"Hey!" I cried.

John eyed me with a frown. "I can't believe, of all of us, you're the one who's buying this haunted island shit."

I said, "It's nothing to do with believing. Except— well, I *believe* it's rude to mistreat someone else's things."

Ignoring me, John lifted the last doll—the one that looked like him—and drop-kicked it, sending it flying. It smacked a tree and fell down into the ferny brush.

"Real mature," I muttered.

Turning back, John said, "We need to set a watch

again. Larry, you're out."

"Huh?"

"Fool me once," John said, "shame on you. Fool me twice…"

"Whatever," Larry muttered, folding his arms. "I didn't fall asleep last night, I'm telling you. I don't know *what* happened."

"Whether you fell asleep or spaced out doesn't really matter, does it?" John snapped. He glanced at me. "You want to take first watch, or second?"

As afternoon burned out across the canal, I looked around at the gathering gloom. I didn't feel remotely ready to sleep. I didn't even trust closing my eyes, lest I opened them to find the dolls in the trees had moved while I wasn't looking, turned to face me, rubber faces twisting into smiles.

"I can take the first watch," I said softly.

John nodded. "If you see anything, you come and wake me up. Got it?"

I rolled my eyes. "I know how a watch works, honey."

John glanced at Larry. "At least one of us does."

We tried to eat berries, but the bushes were picked. With our bottled water depleted, John prepared some fresh water from the canal, boiling it in a metal tin he found under the pavilion and purifying it with his iodine tablet. It still tasted like mud.

John and Larry prepared to bed down for the night under the pavilion. I remained on watch beside the fire, sitting on the edge of the pavilion's wooden platform.

"Here's my flashlight, if you need it," John whispered, leaning over to hand it to me. He paused as another thought occurred to him. Then he unslung Don Julio's crossbow, belted over his shoulder. "Take this, too."

I looked at the weapon uneasily. "John, I wouldn't even know how to use that."

He shook his head. "It's a crossbow. The whole point is it's easy, for pansies that can't use real bows. Seriously, take it, just in case. What if Miguel comes back and tries something?"

I rolled my eyes, but he insisted, pushing the weapon into my hands. "Here. Hold it like this." He set the stock of the bow against my shoulder. "Easier if you stand up."

With a sigh, I took his hand and stood. He stepped behind me, adjusting my stance, then wrapping his arms around me to move my aim.

"Trust your instincts," he whispered. "Don't overthink it. Just aim it like a camera. Point, and… shoot!"

His hand clenched over mine, forcing me to pull the trigger. The bow loosed with a *twang* and the bolt thudded into a doll in a tree, several yards away.

"Hey!" I cried.

"Don't blame me," he laughed. *"You* did it." He took the bow and showed me how to reload. "The crank's a bit rusty. Takes some doing to reload. You'll probably only get one shot, so make it count."

He handed me the reloaded bow. I held it uneasily, as if it might go off in my hands. After a brief consideration, I slung it over my shoulder and tightened the belt to hold it on my back. The weapon made me uncomfortable, but he was right. Better safe than sorry.

John shrugged. "When you start to get tired…"

I sat next to the fire. "I'll wake you up, I know."

It was completely dark, now. Out on the canal, frogs sang. The wind rustled in the trees, moving the leaves, shaking the dolls. I looked out into the night and for a moment I regretted taking the first watch.

Not that I'd sleep anyway.

She never sleeps…

That's what the little drowned girl in my dream had said, but who had she meant?

Nothing heals in death… her madness only grows.

I squeezed my eyes shut for a moment to rid the thought. Then I opened my backpack and fished out my camera.

It was my usual defense mechanism. I'd been playing with cameras since I was a girl, when I stumbled on my mom's old equipment. Some of my earliest memories were making stop-motion videos with my toys and little mock newscasts.

Whenever a boy hurt my feelings or my schoolwork overwhelmed me, I could retreat to my camcorder. It grounded me. *Focused* me. Something about looking through the narrow viewfinder had a calming effect, like blinders on a horse.

I took solace in my camera now, looking down the viewfinder and starting to record. It made me feel safer than any crossbow could.

"It's our third evening on the island," I whispered, filming the dolls in the trees. "About nine or ten at night. Creepy as shit, as usual. We've been doing watch shifts, and tonight I have first watch. John and Larry are trying to rest, so…"

I crept off on my tiptoes, down the stairs to the dock.

Sitting on the steps at the bottom of the dock, I looked out at the dark, still waters of the canal. The water lapped around the pilings of the dock, a wet, disconcerting *plop*, like footsteps moving through the shallows. It was creepy enough by the water that I had to get out John's flashlight, aiming it with one hand, my camera with the other.

The light reflected back off the choppy, wind-blown surface of the water. I saw nothing else there.

I swallowed and said shakily, "I have to admit I'm pretty scared. It'd be bad enough being stranded anywhere, no food, no supplies, but to be stranded *here*, of all places."

My voice held an edgy, irrational note that annoyed me. The sound shocked me out of my fear a little.

"It's just a shitty little island," I told the camera, and myself. "I don't know why it's getting to me, but maybe it's my fault. I keep entertaining these irrational thoughts."

I sighed.

Then I heard another soft splash out in the canal, and I startled. Aiming John's flashlight at the water, I saw a set of concentric circles, fanning out, where something had broken the surface.

As I scanned my flashlight over the water, the light caught something pale, about twenty feet out from the shore. I had to do a double-take, swinging the light back to focus on what I'd seen.

There was something out there, half-submerged and floating along through the tall reeds. It looked like a dingy sack of laundry. It bobbed lazily down the canal from the east, through the part of the canal where Don Julio and the little girl were said to have drowned.

As it emerged through the reeds and swung toward me, I realized what I was seeing. My eyes widened. My breath caught in my throat.

Finally, I started to scream.

It was a human body.

Chapter 19: Things in the Water

I'm not sure how long I stood there screaming. I couldn't control it. The sound seemed to come out of me over and over, like an awful song played on repeat.

The body drifted closer in the canal. It was face-down, half-submerged, but to my horror, I recognized it—the short dark hair, the tattered blue jeans, the tan fishing vest, now bloated and waterlogged.

Distantly I was aware of movement on the stairs behind me as John and Larry hurtled down onto the dock. "What is it?" John yelled, trailing off as he followed the flashlight.

"Oh, my God," Larry whispered. "Is that…?"

He didn't need to finish. We all saw who it was, even if his still, bloated body was floating face-down.

At last, we'd found Miguel.

I whirled toward John, grabbing his dingy hoodie in both hands. "Help him!" I screamed.

"Jesus Christ!" John held me steady long enough to pluck his flashlight out of my hands, aiming it out onto the water till he found the body and saw it for himself. "Oh, Jesus," he said again, softly this time.

"Oh my God," Larry kept whispering. "My God, what is *happening?*"

"Do something!" The shouts burst from my throat as if coming from someone else. "God, help him!"

"What can I do?" John cried. "There's nothing… I don't think we can do anything."

"What if he's alive?" Tears cooled on my cheek in the breezy night air. "We can't just leave him there!"

John's perpetual scowl had become a boyish look of worry. With a heavy swallow, he took off his baseball cap, then unzipped his sweater and peeled off his undershirt, piling it all on the deck.

"Hold this." He shoved his heavy steel flashlight into Larry's hands, with a last solemn look at me.

In my panic, I didn't realize what he was doing till it was too late. My eyes widened and I shouted, "Wait, no!"

But John had already jumped off the dock.

He landed with a splash in the muddy water. To my surprise, it came up only to his waist. The dark, opaque canal looked much deeper—but John was able to wade a surprising distance through the reeds before it rose above his neck. Then he started to swim, his long, muscular arms rowing through the water.

"Be careful!" I cried.

Behind me, the wind picked up, sighing through the dark trees of the island. The dolls started to rustle along with the dead leaves, as if waking up, coming to life.

The waters of the canal started to ripple in the wind. Larry moved the flashlight between Miguel's body and John as he swam toward it through the choppy waters. The light shook in Larry's hand.

I watched through the viewfinder on my camcorder, seeing everything in the monochrome gray of night vision. The canal seemed to grow choppier and choppier, turning into little splashing white-caps. I could feel the flimsy dock—or perhaps the entire floating garden—rocking with the motion of the water.

The howl of the wind was so loud now I had to look up from the viewfinder at the trees behind me. Dolls bounced and jiggled on branches or suspended on wires, seeming to float and dance in the darkness. The campfire was guttering like a flag, licking at the nearby trees and their dry wood, threatening to spread.

Larry cried, "The fuck is *that?*"

Pressing my face back to the viewfinder, I scanned the dark water. John was only a few yards from Miguel's body now, slowing down as he reached it.

But the water was rippling a few yards behind him. Not the same ripple of waves in the wind, but an impact ripple, from something breaking the surface.

Even as I focused my lens, I saw a shadow move under the water and my breath caught in my throat.

There was something in the canal.

I could see its hazy form, distorted by the ripple of the waves. It was *big*, serpentine, stretching out toward John like the long, inky tendril of a deep-sea monster.

"John!" I screamed, my high voice drowned by the womanish wail of the wind. "Look out!"

Sensing something was wrong, John stopped where he was, paddling in place and looking around. The darkened waters all around him had grown violent, as if someone had turned the canal up to a slow boil. John looked back, shielding his eyes from Larry's flashlight.

"John!" I shrieked.

"There's something in there with you!" Larry cried. He waved the flashlight around frantically, looking for the long, snake-like shadow under the churning water.

Ignoring or perhaps not hearing us, John turned and kept swimming the last few yards toward Miguel.

I watched in horror through my viewfinder as a rough wave broke between John and Miguel. Rising from the depths, a long, feathery dorsal fin broke the surface, as some vast unseen thing passed beneath.

The great tail arched up, black scales glinting, and

crashed back beneath the surface. Waves rolled over John in its wake, and for a moment I lost sight of him.

"John! Oh, Jesus…"

Larry focused the flashlight on the great white splash zone where the tail had come up from the water. John was nowhere to be seen, but Miguel's body still floated there, out in the canal.

"Oh, God," I whispered.

I put my eye to the viewfinder and zoomed in.

The waves had turned Miguel over so he lay on his back, floating face up. Even from here, through my blurry, unsteady camera, I could see his expression. His face was fixed in a look of pure terror, his mouth open, his neck strained and stiff with *rigor mortis.*

But most disturbing was his eyes—wide open and deeply, deeply bloodshot. The whites were full red. Thin pink tears trickled down his puffy cheek.

"Miguel!" I cried, tears streaming from my own eyes.

A shadow moved across the water beneath him. Something seized Miguel's body by the feet and yanked him under with one swift jerk, leaving only a circle of waves and scattered bubbles.

Then he was gone.

Something thudded against the pier and I screamed, leaping back. At my feet, a pale hand reached up over the ledge of the dock, dripping and draped in moss. Another hand followed, scrambling for purchase.

Then John's head appeared, his head plastered with mud. His wide eyes found mine.

"Run!"

His thick arms flexing, he vaulted up out of the canal, pulling himself onto the dock. In the same motion he was on his feet, running, not bothering to grab his clothes.

Larry was already halfway up the stairs to the pavilion. I turned to follow, fleeing the churning waters behind me, the crossbow bouncing on my back.

Up ahead, the island was alive, the trees groaning, the dolls shifting in the dark.

As we reached the pavilion, our campfire swirled in the wind and guttered low. Then it seemed to implode in a puff of sparks, as if stamped out by some invisible force.

Instantly we were plunged into darkness, save for the beam of Larry's flashlight. All of us were screaming; the whole world was screaming. Larry's flashlight beam kept bouncing away, and I followed it, thrashing after him into the woods. I couldn't tell if John was with us. We were all separated in the gloom, each of us running for our lives.

Overhead, the rubber faces seemed to move, tracking me through the darkness, their visages watching in silent, open-mouthed horror. Behind us, the whine of the wind over the water sounded like a woman's weeping.

Can't you hear the crying?

Yes, it *was* a woman's weeping, not the wind at all. The sound seemed to chase after us, coming up from the canal. I could hear it, right behind me, closing in fast. I looked back in panic, struggling to see through the gloom.

Then my feet tangled in the brambles and I stumbled, falling down in a wet, soggy ditch. Somehow I managed to keep my arm up, holding my precious camera out of harm's way. Instead I hit the ground hard on my shoulder.

When I lifted my head, I'd lost sight of Larry's flashlight.

I was alone, and something was coming through the trees, coming to meet me with a horrible sound that was half-animal grunting, half-sobbing, all madness.

She was coming for me, coming to pull me down into the water with her, to join her eternal family, because—

Once you hear her, it's already too late.

"Please!" I screamed, sobbing, on my knees. *"Por favor!"*

My cries were lost in the swirl of chaos. Terror overwhelmed me and I pressed my face to the mud, holding my ears to drown out the sounds.

"Please!" I begged, remembering Miguel's prayer. "Have mercy, and give us sanctuary!"

I kept repeating it, finding strength in the words, like a talisman.

"Please, have mercy, give us sanctuary…"

I don't know how long I remained there, shivering in the mud at the bottom of a ditch, expecting some cold darkness to swoop over me.

Eventually, I noticed the wind had died down. I took my hands from my ears and lifted my head. The sound of weeping was gone, as if it had never been.

"Carmen!"

Startled, I looked toward the low, sharp whisper, blinking in the gloom. "Larry?"

Faint moonlight glinted off his glasses, giving him away. He was hiding in the brush, further down the ditch. I crawled to him, breathing in shallow little gulps. He put his slender arm around me.

"Are you all right?" he whispered.

I looked around frantically. "Where's John?"

Larry said, "I don't know."

He started to raise his flashlight and I grabbed his arm. "Don't," I whispered. "What if something's out there?"

He said nothing, breathing softly in the gloom.

Overhead, the dolls seemed still again, quiet. But I couldn't relax. I listened for the distant weeping, but over the whisper of the breeze I couldn't hear it.

The unnatural wind died down and the island grew quieter and quieter, until it was *too* quiet. I kept waiting for something else—whatever it was—to make the first move.

Finally I said, "We need to look for John. Don't turn the light on, but just…" I waved him to follow me, then put a finger to my lips, gesturing for quiet.

I crawled up the embankment, through the leafy ferns, and looked around. My eyes had adapted to the darkness somewhat. I swung my head from side to side, looking for anything moving. The trees were still and silent, now. The wind had died to a mutter.

I put my camera viewfinder to my eye. The camera let me see further in the gloom than I could with my naked eye, but it reduced my field of vision to a tiny square.

"John?" I called tentatively. The silence absorbed my voice, goading me to speak louder. "John? Where are you?"

I could see my own breath frosting in the cold gloom. It felt much colder than it had even an hour ago, as if the strange, unnatural winds had ushered in a terrible chill.

"Oh, shit!" Larry hissed. "What's that?"

I whirled, trying to focus the camera. A few yards away, through the trees, a pale shape stood. I gasped and I nearly fled.

Then I recognized the figure was John. Still shirtless from his attempt to swim to Miguel, his wide, naked back faced us.

"Oh, John," I sighed. "It's you."

But my relief was only momentary. John didn't answer me. He didn't move at all, only stood there with a stillness that seemed unnatural. As I came around to his other side, I saw he was staring into space, his jaw slack, his blue eyes blank. He swayed slightly, breathing in low, shallow gasps.

"John?" I looked up at him.

Slowly, his head tilted toward me; but the cloudiness never left his eyes. He seemed to look clean through me.

"He was right," John whispered, with no intonation. "There is something in the water."

I took his hand. It was ice cold and clammy. I clutched it close to me, trying to rub warmth back into it. "God, you're freezing!"

He was waking from the stupor of shock, and as his mind returned, his eyes widened. His shallow breathing quickened till he was almost hyperventilating. Still, his voice remained flat and emotionless. "We have to get away," he whispered. "Get away from the water."

Pulling away from me, he backed up, shaking violently. He looked very pale.

"There's something in the water."

"I know," I whispered. "I saw it, too."

"It... it *touched* me." His bewildered eyes found mine. "I can still feel it."

I swallowed, staring at him as he clutched his arm, where the thing had touched him.

"We have to get away," John said. "While we still can."

"I'm not going back to that shack," Larry whispered.

I frowned, trying to think through the pounding drum of panic in my ear. "Miguel wanted us to stay in the shack," I whispered. "Maybe we should have. He and Don Julio both thought the dolls would protect them."

"And how well did they protect *them?*" Larry asked.

"John's the one who threw Miguel's doll in the canal."

John didn't respond. He was still eerily distant, barely present at all, his face frozen in shock.

"So it's a *ghost,* then?" Larry demanded. "The drowned girl Don Julio couldn't save, she's haunting us?"

I swallowed. My mouth felt very dry. The moment I saw Miguel's body, floating down the canal, everything had changed. There was no logical explanation for that. No way to blame a prank, a mistake, a coincidence.

Not to mention what *else* I'd seen in the water. I kept picturing that long, tendrilous shadow, under the waves.

I chewed my lip, remembering my dream of the drowned girl. She hadn't threatened me; she'd *warned* me, against some other force.

She never sleeps... her madness only grows...

"No," I said. "I don't think it's the ghost of the drowned girl at all. There's something else here."

I turned to face Larry, frowning. "You said Miguel told you that in some of the legends, *Malintzin* and *Llorona* were the same woman. Right? And didn't he say that La Llorona can take the form of a mermaid creature with a long, snaky tail?"

Larry lowered his eyebrows. "You don't think...?"

I shrugged. "What if that was the *big fish* Fernando saw near the body of Don Julio? What if it was the *mermaid,* calling Don Julio before he died? Calling him to join her?"

I looked away through the trees, toward the canal.

"I think we're dealing with something much worse than a little girl's ghost. Not the drowned girl, but the thing that drowned her. Her, Don Julio, and Miguel."

The thing that's haunted these waters for centuries, dragging down anyone misfortunate enough to hear her cry, to join her in her watery grave.

Dropping my voice to little more than a breath, I looked back at Larry.

"The Weeping Woman," I said. "La Llorona."

Chapter 20: The Weeping

I let the words hang in the air, feeling their power.

Larry looked back at me, his eyes wide. "La Llorona," he repeated in a whisper.

As if summoned by the name, the wind picked up, whining in the trees. The sightless dolls shifted in their permanent fetal positions.

Just the wind was enough to frighten me. I waved at the two guys. "Get down! Come on!"

John was still staring at the softly moving trees with a vague look of shock. In the panic, he hadn't stopped to grab his clothes after pulling himself out of the canal; now he was naked from the waist up, his muscular upper body tense from shivering. When he made no move to follow me, I grabbed his hand, still disturbingly cold after his dip in the canal. Then I led him out of the open into the brush.

The three of us hunkered down together, hopefully out of sight to anything that might be out there. I kept my camera running, setting it aside on a dry patch of grass. Larry's eyes were invisible behind his glasses.

John sat with his legs folded, hugging them to his shirtless chest in an almost childish way and staring into the gloom, still stupefied by what he'd faced in the canal.

I put my hand on John's shoulder to comfort him, and I was shocked by how cold he felt. A patch of his bicep was like ice, cold and clammy and wet.

"John, you're freezing!"

He raised his hand slowly to probe his muscular arm. "That's where it touched me," he said. "I can still feel it."

I stared at it, then glanced at Larry. "Feel his arm."

Larry only looked out into the darkness. "We need to build the raft," he whispered. "We need to build the raft and get off this God-forsaken island. First thing in the morning."

I frowned, unsure about the raft idea. If there was something in the water, going out on a flimsy raft seemed like a bad idea; but I couldn't think of any better ones.

"What do we do till then?" I asked quietly.

Larry frowned, looking around at the tall trees. "I don't want to go back to the camp. Not till morning."

I nodded, relieved. "Me neither. Let's just stay here, okay? Stay real quiet and wait until morning."

I pressed myself to John, trying to warm him up, afraid of hypothermia. He didn't move to put his arm around me or return the embrace. He simply stared into the dark woods, his eyes flicking back and forth as if dreaming with open lids.

Whether it was his swim in the cold affecting him so greatly, or the thing that had touched him in the water, I couldn't say—but I had never seen John like this.

"Need to light a fire." His normally loud and brusque voice had fallen to a hush, whispered through clenched, chattering teeth. "Just let it all burn."

I stared at him, my heart racing. In the dark it was hard to see his face, but it looked as though his lips were peeling back in a grimace—or a grin.

"She's back," he whispered.

Before I could respond, a sudden scream penetrated the night. The sound was faint and distant, but in the quiet it was very clear. Every bone in my body tried to jump out of my skin. I looked over and saw the glint of Larry's glasses as he spun toward me.

"You hear that?" he whispered.

The sound came again, louder and clearer than before. It was a man's voice, screaming in pain and terror. I knew that voice.

"Oh, my God." My hand went to my mouth.

The screams continued, becoming broken, unintelligible Spanish. *"No, por favor! Oh, oh, mi Dios!"*

I started to rise, but Larry held me back.

"Aren't you going to help him?" I looked frantically from John to Larry. "Isn't anyone going to help him? It's Miguel! It's Miguel!"

"No," Larry said, his once-powerful voice now soft and dry. "It's not. He's gone, Carmen. It's not him."

"Please!" the voice screamed. *"Please!"*

I clutched my ears and shook my head, trying to keep out the awful screaming. I could feel tears building at the corner of my eyes, then trickling down my dirty cheek. In spite of what I knew, what I'd seen with my own eyes, I still wanted to run out toward the screams.

Can't you hear the crying?

With a flash of understanding, I sat up, eyes widening. "You're right," I whispered. "It's a trick. It's *her*. Luring us. She *wants* us to come out there."

As if in response, the Miguel-like voice issued a last set of agonized, muffled screams—then the screams were cut short.

Silence followed, heavy as a grave.

Squeezing my eyes shut, I clung to John for comfort in the dark. He didn't hug back, but simply sat slumped and staring into the dark.

For a long time I listened, petrified and shaking. But I heard nothing else. The island had again fallen silent.

There was no talk of watch duty. There was no need. There'd be no sleep for anyone tonight.

The hours stretched on into the early morning as we huddled in the ditch. Occasionally exhaustion mastered me. My eyes closed, my head dipped. Then some sound would make me jump—the hoot of a distant owl or the creak of the trees in the sinister wind. I kept looking out through the brush, scanning for movement in the dark.

At last, I noticed color returning to our surroundings. The dolls seemed to float out of the darkness like bodies washing up from the sea. Their pale, ghostly faces watched over us in the gloom.

All the dolls were facing the dock, I realized. Had they been oriented that way before nightfall? I wasn't sure.

But I didn't think so.

We didn't move until the dawn deepened into gold, bright daylight, filtered through the leaves and dolls above. Then I stood cautiously, stooping behind the juniper tree above the ditch where we hid.

I turned on my camera, but only out of habit. The documentary was now a distant consideration, not even close to my mind.

"All right," I whispered. "We made it to morning."

"Do you see anything?" Larry asked.

"Everything looks normal." I sniffed humorlessly as I realized what I'd said. "Normal as ever, anyway."

Hesitating a moment, I said, "Let's get back to camp."

It was Tuesday, now; the start of our fourth day on the island. Four days of bugs, mud, and fear with no food and no sleep. I could barely put one foot in front of the other.

Wearily, I led the way out into the quiet woods, pulling John by the hand. Larry followed, looking suspiciously at the dolls in the trees.

The dolls only gazed off toward the canal, swaying.

Up ahead, the pavilion appeared, and I gasped.

Our camp site was in ruins. The fire was dead, the ashes and coals scattered, as if kicked, in all directions. The firewood and boards we'd gathered were floating on the surface of the canal, and the gas cans with the gasoline had disappeared altogether.

Someone's backpack had been overturned, its contents strewn on the grass. I recognized the canary yellow bikini top and realized it was my stuff. With a little gasp, I rushed to it, setting my camera down and scrambling to gather up all the cassette tapes and fallen gear.

"What the hell?" Larry cried, moving to his own bag. "What the hell is this shit?"

I ignored him for the moment, hurrying to check my equipment for damage. Aside from being a little damp, perhaps from morning dew, the tapes *looked* okay. The thought of losing all the footage, the very reason we came here, was crushing.

"Seriously, Carmen?" Larry cried. "The hell is this?"

I came over to him. He was squatting over his backpack under the pavilion, staring at the bag incredulously. It was soaking wet and covered in some kind of green slime.

"Algae?" I whispered. "From the canal?"

Angrily, Larry started scraping the green substance off with his fingertips. "My bag's all fucking wet! Where the hell did this shit come from?"

Someone had come to our camp site in the night. Rooted through our stuff. Stolen or ruined our fuel and scattered all the boards we'd gathered for the raft.

I turned to Larry, trying to catch my breath.

"She was here."

Chapter 21: The Offering

We stood there in the soft blue light of dawn. For a moment no one moved or spoke, each of us absorbing this latest violation.

She'd been here.

Then Larry stood abruptly, dropping his water-logged bag in disgust. He whirled on his tall boot heels and stalked into the woods.

"Where you going?" I said, surprised.

"To get more wood," he growled. "So we can start another fire, and then build a goddamn raft. Bitch threw out our supplies, but that ain't gonna stop me."

I frowned. I was still in shock, still distant, curiously void of emotion. With no intonation, I said, "Maybe the raft won't do. It's in the water itself, not the island. What makes you think she'll let us leave?"

Larry said, "Look, all I know is I'm not staying on this island. So either help build the raft or stay out of my way."

He turned and stormed into the woods. I looked at John, who met my gaze with a sleepy, sulky blankness around his eyes. As he stood there, I noticed a fat, black leech, stuck to his bare chest.

"John!" I said, startled. "There's a leech on you!"

He looked down slowly and peeled it off, leaving a red sore where it had been. Then he flicked it away and crouched above his backpack, getting out a spare T-shirt and pulling it clumsily over his head.

"Here." Unslinging the crossbow, I handed it to John. "You should have this again. More use to you, anyway."

John looked at it mutely for a moment, then took the crossbow and tightened the makeshift strap over his chest. His sleepy expression never changed.

I looked at him uneasily. "You sure you're okay?"

He smiled thinly. "Right as rain, sugar cane," he said.

That did little to ease my mind. "I... I guess you're on board with Larry's raft thing?"

He rasped, "I'm on board with starting the fire." Then he drifted past me, following Larry into the woods.

I drew a long, slow breath and exhaled, trying to calm myself. Maybe gathering wood would clear my mind, so I wouldn't keep playing those sounds in my head—Miguel screaming, the wind, and the weeping—the *weeping!*

Besides, the raft *had* to make sense. If that didn't work, I didn't think there was any way we could *ever* escape.

Already too late...

I wasn't ready to believe that. Not yet.

I joined Larry and John, dragging likely lumber out of the woods. Despite last night's violent winds, it was even harder to find good wood today. We'd already found the easy pickings the other day. Now those supplies were at the bottom of the canal, and we were starting from scratch. It was hard to find wood fit for burning, much less for building a raft.

Larry glanced at John as we gathered lumber. "So, what do we need to build the raft?"

At last a small light returned to John's blue eyes and he muttered, "I'll show you."

With John's assistance and most of the morning, we gathered half a dozen large logs of various sizes and laid them out in a row under the pavilion. Then, crosswise to the logs, we placed three parallel rows of longer, thinner juniper branches in matching sets, top to bottom.

"We need a rope or something," said John, "stronger than fishing line, to tie the braces together. A saw would be nice, too, to cut these logs even."

"I think I saw a handsaw back at the cabin," I said. "There might be some rope there, too." I looked over at John expectantly. "I take it you want to escort me?"

He glanced back at me, and my smirk died on my lips. Then he turned away, muttering, "I have to start the fire."

Chewing my lip, I glanced out at the still, empty canal. I hadn't seen a single other boat since the first one missed us. Still, I supposed it was important to keep the fire lit.

"So… Larry?" I cleared my throat, turning to him. "*You* want to come with?"

He frowned at John, but John was squatting over the fire pit, almost appearing to sniff the air—as if he smelled some trace of something there that interested him. Raising his eyebrows, Larry turned to shrug at me. "I guess."

We set out through the quiet, eerie trees. Dolls bobbed on wires, crisscrossing our path overhead. Rubber faces watched from the trees. Yet somehow their presence seemed less disturbing to me than it once had. They seemed to stare out toward the canal. Not watching me, but watching *over* me.

It was a thought that would have brought me an ironic smirk a few days ago. It occurred to me now in earnest.

"What's with lover boy?" Larry muttered, once we were out of earshot.

"I think he's in shock. Can you blame him?" I looked down. "He was much closer to Miguel when it happened."

"When that *thing* pulled Miguel under," Larry said with a shudder. "God, I can't believe this is real."

"I think it's past time we started believing," I said. "Our lives might depend on it."

We'd arrived at the cluster of shanty buildings.

"Anyway," I said, "I'll go get the handsaw in the cabin. You check the other buildings for rope."

He nodded nervously. "All right. Yell if you need me."

He left me next to the rotted barn. Across the yard, the house of Don Julio waited for me, dark and uninviting.

Balancing my big camera on my stiff, aching shoulder, I crossed the yard and climbed the rattling porch steps.

"So, we're back at the cabin of Don Julio." Whispering to the camera made me feel less alone. "Hoping we find some last supplies to finish our raft."

As I reached the front door, I pushed it in slowly. "Hello?" I called, in a joking way. My voice sounded more confident than I felt. The camera gave me strength; with the camera, I wasn't alone. I was always being watched by my future audience, so I had to do my best to perform. "Hello? Anybody home?"

Inside the dark shack, the dolls along the back wall gazed back at me blankly. There was no light save for what came through the boarded, dingy window and the doorway behind me.

I saw the bow saw, hanging above the work bench at the back of the room. There were other tools, as well, on the wall—a sledgehammer, a shovel, a big pair of hedge trimmers. Underneath was a tool box with more supplies.

As I stepped inside, the drowned girl's doll caught my eye. The slanted beam of light from the door behind me fell directly on her beneath her colorful shrine.

The sight of the doll gave me pause. I remembered the ghost of the dead girl in my dream, holding this doll.

"Nobody here," I told the doll softly, "but you."

The doll stared off at the rafters, hung with cobwebs and rotted doll parts.

Cautiously, I came closer to the doll, deeper into the gloom. The earthy air in the cabin was stuffy, hard to breathe. The floorboards groaned with every step I took. Slowly, I sank to my knees in front of the doll. It was cold on the dirt floor, yet I was sweating.

"You were Don Julio's favorite, weren't you? What did Miguel say you were called? Rosita, wasn't it?"

I remembered how Miguel had crouched before the doll's shrine, praying to her and putting a ten dollar bill in her dish as an offering. The money was still sitting there in the dish. Anyone could take it, I thought. *I* could take it. I'd given it to Miguel, after all.

Instead, I found myself setting the camera down on the floor next to the doll and me. Then I reached into my pocket and pulled out my wallet. To my dismay, Miguel had cleaned me out; I'd given him every dollar I had to bring us here. I didn't think I had anything to offer.

Then I reached up to touch my grandmother's topaz earrings, dangling from my ears.

My face hardened. I unclasped the earrings, first one, then the other, and laid them carefully in the dish.

Then I closed my eyes and bowed my head.

"This is all I have," I whispered, remembering how Miguel did it. "Please, *por favor.* Take this offering. Give us sanctum from the restless dead."

I couldn't remember the last time I'd prayed. It must have been when I was little, when my dad still forced me to go to church. It felt awkward, and I wasn't sure I was doing it right, but I figured I might as well try. All I had to lose now was my pride.

"Please. You protected Don Julio for so many years. Save us, now, if you can."

The darkness seemed to thicken around me. A chill

crawled up my spine, and I had to look over my shoulder.

There was no one here; yet I sensed I was not alone.

"Please!" My voice came out as a tiny rasp, barely louder than my pounding heart. "Can you hear me?"

At that moment, a sound came from against the wall that made the blood freeze in my veins.

One of the dolls started to laugh.

It was a low, mechanized sound, the recording warped with time. Just a soft burble, so brief it could have been imagined.

But it wasn't.

Leaping to my feet, I whipped toward the sound. My eyes were drawn to a little baby doll on the floor, propped against the wall. His rubber head was caved in and one eye was missing, leaving an open tunnel into the dark skull cavity. The other eye was closed under a plastic eyelid. Green mold covered one side of his face, like a mask.

"Jesus," I whispered, clutching my chest. Cautiously, holding my camera, I moved closer to the doll, looked down at it from a safe distance. "Am I hearing things, or did you just laugh?"

The doll only sat silently against the wall, its one eye closed, as if it were asleep.

I looked across the room at Rosita in her shrine. She wore her perpetual, cartoonish smile. My eyes widened.

"Are you doing this?" I asked Rosita.

Nervously, I sank to my hands and knees and crept closer to the doll that had laughed. Part of me still wanted to believe it was just some kid's toy with a recorded voice. It wouldn't be the first doll with an electronic voice box.

But something told me if I turned this doll over and checked, I'd find the battery compartment empty.

The door of the cabin banged open behind me, and I barely stifled a scream.

When I turned, it was only Larry, blinking at me in alarm. He held up a length of rope. "I got what I needed," he declared, with a note of impatience. "How about you?"

I stood and went to the shelf, yanking the handsaw off the peg board. "Help me get the rest of these tools," I muttered. "I don't want to have to come back."

Larry stepped up beside me and tucked the shovel, the shears, and the walking stick under his arms.

"Come on," he said. "The sooner we finish the raft, the sooner we get off this God-forsaken island."

I nodded absently, still staring at the one-eyed doll, slumped against the wall. As I turned to follow Larry out of the shack, the doll's one vacant eye watched me go, its expression a soft, easy smile.

Something about it seemed off, and only as I looked back from the doorway did I realize what was wrong.

The doll's one eye had been closed before.

Now the eye was open.

Chapter 22: Out of the Frying Pan

Larry led the way through the woods back to the dock, his oversized Harley boots trampling the ferny underbrush. I followed, lugging the rusted steel toolbox at my side, my breath still short from my eerie experience at the cabin.

A day ago, I might have still tried to dismiss what I'd seen or explain it away with some contrived attempt at a *reasonable* explanation. The doll's laughter was only a recording. Some spring in the eyelid had loosened to open the eye.

Yet there was a simpler explanation, too.

I'd asked for a sign, and something had answered.

As we walked, Larry asked, "What took you so long in there, anyway?"

I shrugged, meeting his suspicious gaze with a frown. Finally I admitted, "I was praying."

His eyes narrowed behind his glasses. "*You*, praying?"

I said nothing, deciding not to mention the rest of what I'd seen in there. Larry seemed deeper in denial than ever, but I knew he was just afraid. Telling him about the laughing doll would only frighten him worse.

As we approached the pavilion up ahead, something caught my eye amidst the brush beside the narrow path. The big fern there was bent, weighed down by something pale in the bushes.

Of course it was a doll—but not just any doll.

This doll had soft brown skin, brown hair in a pony-tail, and a sweet smile. The rubber surface of her flesh was wrinkled and warped, like old leather.

It was the doll that looked like me, lying on her side, where John had kicked her into the foliage.

I stared back at the doll, shocked, then entranced. The resemblance was close enough to be eerie, like looking in a funhouse mirror.

"Carmen?" Larry called.

I made myself look away, following Larry back to the camp. I could feel the doll's eyes—so like my own—on my back.

Up ahead, a plume of gray smoke rose from the camp fire beside the pavilion. John stood over the fire, leaning toward it with his palms on his thighs. The clothes he'd taken off to go in after Miguel were drying next to the fire, and the crossbow and bolts were once again strapped over his tight T-shirt.

At first I thought John was leaning over the fire to blow on it, stoking the flames. But as I grew closer, I saw he was simply staring into the fire, captivated, like a kid looking through a candy store window.

"John?" I said. "You okay?"

Slowly, he straightened, and turned to gaze at me with a mute expression. I frowned uneasily. I'd known John for half my life, but I couldn't read him at all today. I guess I'd never seen him forced to deal with something like this. If Larry coped by denial, John, it seemed, coped with child-like withdrawal.

Larry set down the tools under his arms. "Did any boats come by?" he demanded impatiently.

John's eyes crawled over to meet Larry's, lingered there for a long moment, then slid away, back to the fire. He squatted before it, saying nothing.

"I'll take that as a no." Rolling his eyes, Larry took the rope and went to the half-built raft on the pavilion.

When I touched his shoulder, John looked up at me in sullen silence. "You okay?" I asked again.

He looked back at the fire, and I thought the silent treatment would continue. Then he spoke, his voice soft and raw from disuse. "Just need the fire, is all."

I reached out and felt John's forehead for a fever—but to my alarm, his skin felt cold and clammy still. Could he have hypothermia, from his dip in the water? It was cold here at the end of October, but it didn't seem *that* cold.

"Christ, you're freezing. Here, get by me."

I slid under his arm and hugged him close. I wasn't sure, but it felt like he was shivering. I rubbed his back through his shirt, trying to return some warmth to it.

Then John whispered, "What was it we saw last night? What was it that took Miguel?"

He sounded lucid, his breathing fast. As I'd suspected, he was still trying to process what had happened. I paused, suddenly torn. This was a side of John I'd never seen. He seemed vulnerable. Almost child-like.

I squeezed him close. "Don't think about it. We'll be out of here soon. All right?"

But my words came out hollow. I looked past John to the dark waters beyond the dock. The surface was black, rippled in places by the wind.

A surface that dark could hide anything.

"Whatever it was," John said, "I can still hear it. Can't you?"

Can't you hear the crying?

At this angle, lit by the glow of the fire, I couldn't see his face; but that soft, eerie flatness had returned to his voice, as if John himself were somewhere far away, quite detached from all of this.

My heart raced. I closed my eyes, but that only made

the memories of last night more vivid—the screaming, the splashing, the dark shape beyond the rough waves.

I remembered the sound of the endless weeping—one moment pitiful and blubbering, the next intermingled with mad laughter, then erupting into wails of pure fury.

"Yes," I admitted. "I can still hear it."

They say if you hear her cry, it's already too late.

"I can't stop hearing it," John whispered. "I can't get it out of my head. And the strangest part is, I'm not sure I even want to. It was... *beautiful.* Almost musical."

I stared up at him in horror. "John, please. Try not to think about it. You have to try to not think about it, okay?"

John only stared into the flames, his expression slack.

"Can I get a hand over here?" Larry called.

Eagerly disentangling from John, I stumbled back to the pavilion. My head swam from standing too quickly on an empty stomach, and I felt half in a trance myself. My fear had slipped its leash and run rampant again.

Can't you hear the crying?

Those had been the last words of both Don Julio and Miguel, before the thing in the water called them to their deaths. Now John was saying it, too.

And we were about to challenge those waters head on.

Under the crumbling roof of the pavilion, Larry was wrestling with the rope, tying the last support braces to the raft. "Hold this," he said, gesturing at one of the logs. Then he grunted, straining, to pull the rope taut. He glared past me at John. "Lover boy still too good to help?"

I followed his gaze toward John. "Let him be." I looked at the little hand-made raft. "You sure about this? It doesn't exactly look seaworthy."

Larry shrugged. "Let's just see if it floats." He finished

tightening the last knot, then nodded toward the other side of the raft. "Help me slide it down to the water."

Taking care around the rough-hewn edges, I gripped the raft. Together we pushed it down the shallow stairs to the dock. With a final heave, we slid it with a splash into the muddy shallows, where it bobbed, floating.

Larry grinned at me. "I think I built a raft."

I was impressed. "Yeah. Hopefully it'll be enough."

"Get your stuff," Larry said. "We're outta here."

I followed Larry back to the pavilion, where his things were lying out to dry. As he packed his bag, I turned to John. "You ready?" I called.

He stood, turning away from the fire reluctantly, and started to gather his things. "What about the fire?" I asked.

He shrugged. "Let it burn." With a blank look, he shouldered his bag and drifted down the stairs to the dock.

Scowling, I grabbed the tin bucket we'd been using to filter our water. Then I poured it slowly over the fire, and afterward I kicked and stomped the embers as the steam blew back my hair.

As I lifted my head, something caught my eye.

The mocha-colored baby doll at the tree line, the one that looked like me, was still staring at me innocently. I found it hard to look away.

"Any day now," Larry called impatiently from the dock. Both of them were down there, their backs turned.

"Coming," I called. Then, hardly aware of what I was doing, I hurried over to the doll and opened my backpack.

The island wanted us to have these dolls, I was sure of it. And I wasn't going to ignore that any longer.

Miguel had lost his doll, and now Miguel was dead. It was a coincidence that wasn't lost on me.

"If we're supposed to have these," I muttered. "Maybe you'll protect us out there."

Reverently, I slid the filthy doll into my bag, next to my camera, then zipped it up to hide her.

"Carmen!" Larry called again.

"All right!" I hurried back to the dock. "Just want to make sure I have everything."

Larry was sitting on the dock's edge, easing down onto the flimsy raft. When it held his weight, he looked up at John. "Get me that walking stick."

Larry was pointing at Don Julio's walking stick, leaning against the railing by the toolbox at the top of the stairs. John made no move, so I grabbed it on my way down the stairs, handing it to Larry.

He took it carefully and jammed it into the bed of the canal to anchor the raft. John swung down onto the raft beside him, crouching as it rocked among the reeds.

I looked out at the dark water. It was already past noon, and the late autumn light was starting to change, turning red. But no light penetrated the gray-green waters. Nothing could be seen below the surface.

"The hell you waiting for?" Larry called. "Let's go!"

I handed Larry my backpack, carrying its secret cargo, then I eased down onto the raft. It was already sinking low from the weight of John and Larry; when I joined them, it went fully under. Dark water splashed up through the wide gaps in the logs, soaking my pants. It was surprisingly cold.

I splayed on the bottom of the raft as it buoyed about, trying to hold my bag above the water. Larry put out a hand to steady me.

"This isn't gonna work," I said. "We're sinking!"

"No," Larry insisted, "just riding low. I should've built a platform on top or something."

"No, really." I looked at the water around my knees. "I've been on pool floats sturdier than this."

"Look, there's no way I'm turning back, okay? We'll *make* it work."

On his knees, Larry leaned over to poke the walking stick into the water, pushing off from the dock. The motion rocked the raft and I clung to the rough logs till the ramshackle vessel steadied itself.

As we drifted away from the Island of the Dolls, Larry took a deep breath and released it.

"I ain't *ever* setting foot on that place again," he said. His low voice was a strange mix of loathing and triumph.

"Good riddance," John muttered darkly.

As the forlorn pier and pavilion fell away, I lifted my head and watched it go. I should have felt relief to be done with the island, like the others.

Instead, I felt only a sinking feeling.

They were sure we were escaping the danger, while I kept wondering if we'd just abandoned our only safe haven; our only hope for sanctum from the true danger, which dwelled not on the island but in the water itself.

"Out of the frying pan," I whispered to myself.

Into the canal.

Chapter 23: On the Canal

We floated off, clinging to our crude, half-submerged raft of bundled logs. Larry sat at the back, his boot heels braced in the frame while he poled us along with Don Julio's walking stick. Only six feet long, the stick made a poor rafting pole; Larry had to bend precariously close to the dark water with each thrust just to hit bottom.

"Careful," I told him. "Stick to the shallows, at least."

"Carmen!" Larry laughed. "Stop worrying. We did it! We're free, all right?"

"If you say so," I said. I couldn't relax. Not here. Not until my feet were back on solid ground.

Now that the raft had steadied, I unzipped my bag to get out my camera. Filming always distracted me from my fear. As I slid the camera out, I saw the grungy doll I'd stowed in my bag, and tried to take comfort from her, too, before I zipped my bag to hide her from the others.

Grant us sanctuary, I found myself thinking silently. *Save us from the restless dead.*

"Which way to Xochimilco?" Larry asked.

I thought about it. "That way, I think?" I pointed up ahead, to where our quiet green section of the canal joined a larger thoroughfare. Out of habit, I looked to John for his directional expertise, but he only stared into space, kneeling on the raft beside me and hugging his bag.

"Hey John?" said Larry. "You want to help navigate, make sure I'm going the right way? I don't exactly know what I'm doing."

"John?" I prompted.

"Yeah." He stirred, with a curt nod. "She's right. That

way. Northwest."

I huddled against him, holding my camera on my other shoulder, my bag on my back. The cold water licked at my jeans through the gaps in the raft. The chill radiated through my clothes, through my flesh, into my bones.

We drifted through the grove of juniper trees that grew up out of the shallow water in front of the island. These trees bore the outermost dolls, perimeter sentries, stapled to the tree trunks in grizzled, water-ravaged rot. As the last of them faded behind us and we fell out of their silent gaze, heading deeper into the dark green tunnel of the canal, I began to feel more and more anxious.

A vague sense of isolation crept over me, and suddenly I was certain we were no longer sailing down an old canal in Mexico. Perhaps we were no longer on Earth at all, but some swampy borderland between the waking world and a hellish nightmare where anything was possible—and no one could save us.

Holding my camera above the water in one hand and trying not to rock the precarious boat, I clumsily unslung my backpack, bringing it into my lap.

Suddenly I felt the need to see the doll I had stowed again. To know I wasn't alone.

I opened the top of my backpack. The doll looked out at me with a blank expression. My throat felt very dry as I started to speak.

"Por favor," I whispered. "Give us sanctum from the restless dead."

Larry looked over his shoulder, raising an eyebrow. "Doing your Miguel impression?" His smirk died as his eyes fell to my bag. "What's that?"

Panic flooded me and I tried to close the bag, but it was too late. John reached over and held the top flap open as I tried to close it. His blank face twisted to outrage.

"The hell?" He plucked the whole bag out of my grip as easily as a man taking a toy from an unruly child. He withdrew the doll with one smooth motion, holding her up by the ponytail. His mouth hung open in mute anger.

Larry's eyes widened and he gasped. "Jesus! They're back?" Tucking the walking stick under his arm, he raced to open his own bag, at his feet.

Before John could throw the doll overboard, I grabbed her by the foot. "Don't!" I cried. "Please!"

Finding no doll in his own bag, Larry looked up, his eyebrows drawing down into an accusatory glare. "Wait. Did you *mean* to bring that thing?"

"Larry, let me explain…"

"What the hell are you *thinking?*" he shouted. "We're trying to get away and you're bringing them with us?"

He reached over, grabbing the doll and helping John wrench it from my grip. The raft rocked in the struggle, splashing on the green water. For a moment I thought I'd fall. Then I grabbed John and steadied myself.

Larry held the doll, looking down at her—my image—with a scowl. "Sorry, but we are *not* taking any souvenirs. Definitely not, thank you very much! This shit ends here."

Before I could stop him, he threw the doll out into the water. It landed with a splash and sank into darkness.

"Asshole!" I shrieked, lunging at Larry. John held me back, pulling me down to the gapped floor of the rocking raft. I barely kept a grip on my camera. "We were given those dolls to *protect* us!"

"We're done with all that," Larry insisted.

I twisted my head to glare at John. "Get off me!"

He released me at last. I checked my camera; it had been splashed in the scuffle, but it was still recording, the lens distorted by water droplets. "Idiots!" I shouted.

"Yes, yes," Larry grumbled. "Check your footage. Make sure you got everyone's reactions."

"Fuck you, Larry."

He resumed his seat at the back of the raft and leaned forward, starting to pole again through the water. "Just sit down and shut up," he said. "No more surprises. No more bullshit. Okay? We are *done* with your little *Muñecas* project, and done with Island of the Dolls."

I said nothing, glaring at his back in fury. Slowly, my fury faded into fear; because now we really *were* alone.

That doll was the last talisman, the last protection we held against whatever lurked in the canal.

Before us, the dark, narrow waterway stretched on into green gloom beneath the treetops. The shores to either side were indistinct swamps, the water green with algae slime. Gnarled willows grew up from the depths like great, strange hands, laced in vines and tendrils. Beyond, the half-sunken islands and marshy lands to either side were empty and overgrown, no signs of life.

I remembered passing down this canal the day we came to the island. Hard to believe that was only four days ago. It felt like a lifetime.

This empty land had seemed so peaceful and pastoral on the trip to the island. I remember how optimistic I felt then, filming every detail. Everything had seemed so bright and green, full of possibility, like springtime in autumn.

Now it was only a dismal gray swamp, overgrown and teeming with biting flies. Our bug spray had long since run out and I kept swatting gnats away. Sweaty and filthy as we were, the bugs seemed especially attracted to us—acutely aware of any life passing through their desolate kingdom.

Larry leaned over the back of the boat, poling us along in the shallows, avoiding the deeper, darker water at the center of the canal.

God only knew what could lurk just under the surface.

Quickly, Larry started to sweat, pausing to peel off his now-ruined leather jacket. His slender muscles tightened as he leaned on the pole, pushing us through the reeds. Occasionally some unseen, submerged tree limb tugged the bottom of the raft, but Larry was able to push us free.

"We going the right way?" he asked John.

The further we got from the island, the more color came back to John's face. "North." He nodded. "Yeah."

I dried off my camera sullenly with a towel. It still seemed to work, to my amazement. I wanted to put it away, to protect it from further damage, but I also wanted to keep it well within reach, in case something happened out here that I needed to document. I kept it out and held it close in both hands.

"Sorry about your camera," Larry muttered. "I didn't mean for that to happen."

"Forget it," I said at last. "It's only a camera. If I get out of this with nothing else lost, all things considered I'd say that's pretty lucky."

I pictured Miguel, floating one minute, yanked under the next. I tried to push the thought away.

"I wonder if any of our stuff will still be at the hotel," Larry said glumly.

"Who cares?" John muttered, looking around at the dreary setting with disgust. "I mean, do you even want to go back? Let's get a cab straight to the airport and get the fuck out of here."

Larry smiled slowly. "I could get behind that."

"We'll have to go to the cops," I said firmly. "We'll have to tell someone what happened to Miguel. He said his mom was sick. They deserve to know what happened."

Larry and John both looked away, saying nothing. I

took that for agreement, and figured that settled it; but as I thought about it, I wondered what we'd tell the police.

Something pulled him under. He heard La Llorona crying, and once you hear her cry, it's already too late.

They'd either laugh us out of the building or arrest us for Miguel's murder. That's how insane it sounded.

As we floated, the sky grew more overcast, letting less and less light through the canopy. I thought I recognized some of our surroundings from our first trip, but I couldn't be sure. In the dim light, it all looked the same: a labyrinth of muddy islands, strips of sand, and half-submerged trees.

We passed no other boats.

John advised Larry with increasing confidence, telling him every turn to make. After an hour or so, Larry was drenched in sweat and losing steam. John offered to take over, kneeling at the back of the raft and pushing with the pole in silence. With each yard we put between us and the island, John seemed more and more like his old self.

Larry sat cross-legged on the raft beside me, leaning back to catch his breath. "We must be getting closer," he said. "Don't all this look familiar?"

I shrugged. "I guess so. Don't it all look the same?"

"I definitely feel like I've seen this before," Larry said, looking at the murky swamp passing by on either side.

As evening approached, however, I began to grow nervous again. Had the journey taken this long the first time? It didn't seem like it. Granted, Miguel had been an expert at this, while John and Larry were amateurs, but it still felt as though we should have been there by now.

Just as I started to get anxious again, Larry sat up, pointing. "Look! What's that?"

I followed his gaze. The canal had opened wider. Up ahead, in the distance, a land mass spanned the canal, and I thought I saw buildings through the trees.

"Is that the mainland?" Larry shielded his eyes with a hand to see. "I think I see people. Oh, thank God!"

John didn't react, merely poled the raft along. With each thrust, his face and upper body dipped close to the water, which he stared into with fixed concentration. The red glow on the waves sparkled in his eyes. I frowned. He'd grown quieter the last few minutes.

But Larry clapped his hands and yelled in excitement. I jumped, startled, and met his eyes with a nervous laugh. He grinned. "Man, I hope some of that footage survived. We'll have one hell of a story to tell. All things considered, I still think we should've stayed local for the project."

"Yeah," I said, with a smile. "I agree."

The trip had been the mistake of a lifetime, to be exact. But it looked like we were going to make it, after all. We were going to make it home.

I looked back at the land up ahead, shielding my eyes from the stark, fading light of the setting sun.

My smile faded as the land grew closer. "Oh my God."

"Wait…" Larry muttered beside me, his voice bereft of all force. Squinting through his glasses, he was starting to see what I saw.

It wasn't the mainland at all: the canal wrapped around the landmass to either side. And those pale figures beneath the trees weren't *people*, as Larry had thought. They were too small. Too still.

Larry raised his hands to clutch his head. His face twisted in rage and panic. "It can't be! No, God, *please!*"

The things under the trees weren't people.

They were dolls, hanging from every bough and branch, sitting against the tree trunks, dangling their feet over the edge of the island, as if waiting for us.

Somehow we'd returned to the Island of the Dolls.

Chapter 24: Return

"No," Larry whispered. "This can't be happening…"

I stared, dumbfounded, as we floated closer. This looked like the other side of the island, opposite the dock. Somehow we'd come to the north side, despite traveling straight north all day.

Larry whirled at John, the sudden motion rocking the raft. "I thought you were navigating! You said we were going north!"

Some life returned to John's eyes in the form of anger. "We *were* going north," he growled.

"Well, you fucked up! You think this is a game?"

"Get out of my face!"

John shoved Larry away. Larry's arms pinwheeled and he nearly toppled back into the dark water.

"Stop it!" I hugged my camera with one hand, clinging to John's legs with the other. The raft was shaking wildly, threatening to capsize.

Crouching for balance, Larry faced John, barely inches between them. "If we were going north," Larry demanded, "how the hell did we end up back here?"

"I don't know," John growled. "You must've taken a wrong turn. It wasn't me."

Larry's face was purple with fury. "You were steering for the last hour!"

"Steering *north,*" John replied flatly.

I interrupted, trying to get myself between them on the tiny raft. "He's right," I said. "We were watching him. He was going north. We went north all day."

"Then how the hell are we *back here?*" Larry's desperate voice cracked as he thrust a finger at the island.

Carried by momentum, we were still drifting in toward shore. I chewed my lip as the trees loomed closer, the pale sightless dolls staring out as we approached.

"I told you she wouldn't let us leave," I whispered.

"Thanks, Carm!" Larry snapped. "Really helping."

"You're the one who threw away my doll!" I cried. "What good is fighting doing us? Almost turning the boat over, getting us all killed!"

"Give me that!" Larry tugged the walking stick away from John, who opened his hands to let him take it. Turning to the raft's edge, Larry began to pole away, fighting momentum as the island drew us, magnetically, closer.

"What are you doing?" I demanded.

"What's it look like? I'm going back the other way. We must have made a wrong turn. It's the only explanation."

I sighed. "Larry, it's almost dark. If we couldn't find our way in daylight, how will we get there in the dark?"

He whirled on me, his eyes wide and white, his lips peeled back in a desperate snarl. "Then what? I told you, I am *not* going back on that island!"

I turned and looked pensively at the dolls, white as ghosts under the trees. "I don't think we have much choice," I said quietly.

We couldn't leave because she wouldn't *let* us leave.

Larry winced and sagged with a whimper, as if he'd been dealt a physical blow. "God, no. This can't be happening. God somebody please just wake me up."

I tried to stave off my own panic. "We'll be all right," I said, for my own benefit as much as Larry's. "Maybe it's just like you said. We don't know the area. We could've made a wrong turn. We'll have to try again tomorrow—"

Larry barely let me finish. *"Fuck* tomorrow!" he cried, turning to me. I was alarmed to see tears at the corners of his eyes. "What the fuck good is tomorrow if we don't make it through tonight?"

I knew I should say something, but I didn't know what. All I could hear were the words of the dead girl, bouncing in my head like a nursery rhyme.

Already too late. Already too late.

I put my hand on his shoulder, steadying him. "Larry, we're gonna be okay, all right? We'll try again tomorrow."

My voice trembled with fear. I doubt I convinced him. I wasn't even convincing myself.

Again I had that strange sensation that we were no longer on Earth at all; we had passed through some nexus point along the canal that had brought us to this strange and alien world, where you could travel in one direction for hours straight and arrive back where you began.

Where dolls picked themselves up and moved in the night.

Where there were *things* in the water.

Inexorably, borne by some subtle, unknown current, we bobbed in toward the island. John took the walking stick back from Larry, who offered little resistance. Then, squatting again at the back of the boat, John began to push us along, controlling our approach. His expression was flat, his eyes once again far away.

We drifted past the low, deteriorating wood framework of the island, and I recognized where we were. This was where I'd first seen Miguel's body, floating down the canal. It was also the place where Don Julio and the little girl were said to have drowned. The thought made me shiver. I watched the waters nervously, fearing every ripple and splash.

Up ahead, as we rounded the corner of the island, the old, decrepit dock came into view, its pilings green with algae and rot. Doll heads adorned the pilings and railings of the pier. Only as we floated up to that familiar dock did I grasp the reality of the situation.

She wasn't going to let us go.

Already too late…

The raft bumped to a stop on the piling of the dock.

"Oh, God," Larry was muttering, shaking and holding himself. "Oh, this can't be happening. Please, God. This is a dream…"

John reached out and grabbed the piling, holding the raft in place against the side of the pier. I put my camera up on the dock, then pulled myself up, surprised at how weak I felt after a few days of no food or sleep. I sprawled there a moment on my hands and knees, wet and shaking.

When Larry climbed up, John pulled the raft along the pier using the pilings, till it wedged in the reeds by the shore. Then he sprang up, joining us on the dock. He leaned on Don Julio's walking stick, meeting no one's eyes.

"I guess we'll need to tie the boat up," I said.

Larry uttered a bitter, humorless laugh. "Yeah. That worked real well last time."

"You got a better idea?" I glared at him. "I mean, we could try pulling it up on shore, if you think we can move it. Which of you wants to get in the water and push?"

We all stood there a moment, looking out at the dark canal. Neither of them seemed eager to set foot in there, and I certainly wouldn't. In fact, alarming and bewildering though it was to find myself back on this island, I couldn't help but feel a little relief just to be on solid ground.

Larry rolled his eyes and stomped off up the dock.

"Where are you going?" I asked.

"We need rope to tie the boat, right?" he growled. "I'm getting some fucking rope!"

Grabbing my camera, I hurried after him, looking around at the darkening foliage through the night vision lens. Faces swam up from the gloom, their sightless eyes watching us pass.

"Larry, wait! Stick together!"

But he ignored me, storming up the stairs to the little pavilion above the dock. Everything there was just as we'd left it. The gray ashes in the fire pit next to the pavilion were still drying where I'd doused them. Don Julio's toolbox still sat on a crate under the pavilion, where Larry had built the raft. Larry went to the toolbox now and fished around inside. The rattling of tools was horrifically loud in the island's cathedral silence.

"We used all the rope on the raft," I said behind him. "We'll have to go to the cabin and look for some more."

Larry barked a laugh. "Yeah, right. Nah, this'll do."

He raised a pair of rusty pliers, inspecting them in the fading light. Then he strode out to the tree line, pausing under one of the clotheslines strung between the trees, hung with dolls. My eyes widened as I realized what he was doing, but it was already too late.

"Larry! Don't!"

Reaching up with the pliers, he snipped the clothesline at the tree trunk. The string of dolls fell in an unseemly pile. Trampling them, Larry moved across the path to the other side of the clothesline, cutting the length of rope free. Then he turned and stalked back to the pavilion, dragging the rope, still strung with dolls. They flopped and bounced through the dirt and foliage behind him, like tin cans on a newlywed's car—but instead of cans, these were tiny, human bodies.

I gaped at him, horrified. Finally I managed to croak, "You can't do that."

But Larry had already walked past me, dragging his ghoulish chain of dolls down the stairs behind him. He passed John, who watched on the dock in mute disinterest. At the end of the pier, Larry hopped carelessly onto the raft and wrapped the rope around one of the crossbeams.

"You want to watch me tie it, John?" Larry growled, his voice all bitter hostility. "Make sure I do it right?"

John said nothing.

I came down the stairs, trying to stay calm, though my mind was screaming panic. "Larry, this shit isn't helping."

"Who cares?" Larry cried, springing back onto the dock. "Nothing we do helps anything. So what the fuck does anything matter anymore?"

"That's no reason to push our luck," I replied tightly.

"Whatever. The boat's secure. At least until whatever fucked with our stuff last night comes back again."

The thought disquieted me. I looked out at the canal as night fell over the horizon. I was starting to wonder if I'd ever see another sunset away from this island.

"The gas cans we found are gone," I whispered. "We don't have time to look for more fuel, and I don't think we should stay by the water anyway. As we found out last night, she can get to us here." Preparing for his resistance, I looked at Larry. "I think we should go back to the cabin, like the first night. Nothing happened to us on the first night."

"The dollhouse," Larry growled sardonically. "Literally the epicenter of creepy on the *island* of the creepy." But the fight had gone out of him, evidently. He only threw his hands in the air and strode past me down the dock. "Whatever. I don't care anymore."

Swallowing, I started to follow, then paused. "John?"

John was still staring off at the water. He was like a different person lately—or perhaps more like no person at all. So quiet and subdued, I'd almost forgotten he was with us. But at the sound of his name, he blinked and glanced at me irritably, as if I'd interrupted a critical calculation.

"What?"

I frowned. "You coming?"

He nodded and followed us at last, with a final, forlorn look at the water.

Behind him, something splashed out on the canal, just once. Just a frog or a fish, most likely. Something ordinary.

Or maybe not.

I shuddered and turned away.

Chapter 25: The Séance

As darkness fell, we hurried through the doll-infested woods. Already the trees grew restless in the cold night breeze. From the corner of my eye, the swaying dolls seemed to turn to track us as we passed—but if I looked toward the movement, I saw nothing.

Still, I could feel their eyes on us as we walked.

How many souls had drowned in this canal over the centuries? How many spirits haunted this island?

How many victims of the thing in the water?

Was Miguel out there somewhere, watching through the eyes of a doll?

The claustrophobic trees broke and I saw Don Julio's building, the bleached, rotten wood bright in the gloom. With little time before night arrived in full, I hurried across the overgrown yard. Holding my camera at my shoulder, I looked back to wave at the other two.

"Hurry!"

The screen door of Don Julio's shack clacked open and closed in the growing breeze. I felt oddly eager to be inside, with walls—and dolls—between me and the night. I peered inside with my camcorder, using night vision to scan the darkness. Lifeless faces floated, pale in the dark. Nothing moved but white dust, hanging on the stuffy air.

Satisfied, I stepped inside. John and Larry followed. Larry shut the front door and fastened the chain. But the outer screen door kept clacking, and even with the lock in place, the wind shook the front door in its jamb, as if there were something out there pawing to come in.

Come out, the wind seemed to whisper. *Come back out and play awhile. It's not quite dark yet and there's still so much fun we can have, and by the way, have you seen my children? You can't miss them. They're dead. I drowned them, you see, like I drowned Don Julio. Like I drowned Miguel. Like I'll drown you, too, if you only come out, come out and join us...*

Quickly, I moved to the oil lamp at the back of the room. "John," I asked, "are any of your matches still dry?" When he didn't answer, I turned to look at him. "John?"

He stood behind me, staring at the dolls on the wall with a pensive, mistrustful expression.

Larry scowled at him, his hands on his hips. "Hello? Earth to asshole?"

John blinked and stirred from his trance, reaching into his backpack to remove his box of matches. He handed them to me distractedly, barely meeting my eyes. He kept staring at the dolls in a way that made me uneasy. As if he saw something there we didn't.

Striking a match, I lit the lamp carefully.

As the light bloomed, I noticed the one-eyed doll that I'd heard laugh the last time I was here. I remembered how the one remaining eye had rolled open to look at me, and how disconcerted I'd been.

The eye was still open. Under other circumstances, I might have wondered if it had ever been shut at all, or if that had all been my imagination.

I knew better now than to question my own eyes.

"What's wrong?" Larry asked, his voice tense.

"This is the doll I heard laugh, last time I was here."

Pursing my lips thoughtfully, I leaned closer. Something glinted on the floorboards behind the doll. My mouth started to fall open as a thought occurred to me.

The doll had laughed when I prayed for protection.

What if someone had been trying to get my attention?

I brushed the cobwebs aside, then gently gripped the doll under the arms. The doll's rotten sailor uniform was so cold it almost felt damp.

"Carmen?" Larry said again, with a note of impatience and maybe fear. "What are you doing?"

"There's something here," I whispered. "I should've noticed it before…"

As I pushed the doll aside, I frowned. A square had been cut into the floorboard, with small hinges attached—some kind of tiny trapdoor or hidden compartment.

I looked at Larry urgently. "There's something behind this panel."

At that moment, as if in response, the wind picked up outside. The door of the cabin rattled in its loose frame, and I jumped, startled. Whining through the eaves of the shack, the wind sounded shrill and alive, so much so I could barely hear myself think. What had John said, that first night?

That wind really wails out here. No wonder Don Julio had to sing to the mermaids. How else could they have heard him over the noise?

In the flickering gloom of the lantern, Larry stared at the door, his face aghast with fear. John sat in the corner on his towel, hugging his knees loosely, staring into the dark.

Outside, a soft crying rose through the howl of the wind.

"Something's out there," Larry whispered.

"Don't listen," I said. "It's a trick."

Yet the crying grew louder. It had come with the wind, and at first the sound was indistinguishable from the howl and bluster of the weather—so much so that you might have thought it was only your imagination, a trick of the wind, nothing more.

Now it rose into its own sound, human and yet not human, a morphing chorus of male and female voices, all weeping and moaning, as if some hellish procession of the dead were ferrying down the canal. Some of the voices were so familiar I could picture the faces, floating past. Miguel's voice was there. My father's voice was there.

My own voice was there, calling to me.

Kicking back from the wall, I clapped my hands over my ears. "Don't listen!" I shouted.

Larry followed my example, covering his ears. But John, in the corner, merely sat listening. His eyes looked vacant and he wore the hint of a smile, as if listening to a lullaby. The sight of it disturbed me.

Even with my ears covered, the sounds still pierced into my head. One voice, in particular, stood out from the rest.

The voice of a woman crying.

It wasn't far. On the canal, or somewhere on the island.

And it was coming closer. Closer to the shack with every minute.

The door rattled in the roaring wind. I could hear things moving outside the cabin, trees groaning and dolls clacking together like flat bells.

On my hands and knees, I scrambled across the old warped floorboards, down to the dirt floor on the other side of the cabin. There I fell before the shrine of Rosita, clasping my hands before her cracked, smiling visage.

"Please!" I cried. "Save us!"

The big baby doll only stared into the darkness above my head. Her faint, perpetual smile seemed somehow smug and pitiless.

It's already too late. Once you hear her cry…

I feared we'd worn out our welcome. Kicking dolls, tearing them from trees, dumping them in the canal.

Would the spirits even listen to our pleas?

"Save us!" I begged.

But the crying continued endlessly, coming ever closer. If the dolls heard my prayer, I couldn't hear their answer.

All I could hear was this terrifying, heart-wrenching, maddening sound.

Then a thought occurred to me. If the crying was all I could hear, perhaps it was all the dolls could hear as well.

I turned to Larry and John desperately. "They can't hear me!" I shouted. "You have to pray with me!"

John looked toward me slowly, his face vacant.

Larry held his ears, his face twisted in terror. "She's coming," he whispered. "Oh, God, she's coming!"

"Please!" I yelled at them. "You have to help! The dolls can't hear me alone!"

To my horror, John started to smile.

"She sounds so sad," he murmured wistfully.

Once you hear her cry, it's already too late.

Even I couldn't deny the compulsion, the urge to rush out of the shack to help this poor, weeping woman. But I wouldn't let myself give in. Not now.

"It's a trick!" I shouted. When John didn't respond, I crawled toward him on my hands and knees so I could shake him by the shoulders. "Don't listen to her!"

"It's not just her," said Larry, on his knees behind me. He clutched his ears. "It's… it's Miguel. It's my old man. They're all out there."

"She's *luring* us," I cried. "I don't think she can get to us here. We're safe as long as no one goes anywhere."

"We *have* to go," John whispered. His vacant, staring eyes were growing slowly wider, as if seeing something terrifying. "Can't you hear the crying?"

"No!" I took John's hand by force. He offered little resistance. He was too far gone, entranced. "Please, resist! We're protected here. You have to have faith!"

But even now, I could see the doll in her shrine across the room. The flickering light in the lamp cast her face in sharp shadows, and I thought her smile looked cruel and indifferent. Larry had thrown my doll in the water. Had we blasphemed the spirits too much?

Were we, as Miguel had put it, forsaken?

I refused to believe it. It was simply that the spirits couldn't hear us over the wailing.

Suddenly a thought occurred to me.

No wonder Don Julio had to sing to the mermaids. How else could they have heard him?

"The spirits can't hear us," I said. "We have to *sing!*"

The old man in Xochimilco said Don Julio used to sing when the mermaids called to him. It hadn't saved him in the end, but perhaps if all of us joined together—like a séance—we could summon the ghosts of the island to protect us now. If I was right in my hunch, the spirits that haunted this place were victims of La Llorona, drowned in the canals over the years. Surely they'd help us against her.

If only they could hear us.

"Take my hand!" I shouted, reaching for Larry. John clenched my other hand.

I started to sing.

The tune seemed to come to me fully formed, as if I'd heard it before. Probably I was just fitting my words to the tune of some pop song I'd heard long ago.

"Oh, little spirits, please help us today! Give us sanctum and mercy, I pray!"

I looked from John to Larry. "Sing!" Then I repeated the verse, raising my voice.

"Oh, little spirits, help us today! Give us sanctum and mercy, I pray!"

Outside, the crying grew ever closer. It had started in the water, beyond the dock. Now it was climbing through the pavilion. Moving through the trees on slow, wet feet.

My throat went dry. Was I wrong? Could she come for us on land, after all? Or was it a trick, to shake our faith, to break our wills?

The candle in the lamp wavered. The wind wailed through the flimsy, slat-board walls, shaking the cabin.

And the weeping grew closer—right outside, now, in the yard. Things were moving and groaning and weeping out there, a circle of manias, surrounding the shack. I went on singing, trying to shout it down.

"Oh, little spirits, please help us today! Give us—"

Something banged the door with a *thud,* and I screamed. The old porch creaked under some unseen weight. Expecting something to burst in at any moment, I resumed my chant, louder now, as loud as I could, belting:

"Oh, little spirits! Help us today! Give us sanctum and mercy, I pray!"

Kneeling at my side, John had taken up the song, too, mumbling under his breath. I turned to reach for Larry, begging him to join us. "Larry!" I shouted.

He huddled against the wall a few feet away, hugging his knees to his chest and trembling. His eyes were wide behind his glasses. They met mine, saw me reach for him.

But he only shook his head, refusing to join us.

"We have to get out of here," he whispered, clutching his hands to his ears. "We have to get off the island."

Branches tap-danced on the rusted roof. The candle spun madly in the wind, guttering. In its flashing red light, Larry rose, leaning unsteadily on the wall.

"I have to go *now*. I can't wait."

"Larry, *no!*"

"I'll *swim*, if I must."

His voice was urgent but eerily dreamy. I recognized it all too well. Miguel had said much the same things in much the same way, the night before he vanished.

"Larry!"

As I fell out of the rhythm of the chant, the wind seemed to howl more and more loudly. I heard the porch creaking. Through the gaps in the walls I saw shadows move outside.

Then something banged the boarded-up window in the wall behind us, hard enough to shatter the dusty glass inside and send it tinkling over our heads.

Larry screamed and made a run for it, bolting for the door, sobbing. He wrenched on it repeatedly, forgetting the chain lock in his confusion, till the chain snapped and the door flew open, letting in the night in one cold gust.

"*Larry!*"

My voice was swallowed in the gale, which shook the walls of the cabin. Larry was already gone, leaving the door swinging in the wind.

Releasing John's hand, I grabbed my camera, which sat on the floor behind me, recording. "We have to stop him!"

John sat where he was, staring out the swinging door, unmoved by the noise and chaos. "Let him go," he said, oddly calm. "It's what he wants."

For a moment, I could only stare at John, shocked and outraged. John only looked back mutely, his blue eyes pale and indifferent. There was no time to stand there arguing with him.

I turned and pushed through the swinging door to go after Larry myself.

Chapter 26: Don't Go

Outside, the yard was chaos. The wind roared. Dead autumn leaves spun through the air on tiny cyclones. Baby dolls bobbed and danced on their ropes, crisscrossing through the trees. Some had fallen to lie in the grass, their tiny bodies in heaps.

I saw nothing else snooping outside the shack, but I wasn't about to wait around and find out. With reckless abandon, I ran down the porch steps and into the yard.

"Larry!" I shouted, searching the night for him. My naked eyes saw nothing in the gloom, but when I put my eye to my camcorder's viewfinder, the screen lit up with gray-green faces, pale and floating amid the trees.

As I swung the camera around, I caught the back of Larry's shirt as he fled into the foliage across the yard.

He was heading for the dock, I realized. Like Miguel, like Don Julio, he was being drawn to the water.

He'd heard her cry, and now he couldn't help it.

It was already too late.

My arms and legs pumped as I raced to keep up with him. I tried to hold the camera to my eye, using the night vision to keep my bearings. Even so, I nearly got turned around, lost in the woods. I kept scanning side to side, searching for threats. In every direction, from every angle, the dolls seemed to whisper and sway in the wind.

Something moved in the woods beside me and I swung toward it in the dark. My own breath misted before me in ragged gasps.

There was nothing else there.

Fleeing, I saw the pavilion ahead, the old gray wood shining in the infrared of night vision. Larry, in his dark jeans and boots, was like a shadow against the white. I saw him pause to root through Don Julio's toolbox. Taking something, he turned and descended the stairs toward the dark water with purposeful strides.

"No, Larry! Stop, please!"

I followed him across the pavilion, my heart racing. Was it my imagination in the dark, or was the wooden floor of the pavilion wet in places—little puddles shaped like footprints, leading the way toward the dock?

As I reached the top of the stairs and looked down, I saw the entire dock was drenched in water, as though a tremendous wave had come ashore.

A wave—or something else.

The water beyond was rough and churning, the surface breaking in white sprays like the sea in a storm. There was no light. The sky was veiled in clouds.

On the dock below stood Larry, Don Julio's long walking stick in one hand, a pair of hedge trimmers in the other. Even as I watched, he turned to the piling where the raft was tied, raised the rusted trimmers, and violently hacked the rope, severing it after several attempts.

"Larry," I shouted. "Wait!"

The wind howled, rippling through his jacket, but he didn't stop or turn back. Tossing aside the trimmers, he sprang down onto the raft, sprawling flat as it bounced on the waves. Balancing on the edge, Larry pushed the stick down into the mud and began to pole away from the dock.

My camera glimpsed his face. The spray of the rough water splashed down his frizzy hair, matting it to his forehead. In the stark infrared light, his eyes were blank white, without iris or pupil, stretched wide in terror. His lips were peeled back in a grimace, baring his teeth as he strained with the effort of his desperate poling.

"Larry! Don't go!"

Even if he made it, John and I would be left behind, and that was bad enough.

But I didn't think he'd make it.

She was luring him into a trap.

I fell to my hands and knees on the damp, green dock, watching him go in helpless terror. He was beyond hearing me. Already too late. All I could do now was bear witness.

Larry poled out further from the dock, fighting the roiling waves. The wind wailed all around us. Through the wind, I could hear the trees rustling. When I looked back, all the dolls were shaking, dancing on the branches like hellish living fruit. Their heads turned toward the canal the way flowers find the sun.

Something splashed and I spun to point the camera at the waves, looking for movement. Wide, concentric circles spread from the center of the lake, where something had broken the surface, about ten feet behind Larry's raft.

"Larry!" I shouted, my voice breaking. "Don't you get it? She's in the water! She's in there with you right now!"

I could see the shadow moving under the water—impossibly long and serpentine, rising from the unseen depths, propelling its sinuous body with deadly curves as it reached toward Larry. She came on slowly, with all the smug leisure of a spider toying with a fly in the web.

"Look out!"

But it was too late, already too late, had always been too late.

Something slammed the raft from underwater, lifting one end and nearly tipping it. Larry flew back, clinging to the boards with one hand, the walking stick in the other.

From where I stood on the dock, twenty yards away, I could see the faint outline of the long, snake-like creature, surrounding the raft in an ever-tightening spiral under the water. Its movements churned the lake, sending out circles of rolling waves. The pier rocked and groaned, buffeted by wave after wave. I could barely keep my camera on Larry.

"Oh, Jesus," I whispered. "Oh, God, no."

Even as I watched, a set of pale, skeletal hands reached up from the water beside his raft. They moved with a slow, stop-motion jerkiness, nightmarish, almost insectile. Seizing the edge of Larry's raft with enough force to rock it again, the hands began to claw upward, dragging some immense form up from the water. First an algae-covered head, then a slender feminine body, no more than a shadow of darkness and mud. Through my bouncing camera lens, I could barely make it out.

Screaming, Larry kicked away, beating at the hands with the walking stick. The thing recoiled with an inhuman screech, tipping the raft as it slid back beneath the waves.

Larry spilled forward again, this time losing his grip on the walking stick. It bounced away into the dark water, sinking. As Larry clung to the raft, the churning surface broke beside him. A vast, scaly tail arched up, slamming down on Larry and the raft.

Twenty yards away, I heard the raft splinter. A splash erupted from the impact, sending shockwaves through the water. I searched wildly for the raft with my camera, but it was gone, disintegrated. Where it had been, I saw only bobbing sticks and logs, spread across the surface.

My breath caught in my chest—then Larry resurfaced, wet and bedraggled, his long tendrils of curly hair damp across his scalp. Clinging to a log, he tried to scream, and instead gurgled up black water.

At the last moment I looked around desperately for something, anything I could do to save my friend.

All I saw were dolls, watching from the pilings of the dock, shaking in the trees behind me, seeming to whisper under the noise of the wind.

Already too late. Already too late.

Larry was screaming, now. I could hear him shouting over the wind.

"Help!" he screamed, spitting up water. "Oh, God!"

As I refocused my camera on him, I saw he was wounded. A long splinter of the raft had pierced his shoulder, sticking through his arm pit and emerging from his back. Crying, clutching the wound and shaking in shock, he struggled for purchase on the piece of flotsam, gasping for breath, appearing ready to faint.

Then I saw the shadow cut through the water toward him. Saw the thick, finned tail rise behind Larry, slow and supple. Saw it snake around him, tightening before he'd even realized it.

"No!" Larry's deep voice was gone, replaced with a high, desperate screech. "Please!"

Then the tail squeezed around his waist, and all the breath went out of him. Gasping in panic, he tried to push away, but the tail only slithered up around him, tightening over his wrists and holding him in place. Like a vine it wrapped around him, constricting. I could see his mouth working, trying to cry out, but there was no air left for him to scream. Slowly he began to turn purple.

A yard in front of him, something rose from the canal in the guise of a woman. Long, dark hair, draped with moss and algae, hung before her face, spilled down her slender shoulders. A white slip of dress covered her, the wet fabric transparent over her breasts and shapely hips.

With a silent, choked gape of terror, Larry looked at the creature, his eyes wide and bloodshot. His dark face turned blue as the forked tip of the tail encircled his neck.

The woman floated closer to him. A long, bone-thin hand reached out to move his wet hair out of his face. When he met her eyes, the terror started to fade from his expression and he stopped struggling.

For a moment she studied him, her head tilting under the curtain of wet hair—seeing if he was one of hers. Then her ghastly, skeletal hand clenched into a fist in Larry's hair and an anguished moan erupted from her cracked blue lips. Her tail twitched and I heard a crunch, saw the angle of Larry's neck change. A thin trickle of blood ran down his chin, and I hoped by then he was already dead.

But still the tail kept squeezing.

More bones cracked in Larry's body, with a sound like paper being crumpled for the garbage bin. It was crushing him, popping him like a zit. His face turned blue, then purple, then red. His swollen tongue trembled in his slack, open mouth. His eyes bulged out from beneath their lids, protruding more and more as the pressure increased in his skull, till blood ran in red tears down his puffy cheeks. The whites of his eyes turned red and blood poured from his ears. Finally, with a quick succession of popcorn *pops* and a spray of red, his eyes burst from their sockets, leaving only empty, gaping holes, staring in blind horror.

Then the creature dove beneath the waves with a shriek, pulling Larry's ruined body with it, vanishing into the unseen depths of what I'd thought was a shallow lake.

As quickly as that, they were gone, leaving only circles rippling from the center of the lake. The water darkened as an inky cloud of blood unfurled under the surface.

On my knees, I stared out at the water through my

camera, the only way to see anything. Tears streamed down my cheeks, blurring the glass of the viewfinder.

It had all happened in the span of a moment, though it had seemed endless. I was still trying to comprehend what I'd seen. What it meant.

But I wouldn't be given time to mourn.

Another splash on the lake broke me from my stupor. I looked up from the viewfinder to see long, hook-like fins breach the surface as the thing resurfaced, waves fanning out from its unseen immensity.

And it started to slither toward me.

Chapter 27: Alone in the Dark

The creature came on, cutting through the water with swift, sinuous curves. Waves crested in its wake, rocking the flotsam and debris on the surface—all that remained of Larry and his raft.

For a moment I could only stare at the churning water, rooted where I knelt on the dock. Part of me wanted to run, but another part must have realized how futile it was to keep fighting, because my legs wouldn't seem to work.

What was the point if this was fate?

It would hurt, but only for a little while. Then it would all be over, and I'd be at peace. Down in the endless depths of the canal, with Miguel, Don Julio, the little girl and a thousand others—and Larry, now, too.

I was almost ready to give up and let her take me. Then the image of Larry's head blowing up and bursting like an overfilled balloon floated in my vision, and terror broke the spell.

She was coming at me like a torpedo now, skidding through the water, aimed at the dock.

"John!" I screamed. Leaping to my feet, I spun and lurched for the stairs. The entire flimsy pier seemed to rock beneath my feet. Hugging my camera, I bolted up the steps. The banshee wind wailed in my ears, tugged at my muddy clothing.

To my horror, the dolls were dancing in the trees, not just swaying in the wind but *shaking* with a life all their own, and the sound created a buzz like the hum of cicadas on a summer night.

Unsettling as it was, it was nothing compared to what

was coming from the canal. Breathless, I fled through the shadows of the pavilion, not looking back.

Then I plunged into the moving forest, trying not to look at the dolls shaking and chattering in the trees. The ones on the lines overhead bobbed and clacked together. The ones in the trees swayed and moved their limbs.

As I passed a black baby doll staked to a tree trunk, he turned his burnt head to watch me with an eyeless gaze, and I wondered if Larry was already here—already part of the island's menagerie of horrors.

Through the wind, I heard a woman's soft weeping behind me. Her crying sounded almost mocking, somehow one slip away from mad laughter.

But the sounds faded into the distance behind me. The chattering and movement of the dolls in the trees formed a cover over the noise, protecting me from the compulsion of her crying.

Still I heard her weeping, far away, as if imagined, and not just her—others joined their voices to hers. Miguel and now Larry wept along with her. The sounds rose from behind me, echoing and bodiless, one minute far away on the canal, the next right on the shore behind me. Distantly I knew it wasn't real. It was all her illusion, all to flush me out. But still it was disturbing, listening to their moaning, screaming, and wailing.

And *her* voice—her voice seemed to echo within my own head, like a catchy tune I couldn't shake. The weeping was so pitiful I had to resist the urge to stop and go back to her. Like an infant's cry to a mother's ear, the sound was impossible to ignore.

I stumbled through the woods, almost blind in the darkness. In my panic it no longer occurred to me to use my camera's night vision, and I would've been too scared to narrow my field of view to the viewfinder. Hidden roots and snarls rose from the rotted floor of the floating garden to tug at my feet. Doll faces floated out of the gloom, glowing like ghosts in the veiled moonlight. And I thought I heard things roving in the foliage around me, their tiny footfalls subsumed in the noise, their soft rubber bodies quiet as the dead.

Then the trees broke up ahead and I saw the buildings of Don Julio. The ferns waved like tattered banners. Leaves and sticks rattled over the tin rooftops, shaken loose from the trees in the gale.

"John!" I shouted desperately. *"John!"*

Passing between the buildings, I ran to the slumping shack across the clearing. The screen door clacked open and closed in the wind. I sprang up the stairs of the porch, feeling the living, hungry night hot on my heels.

Throwing open the door, I leaped inside, spinning to slam it. The wind pushed at the door like a living thing as I leaned against it, holding it closed.

The shack was completely dark inside, the candle in the lantern long since burned out.

"John?" I blinked in the darkness, alarmed. "John!"

Still leaning on the door—since Larry had broken the lock—I brought my camcorder to my eye and scanned the tiny room.

Aside from a hundred dolls, I was alone.

John wasn't here.

My panic growing, I stepped away from the door, looking all around again with the camera, checking the floor, even the web-draped rafters. All our bags were still on the floor, including John's and Larry's. The towels were still laid out as makeshift bedrolls.

In my urgency to save Larry, I'd rushed out without

paying much attention to what John did. Since he hadn't followed me, I'd expected to find him back here.

But no one was here.

"John! Where are you?"

Though I shouted at the top of my lungs, the roar of the wind swallowed my voice and shook the walls of the flimsy cabin.

And under the wind's tumult, I heard the sound of a woman weeping—or at least, what *sounded* like a woman. When I pictured the half-snake, half-woman thing that I'd seen in the water, with its ghastly mop of hair, its gaunt female torso, and its endless, serpentine tail, it was hard to think of it as a woman. But it had the voice of a woman, crying endlessly.

And her crying grew ever closer.

The door rattled in its jamb and I rushed to hold it closed, starting to cry myself. I sank to the floor with my back against the door, digging my heels in to hold it shut.

"Leave me alone!" I wailed. "God, make her go away!" Turning to the doll, Rosita, I whispered, "Please. Please, make her go away."

My voice strengthened as I spoke. I found the courage to close my eyes, giving myself to the darkness. The dolls in the shack would keep look out while I prayed.

"Please!" I lifted my voice until I was singing. *"Spirits of the island, help us today! Give us sanctum and mercy, I pray!"*

I kept singing the same refrain through my tears, my voice unwavering amidst the noise. I raised my voice until I was screaming, the words rasping from my throat.

The cabin shook and the door rattled behind me. Outside, Miguel and Larry wept along with the shrieking cries of La Llorona and countless others—all the new children she'd found to replace the ones she'd killed, to join her in her watery grave.

The dolls moved in the trees, as well. I could hear the strange, cicada-song of them shaking in the trees, all at once, like a single entity.

I kept praying, over and over, while I covered my ears and squeezed my eyes shut.

Slowly, slowly, my singing combined with the buzz of the dolls began to drone out the weeping. The sounds fell back further and further, retreating to the canal.

Finally, when my voice was raw and the dolls, too, had fallen quiet, I stopped chanting, lowered my hands from my ears, and opened my eyes.

The night was silent. I heard only the gentlest wind— the sort of breeze you expect on an autumn night, not the supernatural gale from before. There was no other sound, not a frog nor an insect. I heard no dolls whispering in the trees, and the weeping voices were gone.

Raising my camera, I peered around the darkness of the shack, the doll faces glowing in the infrared light. I saw nothing. No movement. No one else.

Still, the silence felt dangerous, alive with threat. *Was* I alone, or was something waiting out there?

Waiting, and watching?

I didn't want to find out. Didn't want to move or make a sound. I just wanted to sit there, hugging my knees to my chest. Perhaps if I didn't move, I could wait it out.

Wait *her* out.

Finally, after what seemed like a lifetime, I gathered the courage to rise to my feet. The first thing I did was push the big work bench in front of the door, barricading myself into the shack.

Then I crawled to John's backpack and searched it for the box of matches, hoping to relight the candle. But I couldn't find the matches. Probably for the better, I thought. The light would only draw attention.

Instead, I sat in the dark with my camera and the awful visions still playing in my head.

For a time, I hid my face in my hands, and the sound of weeping again filled the silence—this time, my own.

Now, alone in the dark, I broke down. The tears kept coming uncontrollably. It reminded me of the strange crying spell I'd experienced at home, the night before my trip. Only now did I understand what that had foreboded.

Out of loneliness and habit, I turned my camera to face me in the dark. The red light stared back at me like an eye, the only thing visible in the room. Wiping tears from my cheeks, I tried to catch my breath, and started to speak.

"It's been a few hours," I said, "since what happened to Larry. I'm back in the cabin. I'm all alone now. I don't know where John went. I don't know if he's okay. I-I don't know if he's alive."

My voice trembled. I could feel my chin quivering as I fought back sobs. I clasped a hand over my mouth.

"The way it took Larry… oh, God. I don't want to die like that. Please. I don't want to die…"

Larry hadn't wanted to die, either. Larry, John, Miguel. All of them had only come here for me.

"I'm so sorry," I whispered, through the tears. "I didn't listen. My dad, the townsfolk and the boatmen, they all warned me, but I didn't listen. And now… now my friends are dead and it's all my fault."

I bowed my head, unable to fight the tears any longer.

"I'm sorry," I moaned. "I'm so sorry."

I heard a sudden sound off in the distance, like a splash in the water, and my head snapped up, trembling as I stared into the dark. When the sound didn't come again,

I swallowed and looked back at the camera.

"She'll come for me next," I whispered. "I know she will. And I don't know if I can resist. And I don't want to die here. I don't want to die…"

My voice grew smaller and smaller. The unearthly wind howled outside the shack.

Then I heard another sound, this time much closer—like fingernails, drawing slowly down the wood outside the shack. I froze, staring into the darkness.

"What's that?" I could hear the desperate pleading in my own voice. "John?"

Nothing answered. Of course it couldn't be John out there—that would be too good to be true in this cursed place. No, it was something else.

I seized the camera, putting my eye to the viewfinder so I could see in the darkness. There was nothing moving in the shack. The dolls along the walls looked back at me in silence, pale in the infrared light.

Holding my breath, I listened for any further sounds outside the door, straining to hear over my own thudding heart. But now I heard only silence.

I imagined whatever was out there was also holding its breath, listening for *me*—and waiting. Waiting for the right time to come in and meet me, grinning beneath its mop of black hair, festering with slime and barnacles, raising its skeletal hands to engulf me in a cold, tight embrace.

"Please," I whispered at last, through a hyperventilating gasp. "Please, I don't want to die."

For a long moment I heard nothing but my own short, shallow breathing. The silence lasted long enough for me to start to think I was alone again.

But you're never *really* alone on the Island of the Dolls.

As I let out a slow sigh, releasing the tension in my

neck, I heard another sound—this time closer still.

This time it *was* inside the shack with me.

Eyes widening in horror, I turned toward the other side of the cabin. I wanted to whip my head around, but everything had slowed to a dreamy, ballet rhythm. It seemed to take a lifetime just to turn around, to focus my camera, to *see* it.

As the camera focused, the pale blurs transformed into dolls, pinned up on the walls. And as I realized what I was seeing, before I could stop myself, I started to scream.

One of the dolls was moving.

Chapter 28: The Journal of Don Julio

The movement came from across the cabin, the side with the wood floor. The wall there was covered with dolls from floor to ceiling. One of the dolls, hung toward the bottom of the wall, was moving by itself, its leg swinging.

As I watched, the leg stopped swinging and the doll went still, and I realized it wasn't the doll that had moved. Rather, something else must have brushed past the doll, causing its leg to swing in passing.

That meant there was something else in here.

Panic surged through me. I spun around with the camera, trying to take in my full surroundings through the narrow lens, breathing in tiny gasps.

Something rustled across the floor behind me, tiny feet padding on wood, but when I turned, I saw nothing.

Slowly, I backed into the corner of the room, scanning the walls with my camera, darting from doll to doll.

Then something brushed my leg, and I yelped, kicking.

The black cat yowled and scrambled away from me. I caught a flash of its fat, black tail, and then it was gone, leaping behind the dolls piled against the back wall. I found it there in my camera sights, licking a paw.

"Jesus!" Sobbing in relief and laughing through my tears, I fell to my knees. "Oh, Jesus. Just that stupid cat."

It looked at me, its eyes glowing white in the infrared.

"I'm sorry," I told the cat, smiling through my tears. "I didn't hurt you, did I?"

On my knees, I reached toward him with my free hand. I didn't expect much. By the look of him, the rangy old tomcat had lived feral on the island for some time. For all I knew, he'd forgotten humans, or had never met one at all. He could've lashed out at me, attacked me.

But none of that occurred to me. I was too desperate for comfort, and the sight of the cat had relieved me. I was so grateful I wasn't alone after all.

"Here, kitty." I smiled, sniffling. "I won't hurt you."

He only watched from his hiding place behind a doll. After a moment, he resumed licking his polydactyl paw with deliberate ambivalence.

I started to scoot closer across the cold, warped floor, reaching out with the back of my hand. "You're not scared of me, are you? Did you belong to Don Julio?"

He let me within a foot of him—then he turned and bolted, knocking over one of the dolls. He was too fast for me to track with my camera and I lost sight of him.

As I spun, searching for him, I noticed for the first time which doll the cat had been hiding behind. It was the doll I'd heard giggle earlier, when I prayed to the drowned girl for help. The cat had knocked it over as he sprang away; now the doll lay on its side in a fetal position, one eye missing, the other closed by a mechanical eyelid.

And there was something in the floor underneath it.

Raising my camera, I saw it was a panel, cut into the floorboard. I frowned. I'd noticed it earlier, but hadn't had a chance to open it before the crying sent Larry screaming from the cabin. I'd forgotten all about it.

Now I slid over to the panel, inspecting it through my camera. I ran my fingers over the small hinges on one side. Then I went to John's supplies and fished around inside until I found his pocket knife. Opening the blade, I slid it into the crack between the panel and the rest of the floor.

Meanwhile, the black cat sat on the floor across the

shack, his golden eyes fixed on me, seeming to watch what I was doing. I felt somehow better in the cat's presence. Not only less alone, but protected.

Again I had the eerie feeling that someone wanted me to open this panel.

It took several careful pushes, leaning on the knife as a lever with more and more force, to unstick the panel from the dusty floor. I used only one hand, holding my camera to my eye with the other.

Then the panel popped open so suddenly my hand slipped on the knife and I cut myself on the blade.

"Ah!" I winced and studied my palm, watching as lines of blood opened on the lowest joints of all four fingers. I fanned my left hand in the air, trying to shake off the pain. Instead I shook away droplets of blood, running fast down my fingers. It looked very dark in the stark lighting of night vision. The pain bloomed slowly into a hot throb.

Through gritted teeth, I grunted, "Damn it!"

I slid back to John's backpack and set the camera down, feeling in the darkness for the first aid kit. Clumsily, one-handed, I opened a series of Band-Aids and wrapped them around each finger. The blood kept coming, soaking through the fabric to run down my fingertips. The cuts must've been much deeper than I thought. I wrapped a cloth bandage around my hand, squeezing it tight.

Wanting to light the lantern, I looked again for the matches in John's backpack, but for some reason I couldn't find them. Could he have left them by the fire pit, at the pavilion? I was sure we'd taken everything with us when we left on the raft this afternoon.

I went to Larry's supplies and found the flashlight there instead. When I turned it on, the beam flickered a little. The batteries were getting low, I suspected. The light seemed dim, overwhelmed by the gloom.

Holding the camera by my shoulder in my good hand and gingerly holding the flashlight with the other, I turned back to the panel in the floor.

The little square door was open now, and I could see that underneath it was only a small cubby hole, dug out of the earth and lined with slate. I shone my light into the hole gingerly, afraid something might pop out to greet me.

But inside there was only a small shoe box, filled with coins, rings, buttons, and trinkets—a hoarder's stash, as dirty and worn and ruined as the rest of the island.

I almost missed the small, leather-bound book, buried at the bottom of the hole. Curious, I tucked the flashlight under my arm and pulled the book up, blowing off layers of dust from the cracked leather cover.

"This stuff must've belonged to Don Julio. I guess no one found it when he died?"

I looked across the room to the black cat, as if for confirmation. The animal only stared back, unblinking.

Carefully, I set my camera down so I could use both hands. With my throbbing left hand, I held the flashlight, using my good hand to hold and open the book.

The spine creaked and the pages peeled apart in clumps, green with mold and rotted beyond reading. The pages felt brittle and dry as autumn leaves, the ink was blurry, the pages misshapen by old moisture.

Toward the middle of the book, the pages were less damaged and I could make out words. It was in some kind of pidgin-Spanish, filled with misspellings and grammar errors—like the letters I get from *mi abuelita,* who lived on a farm and wasn't taught to write until she taught herself, copying out passages from a *Reina-Valera* Spanish Bible.

Surprised, I realized what I held.

"It's his journal," I said. "The diary of Don Julio."

With new interest, I flipped back to the beginning and tried to decipher the ruined pages. The first several pages were illegible, but I could make out the dates on some of the entries. The earliest were from the 1950s, years before Don Julio witnessed the little girl drowning.

"...Owner doesn't want it," I read out loud, tracing the legible snatches of text with my finger. *"Says it's haunted by a Nahua spirit named Maria. I buy it anyway. The spirits are my muse, the Lord God my Shepherd."*

I blinked. "He's talking about the island."

For a moment, the thrill of discovery overpowered my fear. I moved on to the next page, enthralled.

"September 20, 1959. Today marks one year on the garden. It's peaceful here. I fish in the water. I plant in the earth. I read my Bible and I talk to God without trouble."

The text faded out. I picked carefully through several pages, till I found the next section. I couldn't tell the date of the entry, but the writing looked different, more hurried and inelegant.

"...this was an important island to Cortés. That's what the last owner said, and the carving backs it up. She lived and died on this island. How fascinating, to own a piece of history! I love this land more each day. It feels as if God wants me to be here..."

He had to be talking about Doña Marina, I knew—the temptress who'd seduced Cortés. Don Julio must have found the carving on the heart tree.

"I contacted the former owner of the island to learn more about it, but he won't respond. When I send my cousin to deliver him a letter, the man tells Fernando he can't help us. I think the solitude drove him mad, maybe. Some men aren't made for such solitude."

Don Julio must have been a young man as he wrote this, in his twenties or thirties. When I pictured him, he looked like my father did when *he* was young—dark-skinned, dark-eyed, grinning behind a thick mustache. I imagined him wearing the straw sombrero he was wearing in his portrait here in the cabin.

"It's very different, living here. In the city there was noise and light and people all the time. Here there's quiet and darkness and solitude. I feel I could be the last man on Earth. Some days I see children from up the canal, fishing and swimming, but mostly I'm alone.

"Sometimes I'm frightened in the night. I'm not used to the sounds here…"

The deeper I got into the book, the more water-damaged it became; the back cover had lain in the mud and the moisture had wicked up through the paper over time. Now entire pages—representing months or years of the man's life—were lost to history.

In the next surviving section, his handwriting looked even messier and more hurried, but the writing itself seemed more literate. He'd been studying.

"…can always count on Fernando. He brought me books to the island. History and legends. I am certain Doña Marina lived on this island. I believe she was betrayed by Cortés and his men, who killed the children she'd borne by Cortés to make room for his trueborn heirs. Then they put the blame on Doña Marina…

"She was driven mad. Perhaps she even came to believe the lie they had told of her—that she had killed her children herself. For the final years of her life, she roamed the canal, searching for her lost children. Finally she drowned herself in sorrow, but her spirit lived on, always weeping, always searching.

"Doña Marina became the Woman in the Water.

"The Weeping Woman."

That entry was all I could make out for several pages. When I saw the next legible entry, I gasped at the date.

October 30, 1960. Today's date, fifty five years ago.

"October 30, 1960. Today I saw her for the first time.

I was on the pier, fishing. Then something moved in the water, too big to be a fish. I heard something crying softly, and I sang to God until it left me alone. I still hear it, even now, in my head."

The next surviving section was scrawled in even more furious handwriting, almost as if someone else altogether was writing now. I could see his mindset deteriorating in his handwriting.

"...told her and her friends not to swim in the canal. I told them there were things in the water, but they didn't listen. Oh, why didn't she listen?

"If only I had been able to save her, but I was too afraid. We weren't alone in that water. That girl didn't drown alone..."

The next sentences were illegible, but the same entry seemed to continue below.

"...I think Doña Marina is still here. She never left the island. She's drawn to it, and I think I know why. Something is buried by the heart tree, in the vault beneath it, where I found the crossbow. Something she's been seeking for a very long time.

"They blamed her for killing her own children, and it drove her mad, twisted her into a monster. She's still mad now, in death, still monstrous, still searching. Nothing will sate her thirst for blood and vengeance. Even if she found her children, I don't think it would appease her restless soul. In fact, I think it would be catastrophic. Right now she is fixed on this island. The malevolence of her spirit wanders the canals, but never far. But if they were to be reunited... what would keep her here anymore? What would keep her rage from spreading over all the world?

"...So I must stay, as frightened as I am. I must protect this place...

"But I fear, one day, she will come to take me, too."

After this, nothing was legible. The pages were rotted

together, like mushy paper towels, and where it remained at all, the ink was no more than splotchy blurs.

I stared at the water-logged journal in open-mouthed amazement.

"It wasn't her," I whispered. "She didn't kill them. They took them from her."

By Don Julio's account, La Llorona—known in life as *Doña Marina*, courtesan and translator to Don Cortés— had not killed her own children in a spat of jealous rage, as the legends said. No; her children had been taken from her and killed by servants of Cortés himself, leaving her to take the blame for all of history.

Suddenly I remembered where I'd seen the coat of arms of Cortés, aside from the crossbow. I'd caught a glimpse of it earlier, on the strange wooden box under the heart tree. My eyes widened as I realized what that meant.

"They were buried on this island," I said. "Is that why she won't leave us alone?"

I felt a curious mix of hope and compassion. That had to be right. This was the truth, at last. The reason she was so focused on this island, and on us. Her children were all she'd been searching for, all these years.

Don Julio had wanted to keep Llorona away, to keep her from finding her lost children. He'd feared there was no hope for her soul; that if she were ever unbound from the island, she would only spread her malice everywhere.

But maybe he was wrong.

Maybe it *was* possible to bring peace to La Llorona, if only someone was brave enough to try—brave enough to face her, eye to eye, and reunite her with what she'd lost.

"The poor thing," I whispered. "To have your children taken from you, and blamed for it all of history. She only became the monster they made her into."

I could feel tears at the corner of my eyes, but my face was hardening at the same time.

"If they're here, and I can bring them together..."

The black cat uttered a low yowl in the corner, staring at me, the pale white glow of its eyes eerie in night vision.

"Maybe when her search is over, she'll be at peace—"

Something banged outside the cabin and I jumped. It sounded like metal clanging against metal, loud and resonant as a church bell at a funeral. My eyes widened and I stared into the gloom.

"What was that?" I whispered.

The black cat yowled again, flattening his ears to his head. Then he turned and slunk into the darkness, hiding behind the dolls. Suddenly I was alone.

But not *quite* alone, I realized, as the sound out in the yard came again.

Someone had arrived outside.

Chapter 29: The Break-Up For Real

When I heard the sound, I froze in terror inside the cabin, on my knees and clutching the journal of Don Julio in my right hand. In my left hand, wounded from the pocket knife, I held John's flashlight. My camera sat on the floor beside me, pointing at me and still filming.

"Is someone out there?" I called, my voice shaking.

The wind rose, as if in answer, but I heard the noise again through the roar, loud and resonant as the toll of a church bell. Again and again the sound came, faster and more furious, growing into a clang.

Someone was banging metal on metal out in the yard.

Instinctively, I turned off the flashlight, dropping the book and scrambling for the camera, using the night vision to see in the hopes that this would draw less attention. Then, slowly, I rose to my feet.

I looked through the hole in the opaque window by the door, where Larry had smashed the glass to let us in, what seemed like a lifetime ago. Through the hole, I could see the yard in front of the house. There was nothing there. Yet the banging continued, somewhere out of sight, incessant as the wind.

Then, through the din, a familiar voice rose.

"Carmen? Carmen, where are you?"

I froze. Tears welled in my widening eyes.

"John?" I whispered.

I wanted to cry out to him, tear open the door and run, screaming, to his arms. Fear held me back—fear that what I heard out there wasn't really my boyfriend at all.

"Carmen?" He kept calling, banging on the metal thing between the words, like a drum. *"Can you hear me?"*

I shut my eyes, squeezing tears down my cheeks, and took a deep breath. I couldn't help but answer.

"John?" I called through the broken window. "Is that really you?"

The banging stopped. After a momentary pause, John called, "Thank God. I thought you might be here. Come on out, honey. I need your help."

He sounded strangely calm. Something in the pit of my gut told me to beware, and yet I could hardly ignore him.

I pulled the work bench away and opened the door.

The metal banging noise resumed as I leaned my head out, then stepped fully into the night. I held my camera in my wounded hand, looking through the viewfinder to guide my way in the dark. In my right hand, I held the heavy steel flashlight like a club, the light turned off so I wouldn't be seen. Carefully, I crept across the rickety porch, down the creaking stairs. The wild wind tugged at my hair and shook the trees around the house, moving the dolls like soft *maracas*.

In the stark black and white contrast of night vision, I saw the corner of the shack, up ahead. As I came around the corner, the metallic banging grew louder.

John came into view in the overgrown clearing behind the house, hitting the rusted generator repeatedly with Don Julio's sledgehammer. The crossbow slung over his shoulder bounced with each mighty swing.

When I saw him, I turned on my flashlight and broke into a run, breathing in fevered gasps. "Oh thank God, it's really you! When you weren't in the cabin, I thought…"

I trailed off as I reached him. Several red gas cans sat on the ground beside the generator. A length of garden hose ran from the can to the opening of the generator's tank, siphoning gas.

John kept hammering the side panel of the generator, denting it more and more with each blow. The wrinkled edges of the thin metal plate were prying up from the bolts that held them at the seams.

Stopping several feet from him, I lowered my camera and whispered, "What are you doing?"

He paused to look at me, then smiled, wiping sweat from his chiseled jaw.

"There's a little fuel in the drip pan," he said, "maybe some more I can soak off the machinery. I don't have any tool to get through these bolts, so..." In one fluid motion, he spun and swung the sledgehammer at the generator. The black head of the sledge rang the steel, deepening the dents in the metal.

"Isn't that dangerous?" I cried, appalled.

"Dangerous?" He laughed in genuine amusement. "You really think that matters now?"

His demeanor confused me. He seemed jovial, almost happy. His eyes flashed with a wild light with each swing of his hammer.

"Where'd you find the gas cans?" I asked. They'd been missing since last night, when our camp was sabotaged.

He didn't answer, swinging away at the old generator. I covered my ears, annoyed and frightened by the racket.

"John," I said, looking around the darkness. "John!"

He stopped, glancing at me and panting. His lips peeled back like a sweating dog; I couldn't tell if it was meant to be a smile.

"Listen," I said. "I think I know what she wants."

"I *already* know what she wants," John replied.

I shook my head. "Not us! She's here for her children. They're here, John. They're on the island."

John's sleepy grin widened and he murmured, "Yes. That's why we need *fire.*" He nodded at the gasoline cans.

"The signal fire?" I said, confused and afraid.

He shook his head, and his placid smile drifted over my head to the dolls in the darkness above. I followed his gaze with my flashlight. The dolls looked back in silence.

"No," John said. "*Purification* by fire. It all has to burn."

As he spoke, his voice tightened. Tears streaked his face, despite his joyous grin. I took a step back.

"It's the only way she'll find them," he whispered, his voice almost child-like. "The only way she'll find *us.*"

Slowly, his head turned back to me, and his staring, weeping eyes found mine. His smile looked rapturous.

"And you're wrong. She *does* want us. She does. Can't you hear her crying?"

I looked at John with widening eyes—only it *wasn't* John, was it? I recognized nothing of him in this vacant, grinning creature. His body was here, but something else was behind the wheel.

She's irresistible, a seductress, Miguel had said. *She can make any man do her bidding. She can make you fall so madly in love that you'll kill your own family for her, just as she did...*

And she'd *touched* John, in the water.

I took another step backward.

John, in turn, moved closer.

"She's crying for us," he whispered again, smiling through his tears. "I know you hear her, too."

All around, the wind had risen once more into a wail. The trees shook. The dolls danced. And from somewhere, out on the canal, I heard a soft crying.

"She wants us," said John. "She wants them, but she wants us, too. The whole island. Everything." His smile widened and his face tilted downward. The harsh light of my trembling flashlight brought sharp, skeletal shadows to his features. "And I'm going to give it to her."

I started to sob. "John, please. You have to resist her."

He scoffed. "Why would I want to *resist?*"

For every step back I took, he advanced another, still holding the long, heavy hammer. The black, square head of it trailed through the foliage behind him. The crossbow bobbed over his shoulder.

His blue eyes were eerily empty, his smile impersonal, like a doll—and in that moment I knew John was gone.

With a scream, I turned on my heel and bolted for the woods, but I didn't know where to go. The cabin? That sledgehammer would break the crooked, rotting door like glass. The pavilion? There was no shelter there, no safety from John, no buffer from *her* and her cries. The canal? God help me, that was my instinct—to flee to the water, maybe try to swim for it like Miguel and Larry, but of course there was no escape that way. No escape anywhere.

There was nowhere to go.

I ran anyway, passing the edge of Don Julio's shack, weaving between the buildings in an attempt to shake John from my trail. But when I looked back, to my horror, he was chasing me, holding the sledgehammer before him in both hands. His thick legs pounded the turf.

"You can't disobey her," he said. "It's her way or the highway. If you're bad, you'll take your medicine!"

Emerging from the cluster of buildings, I stumbled toward the trees. My flashlight bounced over the pale faces of the dolls. As I passed, I could see them turning their heads to track me with dead, vacant eyes.

"Help!" I screamed, sobbing. "Someone, please!"

Only the wind wailed in response—and under it, ever-present, her soft weeping, ringing in my ears. I could hear it in my head at all times now, so permanently a part of me that I could no longer be sure when I was hearing the echo in my memory or the real thing.

It sounded like I was running straight toward it.

Yet John was right behind me, herding me on. When I looked back, he was charging me like a football player, his head lowered, the thick veins bulging in his muscled neck, his eyes wide and his mouth hanging.

As I looked back, I didn't see the gnarled root coming up from the mossy earth in front of me. My foot snagged and my momentum slammed me down to the dirt.

My camera landed beneath me.

I heard a loud *crack*, but I was beyond caring and it barely registered. Leaving the camera, I picked myself up, my panic so powerful I barely felt my twisted ankle.

When I looked back, John was no longer there.

I paused to wave my flashlight around, scanning the dark, whispering trees. He was nowhere to be seen.

Breathing in shallow gasps, I kept running.

"You're only making her angrier," he called from the trees, his voice desperate. "Making it worse for us both!"

I couldn't tell where his voice was coming from. It seemed to come from all around me—just like hers. The sound of her piteous weeping was maddening, seeming to circle around me, tightening like an invisible snake.

Clutching my ears, I screamed, *"Shut up!"*

When I looked up, John stood before me, holding the hammer in both hands. My breath froze in my lungs. I wanted to move, but I couldn't.

He looked at me with the hint of a smile, tilting his head a little. "Don't fight," he shouted over the wind and weeping. "You know it's already too late."

"John, listen to me! That's not you talking."

"How would you even know? When was the last time you listened to me?"

The words stung. "I was always there for you, John. I'm still here for you." I shook my head, fighting back tears. "But you can't do this. You can't burn the dolls!"

He drew a long, patient sigh, then weighed the head of the hammer in his hand. My heart started to pound as his blue eyes returned to mine, pale and cold. His smile was very sad.

"If you can't support my goals," he said, "Maybe we shouldn't see each other anymore."

His almost casual tone chilled me.

"And if you're a bad girl," he whispered, still fondling the hammer, "then you'll take your medicine. I may as well give it to you. Yes, I think she'd like that."

"John." Tears welled in my eyes. "Please."

"The dose," he said softly, "was always forty whacks."

I started to step back.

Then he swung the sledgehammer.

The only warning was his twisting face, but it was enough. I leapt aside as the hammer whistled down where my head had been, wedging in the fork of a juniper tree. John tried to wrench it free, grunting like a wild animal.

Getting to my feet, I fled, looking back over my shoulder to see if he'd pursue.

With a final tug, John pulled the handle of the hammer free of the head, stumbling back. He examined the long wooden handle left in his hands, decided it would do, and sprinted after me.

The weeping had picked up again. It was all around me, seeming to encompass me.

As the trees cleared up ahead, I saw the pavilion and the dock, and the dark waters beyond.

I'd reached a dead-end.

The waters were broiling and foaming, turbulent with the movements of some vast monster in the depths. She was waiting for me. Waiting for John to bring me here.

Her shadow pooled under the water, rising toward the surface.

I was screaming but I could no longer hear my own voice. Everything was weeping. The trees were shaking. The dolls moaned and danced and I fled from the shoreline, back into the woods—

But there was nowhere to go.

When I turned, John stood before me, his handsome face empty as a doll's. He held the broken handle of the hammer like a ballplayer at bat.

I looked up in time to see his thick arms cord as he swung.

Then pain exploded against my left temple, knocking the light from my eyes. I felt myself hit the ground.

Slowly, the weeping faded into black.

Chapter 30: Purification by Fire

As I woke, I became aware of a dull heartbeat; it was the first thing I noticed, like an infant in the womb. Later I realized this dull throbbing was inside my own head, filling it to the brim.

And it was accompanied by pain.

"Carmen... you have to wake up, now."

It was a woman's voice, but not Llorona's, I knew. I'd never heard this voice before, and yet it was familiar—somehow like my own.

"Mom?" I whispered.

But when I looked up, it was the drowned girl who stood over me. Her brown hair hung around her pale face. Her blank, sightless eyes welled with tears of blood. She held the doll Rosita in her arms.

The drowned girl stared straight ahead, expressionless; but the doll, Rosita, looked down at me. Her head and eyes moved with the stiff, mechanical jerkiness of a ventriloquist's dummy.

"You have to get up," said Rosita, her plastic mouth unmoving. "You don't have much time."

Now I thought I could smell something, burning. It seemed like a distant concern, next to the pain.

"It doesn't matter," I rasped. "You said yourself, it's already too late. Why help me?"

The doll's head swiveled back and forth. "You know what she wants. Julio's faith was strong, but he was too afraid. Too weak to her charm. You must be stronger."

The smoke stung my eyes and my vision blurred with

tears. I didn't *want* to keep fighting. John was right. There was no use in fighting.

Even now I could hear her calling to me, so sadly.

Come to me, my love. Join us down here in the water. No weight, no pain, no light…

"I can hear her," I whispered. "Crying and calling."

"Be strong, Carmen. Have faith."

I blinked away tears, and when I looked up again, the girl and her doll were gone.

For a moment I swam alone in darkness. As my eyes adjusted, I saw other faces, doll faces, watching in the gloom, and I recognized where I was.

I was lying on the floor inside Don Julio's shack.

It was hard to breathe, and the air stank of smoke and fire. My breath came in shallow, painful gasps. There was no light in the room save for the tiny glow of dawn through the boarded windows.

I frowned, forcing myself to sit up, despite the pain. My head seemed to weigh a thousand pounds, throbbing, as if some monster incubated inside my skull. I raised a hand groggily to touch my forehead and winced at the wet gash I found there. My dark hair was stiff with dry blood.

By instinct, I looked for my camera groggily, then I remembered—I'd tripped while running from John and fallen on my camera. I could still hear the awful crack of the glass, shattering beneath me.

The loss of it hadn't registered at the time, but now I felt a different kind of pain. Not only was the footage gone—our entire reason for being here—but I'd lost my mother's camera, too. I felt naked without it.

Not only that, John had lost his mind.

He'd knocked me out. He must have brought me here, to keep me out of the way of what he was about to do.

As the memory of how I got here returned, tears welled in my eyes—but not just from sadness. Something was stinging my eyes.

The shack was filled with smoke, I realized, thickening by the second.

Shocked from my daze, I lurched to my feet, limping to the window. I'd twisted my ankle when I fell on my camera, and now it was swollen, throbbing. I couldn't put any weight on it.

When I looked out the window, I gasped. The red glow outside wasn't dawn at all. Dawn was far away, the sky starless and black.

At the center of the yard, a massive fire blazed. Logs, wooden panels, and rotting dolls had been piled in a heap and engulfed in flames.

A shadow in the shape of a man stood between me and the fire, his thick back facing me, the crossbow still slung over his shoulder. Over the roar of the fire, I could hear him humming as he poured on more fuel from a red gas can. The flames licked up higher where his gasoline splashed.

"John?" I cried. "John!"

He didn't turn toward me. I made for the front door, threw it open—and stared, dumbfounded.

The screen door had been boarded shut from outside, using plywood from the other buildings. The boards were placed very closely together, leaving only the slightest gaps to peek through, like the windows. I could see the crooked nails driven into the doorframe.

He'd boarded me inside. I was trapped.

Starting to panic, I threw myself against the screen door, tearing the screen mesh and slamming the boards. It was no use. They didn't budge.

"John!" I banged the boards with my uninjured hand. "Let me out of here!"

But only the wind answered, and the dull crackle of flames outside. Returning to the broken window, I peered out through the boards. The smoke was coming in thick, now, so thick I had to hold my sleeve over my mouth. My eyes burned, watering continuously.

"John!" I cried. The oxygen was growing short and it was hard to raise my voice. "Why are you doing this?"

He paused, looking back at last. The wind tugged his orange sweater. I could see him smile beneath his hood.

"I told you," he said. "The dolls, the island, everything. Even you and me. It all has to burn."

He threw the empty gas can and grabbed another.

"It'll all return to the water. It'll all return to *her.*"

"John," I said, as sweetly as I could. "You have to let me out. Think about what you're doing. Come on, honey. Just let me out. Just let me out to talk about it. Please?"

Ignoring me, he poured out more gasoline, dousing the dry, brown grass in a great spiral out from the fire. He was trying to hum again, but he couldn't keep the tune. It sounded like he was crying.

"What are you gonna do?" I asked. "Burn me alive?"

I added a high, nervous laugh, to make it sound ridiculous, a joke, because that couldn't really be his intention.

But John didn't answer. He no longer seemed to hear me at all, weeping as he poured out gasoline.

I tried to shout, but the smoke billowing in made me choke and I broke off in a fit of coughing.

When I looked back through the window, I no longer saw John by the fire. The flames roared along merrily, starting to spread along the spiral lines of gasoline like an eerie light show.

"John?" I called. Tears ran from my burning eyes. Had he left me?

Then I heard the porch stairs creak outside.

He was coming closer, a gas can sloshing in his hands.

His shadow passed the window and I stepped back, my eyes widening. "John." My voice was soft, breathless. "Listen, I'm sorry about what happened. I never meant for things to get so fucked up, okay? I shouldn't have invited Larry here. Hell, I shouldn't have come here at all."

"No," John said finally.

I turned my head toward the boarded-up door. He was standing just outside it, now. His hoarse voice strained through tears.

"No, I'm *glad* we came."

Moving to the door, I peered out at him. Our eyes met through the gaps in the boards. His blue eyes squinted, endlessly watering, the whites tangled with red veins. They seemed to stare through me into some other world.

His lips turned in a twitching smile, fighting the tears.

"If you hadn't brought me here, we wouldn't have met *her*. Don't you see? This is fate, honey."

"It's not fate!" I shouted. "It's *not* too late, John!"

"When she touched me," John whispered, "I felt... *wanted*. Loved, in a way I never felt, not from Dad, not with you, not with anyone."

Behind him, the red firelight spread on the undersides of the trees. Over the growing roar of the flames, I heard her weeping, carried on the wind. John closed his eyes, as if savoring the sound.

"She's so sad. So sweet."

He turned over the bright red gas can in his hand, and gasoline drenched the old bleached wood.

"I'm sorry, Carmen," he sniffled, smiling through his tears. "I have to give her what she wants."

Through the wind, the weeping grew closer. I clasped my hands over my ears, trying not to listen.

"No, John!"

John finished emptying the gas can, shaking out the last few drops outside the door. Then he threw the can down at the corner of the porch.

"John, please, no! *No!*" I wailed.

He winced, then glared at me, like I was talking at a movie theater. "Shh, *shut up!* I can't hear her!"

"Please!" I closed my eyes, and sucked in a breath, my lungs fighting the crush of smoke and panic. *"Please, little spirits, help us today! Give us sanctum and mercy, I pray! Spirits of the island, please help us—"*

John slammed the boarded door with both hands, startling me. We stood eye to eye, separated by the boards, and I glimpsed something of John's old self in his bleary blue eyes—a hint of cool contempt.

"It's not going to work, Carmen." He sounded almost weary. "Why can't you ever just trust me?"

I searched his eyes, hurt and confused. "This isn't *you*, John! It's *her!*"

I had to shout over the sound of her endless weeping. I clasped my hands over my ears, trying not to hear it, but still it penetrated my skull.

John only studied me a moment through the boards. Then he spoke softly, barely audible over the din.

"You'd do anything for *your* mother, wouldn't you?" he asked. "Even in death. You brought us here for her."

My eyes widened slowly. John stepped back from the gas-soaked door, smiling sadly.

"Now *she's* calling the shots," he said, nodding over his shoulder at the awful sounds in the woods. "And she's crying for this shack to burn. Can't you hear her crying?"

He raised his hand, and I saw the red box of camping matches. I'd looked for them in his bag earlier and they'd been missing—he must have had them all along.

He took out a long matchstick and held it up, smiling as fresh tears streaked his dirty face.

"Please." He sniffled. "Don't make this any harder. You have to take your medicine, honey. But don't worry. She says it's *cool* in the water. So cool. Once we're down there, you won't feel a thing."

He struck the match against the side of the box, and the flame sparked to life, bright in my widening eyes.

"Good bye, Carmen."

Then he threw it down.

Chapter 31: Mother of the Dead

The match hit the gas-soaked floorboards of the old porch and lit up instantly with a hungry growl.

Screaming, I slammed the boarded door. Crooked nails slashed my shoulder and I fell back, panting.

Through the gaps in the boards I saw John turn his back and walk away. The air shimmered with heat and I had to step back, clutching my bloody shoulder.

Meanwhile, the flames grew higher outside, the warm glow unfolding through the boarded door, filling the room behind me. Fire crackled as it climbed the boards and the doorframe.

For a moment I stood in the burning cabin, watching the fire rise over the doorway, engulfing the boards. Panic gripped my mind and I clutched my head.

I was scared, but I wouldn't let my fear win over me. I knew what I had to do, and I couldn't let anything stop me now. I was going to save myself *and* John, whether he wanted me to save him or not.

But for that, I had to get to the heart tree.

Heart quickening, I looked around in the darkness for something I could use to free myself; but I saw nothing. I'd made a point of taking every tool down to the dock, so I wouldn't have to come back to this cabin. *That* had worked out well. Now there were no tools, no weapons.

I slammed the front door closed to try to shut out the flames, but it was no use. Smoke billowed through the crack under the door, and the red glow climbed the gaps along the jamb.

Then I heard a soft yowl and looked over. Don Julio's cat was still inside with me, standing at the back of the room and pawing at the wall desperately. His tail was thick and fat as a raccoon's.

"Don't worry, boy," I coughed into my sleeve. "There must be a way out!"

Grabbing a doll from the wall, I started to bludgeon the window beside the door. The glass shattered, but the boards didn't budge. Finally I started banging the boards with my shoulder, barely aware of the shards of glass shredding my skin through my sweater.

The room was heating up slowly, like an oven. Sweat slicked my brow. I could feel the oxygen being sucked out of the room. There was no way out, nowhere to go.

With a tremendous *crack*, a burning rafter peeled down from the ceiling, crashing through the floorboards in a blast of sparks and cinders. I barely leapt aside, rolling over the floor.

I came up next to the black cat, still pawing at the floorboards at the edge of the wall. Even as I watched, the cat nudged a loose floorboard aside and squeezed through the gap, disappearing below the floor.

Eyes widening, I scrambled to the loose floorboard as the ceiling fell around me. I tugged it as hard as I could, ripping my fingernails, but couldn't pry it up; so I stomped on it till my foot went through the old, dry wood, kicked away the pieces, and eased head-first into the dark crawlspace under the floor.

In the darkness under the house, I dragged myself through hard, dusty gravel. I could feel fire on my back through the floor, hear the series of crashes as the ceiling collapsed. It was dark, and my eyes were half-blind from smoke. The cat was nowhere to be seen. There was only a dull red glow up ahead where the crawlspace met the outer world, and I willed myself toward it, despite the pain.

Finally, I emerged from under the cabin, panting. As I lurched to my feet, I had to shield my eyes from the glow.

The whole island was in flames.

Already John's fire was raging out of control, sweeping over the dried-out trees, leaping from branch to branch. The dolls burned and melted, their tiny bodies twisting, contorting, shriveling. Glass eyes cracked. Oxygen hissed from their rubber bodies like screams.

Even the floating garden itself, built on rafts of old rotted wood, had started to splinter up into the canal. Through the red haze, I saw trees toppling in the distance, splashing into the water as their land support fell away.

I winced at a loud *crack* behind me and looked back in time to see the wall of the cabin coming down. With a yelp I leapt aside, rolling out of the way as the burning wood planks clattered to the ground. The rest of the roof fell with a deep, bellowing *whoomp,* like a bomb. Sparks and smoke flew from the smoldering ruins.

Lifting myself from the ditch, I took off running—or tried to. My swollen ankle made every step an agony, reducing my sprint to a lurch.

With my mind awhirl in panic, I was acting on instinct.

I headed for the heart tree, at the center of the island.

The flames seemed to race me there, hopping branch to branch, roaring, all around. Burning leaves and cinders rained through the air. The dolls screamed as they burned, their rubber and plastic visages melting away. The ground itself was rumbling, splitting open to reveal the steaming swamp underneath.

Behind me, I heard the sound of a woman weeping, drawing near as the island shrank. When I looked back, the burning trees seemed to form a tunnel, dark with smoke and swirling cinders. The trees fell one by one, like dominos, bringing the darkness at the end of the tunnel ever closer.

When I looked forward again, the ground was opening up at my feet.

It was too late to stop; I'd already stepped into open air as the fissure widened beneath me. For one desperate moment I balanced, arms pinwheeling, on the edge.

Then the edge crumbled and I fell past the rotted, broken planks and bone-white roots that made the fabric of the island.

Next thing I knew, I hit swampy water with a splash. My legs sank. I couldn't feel the bottom. The water was spinning, pulling me down like quicksand. The wood frame foundation of the island splintered around me, coming down on top of me even as I reached for a handhold. Suction pulled me down and I went under.

The roar of the island's destruction muted to a low drone as water rose over my head. Yet I could still hear her weeping. As the other noise fell into a hollow drone, her voice became all the clearer, warbling up out of the depths. I was exposed to it, laid naked to it. In the darkness under the island, I could see nothing. She could be anywhere, closing in, tightening her sinuous length around me to drag me under.

Frantically I fought the current, but I could no longer see which way was up. I turned over and over, my lungs burning, ready to burst. All the while the weeping came closer, seemingly everywhere, all around me in the water.

A pale hand reached for me and I gasped involuntarily, sucking water into my lungs.

But the hand was reaching in from *above* the water, not

below. Reaching in to help me.

Drowning, I had no time to question it. I seized the hand and pulled myself up, breaching the surface with a huge, rasping gasp that immediately became a fit of wretched coughing, spitting up water.

As I caught my breath, I saw whose hand I'd taken, and my eyes widened.

Blank blue eyes looked back at me, rimmed in deep, dark circles, set in a face as pale as milk.

The dead girl squatted on the ledge up above, Rosita tucked under one arm as she pulled me up with the other, using all her weight for leverage. Her wet brown hair draped her face in stringy strands, almost green with moss. Flames swirled in the treetops behind her.

Under the girl's arm, Rosita turned her head toward me, her rubber face twisted in fear.

"Hurry!" the doll cried, stiff rubber lips barely moving.

There was no time for shock. Tightening my grip on the drowned girl's hand, I let her pull me up onto solid ground with supernatural strength.

As I stood, my legs shaky, my hair as wet and ragged as the girl's, I realized she wasn't alone. Other figures stood under the trees, amidst the smoke—more ghostly children, each holding a doll, their features indistinct as shadows.

"You don't have much time," Rosita told me. "Go!"

Like a runner at the starting gun, I ran. I could no longer feel the pain in my ankle. All that was gone now.

The spirits watched me from the trees as I passed, but I felt no fear. They were no danger. Only more victims of La Llorona's madness.

They stood in a line to either side of me, forming a corridor, and I saw the fire wasn't moving past them. I could see their dolls burning, melting in their hands, but the flames remained parted.

They were helping me, I realized. Parting the flames and protecting me to the last as best they could. As the dolls absorbed the fire, burning in their arms, the ghosts became more and more featureless, fading in the smoke.

Tears of gratitude streaked my face as I ran.

When I wiped my eyes, there was no one there but the smoldering remnants of dolls, wilting and writhing in the trees, swinging from torn, burning strings. The spirits were gone, and I was alone amidst the raging flames, closing in.

But they'd bought me just enough time.

Up ahead stood a familiar clearing. I could see the heart tree rising from the dry, dead grass. For an instant, I felt a flash of relief at reaching my destination.

But as I burst into the clearing, my wet hair singed, my clothes black with ash and mud, I saw I wasn't alone.

A shadow stood beneath the heart tree.

At first I thought it was one of the ghosts, but they were gone, dissipated into the smoke. I froze where I stood, my heart stopped cold. This was no ghost.

It was John, already here, waiting—not for me, but for *her*.

For a long moment, he stood there, his broad back turned to me. His shoulders hitched slightly, and through the hellish din and crackle of the fire, I could hear him, weeping.

Slowly, he turned his head. Tears stained his cheek, the moisture red in the light. His dry lips twisted in a quivering smile as his eyes met mine.

"Carmen." Despite his vapid grin and endless red tears, his voice was void of emotion. "You're supposed to be dead."

As he turned to me, I saw the glint of steel in his hand. He was holding Don Julio's antique crossbow, loaded with a long, rusty bolt.

Shaking my head, I took a step back. "John," I started to plead.

He moved closer, crossing the clearing. "You get so stubborn when it comes to your little films," he rasped.

I took another step back, but there was nowhere to go. The perimeter of the island had collapsed, shrinking into a tiny circle, the outer trees either fallen or still poking up from the water, burning as they sank. The ground behind me split apart with a *crack* as the dry foundations broke with a groan.

John stopped a few yards from me, the crossbow held casually across his abdomen. His once-clear blue eyes looked like weeping red sores, oozing bloody tears down cheeks twisted in a horrible, unnatural smile. His shoulders hitched as he sniffled compulsively.

"Please, John," I begged him. "You have to stop."

"No stopping it. Llorona is coming. The mother of the dead. And you know what happens to girls who disobey their mothers?"

"No!" Despite my fear, I stepped closer in defiance. "I won't let you do this!"

"I won't let you stop me." He shrugged lazily. "I'll give anything to be with her. And you're just in the way."

He raised his crossbow, aiming it at me with slow, careful precision. His awful ruined eyes never left mine.

"You'll take your medicine," he whispered, "if I have to give it to you myself."

I screamed—and John pulled the trigger.

Chapter 32: Landfall

The dark iron bolt whistled through the air and I heard a soft *thunk*, like a blade lodging in a tree trunk. In the same instant my leg went out from under me as if kicked and I fell over on the shaking ground.

The pain didn't even register until I looked down and saw my leg. Even then, I only stared a moment, shocked.

The crossbow bolt was sunk deep into my upper thigh. As I watched, a circle of blood spread through my wet jeans, growing with alarming speed.

The pain hit like a second arrow a moment later. Arching my back, I screamed, clutching my leg in both hands and writhing on the edge of the disintegrating island.

A few yards away, John watched for a moment, his twisted grin never wavering. Calmly, he retrieved another crossbow bolt from the belt over his shoulder and began to reload the weapon.

Panic kicked in, overriding the pain and shock.

"You… you shot me!" I cried.

Saying nothing, John raised the bow for the final shot, and I forced my body to move. With my last strength, I rolled backward over the edge, sliding down the muddy bank behind me into the water. Melted, blackened dolls floated and burning trees cracked and toppled in the canal behind me. A skeleton bobbed up beside me, its skull hanging in a slack grin, and I screamed.

Above, John loomed over the ledge, barely keeping his balance as the ground continued to break up. His red eyes squinted in the dark, searching for me amidst the dolls and bodies in the canal.

Then his face changed. The awful grin faded, and he looked suddenly solemn, on the verge of epiphany. Even the island seemed to stop shaking, the waters to still.

"She's here," he whispered. "She's come."

John turned away, vanishing from the ledge. I could hear him up above, moving closer to the heart tree, still laughing and crying madly. His voice grew louder and more jubilant, hailing the arrival of La Llorona.

"Llorona!" he cried. "Oh, God! It's you! *It's you!*"

My leg throbbing, I dragged myself up the muddy, sinking bank. As I lifted my head over the edge, I saw John standing by the burning heart tree as the island crumbled to a tiny circle around it. There were no dolls left, nothing left to save us.

And John was no longer alone.

On the far shore, like a hurricane, she'd made landfall.

To my horror, I saw her clearly for the first time. She was pulling herself up from the dark waters of the canal. Lank, black hair hung over her face. Her body changed as it rose above the surface, becoming the torso of a shapely woman, beautiful, loosely clad in soiled white rags. As she dragged her dark, serpentine lower body from the water, it transformed into a pair of slender female legs. Her feet were worn with red sores from ages of wandering. The world seemed to shimmer around her, and she moved with swift, sudden jerks, like stop-motion film.

She stood on the shore, weeping softly, hiding her face in her long, lovely hands. Wet, dark hair fell like a curtain before her.

John dropped the crossbow, forgotten. The weapon hit the broken wood platform around the heart tree with a clatter. Slowly, John's feet stirred, and he began to walk toward her.

"You've come for me." His soft voice shook with joy. "Haven't you? Tell me you've come for me!"

Despite the pain, I lifted my head. I had to try to save him. "John!" My voice was choked and rasping, almost inaudible, drowned out by the soft weeping. "No!"

"I've loved you." He stepped closer to her. "Since the moment I heard you. So much beauty. So much pain."

Barely feet away from the bent, weeping woman, John reached out with a shaking hand to touch her.

She lifted her gaze with a scream, her hair flew back, and I saw her true face. Her eyes were gone, only sunken red sockets left in their place. The flesh was torn to shreds all around them where she'd gouged her eyes out, blinding herself in her mad agony. The empty holes bled red tears down her ghastly, milk-white face.

"John!" I screamed.

But John recoiled only slightly before Llorona's wail, falling to his knees before her.

"Take me," he whispered. "Let me be the one you've searched for, all these years…"

Her mouth was vast, lined with white fangs, her jaw unhinging like a snake to take him whole.

Terror crushed my heart. Pain held me to the ground. Despite it all, I made myself raise my voice.

"*Doña Marina!*"

At the sound of her real name, the spell was broken. Llorona's mouth closed, shrinking back to human size.

Slowly, the empty, weeping eyes turned toward me.

The maddening sobs resumed, transforming into wild laughter—and as I looked into those empty holes, I felt my mind slipping away, and I realized the laughter was my own voice, high and frantic. I made myself rein it in—but God, John was right. She *was* beautiful.

My heart swelled with love and sorrow.

I staggered toward her, my left thigh stained in blood, the bolt still buried deep, but I no longer felt the pain. I no longer felt anything except a *need* to be with her, to walk into the arms of the dead and be dead with her forever. Somehow it would be like returning to my own mother's arms, feeling her embrace, just once.

A mother always loves her children.

My dad's voice rose in my mind. I remembered him talking about Mom, the night before I left. Somehow it gave me strength, snapped me out of the trance.

At the center of the island I stopped, wavering on my wounded leg as I fought to resist her.

"Doña Marina," I said again, giving the words force, like a curse.

Llorona wailed, hiding her face in her hands with an awful, echoing sob.

"That was your real name." I made myself go on. "I know who you are. And I know what they did to you. Please. Your search is over, Marina. You can be at peace!"

I leaned on the heart tree for balance, burning leaves and ashes raining down around me.

"Your children, Marina. You never killed them, did you? They were taken from you, to protect Cortés's name, because they were *his*, weren't they? Born out of wedlock, while he kept you as his slave. That's why he feared for his legacy if they lived. That's why their coffin bears his mark. That's why they killed your children—and you were blamed, for all these years. But you've found them! You've found them!"

Llorona ripped her hands away from her face to scream at me, fixing me in her awful, empty gaze. I stepped back, nearly toppling on my bad leg.

"That's what you want, isn't it?" I whispered breathily. "Your children, Marina!"

But it was useless. It was just as Don Julio had feared. Because La Llorona *wasn't* Doña Marina. Not anymore. She no longer knew reason, no longer knew love, no longer knew herself. The monster they'd made of her had taken over, and she knew only vengeance and destruction.

"Listen," I begged. "They're here! They're—"

Llorona let out another wail, this one ear-splitting. My hair blew back in the wind of it. I shoved both hands to my ears to keep it out, but it was no use. The sound drove me to my knees in agony.

From the corner of my eye, I saw the crossbow, still on the ground where John discarded it—my only chance.

But before I could lunge for it, the ground split open at the dead woman's feet with a rending *crack*. The fissure cut through the island like jagged lightning, right between my legs. The wooden rim of the heart tree cracked with a puff of dust, and the tree itself toppled over with a crash.

Suddenly the ground was shifting beneath me, as the last remnants of the burning island split apart down the middle. The dolls had burned; the spell was broken. On my hands and knees, I tried to cling to the shattered wood foundations, but they, too, were shifting, unbound. The small fragment of island was sinking, like a broken ship, and it could no longer hold me.

In desperation, I threw my battered body at the cross-bow, landing on it and searching for the handle; but it was too late.

With a final splintering crack, the floating garden broke beneath me, and I felt myself falling *through* it, through the earth itself.

Then the cold canal seized me.

Chapter 33: The Last Stand

The gravity of the sinking island pulled me under with it, and for a moment I spun, struggling to find the surface. With my uninjured right hand I gripped the crossbow, paddling with the other arm and kicking with my good leg.

Gasping for breath, I burst to the churning surface.

The island was gone. A few of the juniper trees that had anchored it remained, rising from the water in flames. Aside from that, there was only debris—burning wreckage and blackened dolls and dislodged skeletons, bobbing on the rough waves.

I spun in the water, looking around desperately, but La Llorona was nowhere to be seen. Her absence did nothing to calm me. The dark depths could hide anything.

With a sudden *whoomp*, something burst to the surface beside me, and I nearly screamed.

But it was only a piece of the island—a big, rectangular slab of wood that seemed to want to float on the surface.

Then a cold, firm hand gripped my shoulder, and this time I *did* scream.

"Carmen?"

As I spun and kicked away in the water, I saw it was only John. His eyes were still bloodshot, but the water had washed the bloody tears from his face. His expression was a mix of fear and confusion.

"Where is she?" I shrieked.

"What…?" John rubbed his sore, red-rimmed eyes.

"La Llorona!"

Even as I said the name, my eyes widened and I saw a

disturbance under the surface, just behind John. The water churned, rolling over in little white-caps.

"John!"

His eyes widened and he started to turn—when a vast, prehensile tail whipped up from the water and slammed down on his head with a sick crunch. Blood sprayed the surface as the serpent pulled him violently below.

"No!" I tried to aim the crossbow, but they were both already gone, underwater. I couldn't see them. "John!"

With another sudden splash, John emerged from the water, gasping and spluttering. His scalp was split open from the blow, his face dazed and masked in blood down one side. He tried to swim away in a clumsy doggy-paddle toward me. His bleary, blinking eyes found mine. I'm not sure what I saw in his eyes in that moment. Fear, of course, but sadness, too, and regret.

Then the tail coiled around his waist, lifting him clean out of the water. The black, muscular monstrosity waved him around in the air as he kicked and screamed, seeming to toy with him a moment.

Shouting in wordless panic, I raised the crossbow, tried to find a clean shot—but it was too late. Everything happened in the span of seconds.

The muscles under the scales flexed visibly around John's waist, and several bones in his spine and pelvis cracked. His scream rose an octave, then broke off as blood spilled from his mouth, his body limp as a doll.

Then the monster pulled him under the surface with enough force to make waves, knocking me back.

"John!" I wailed.

Feebly, weakened by my injured leg, I kicked to where he'd been, trying to see under the water, trying to aim the crossbow, but it was no use. I couldn't see anything, and anyway it was too late.

He was gone. John was gone.

No one left but me, and *her*.

Fear overpowered my sorrow and pain, and I looked around again, aiming my crossbow. My finger itched to fire at the slightest ripple on the water, but I had only the one bolt. I had to make it count.

Something brushed my foot and I kicked away with a squeal. John's torso bobbed to the surface, his body torn apart at the waist, leaking inky blood and guts that spread like tiny snakes on the surface. His sightless, bulging eyes met mine, and I screamed.

Then a firm, cool grip entwined my calf, squeezing with instant tightness.

Next thing I knew I was underwater, before I could even hold my breath. Water flooded my mouth and I choked, even as Llorona pulled me deeper into the abyss. Her tail slithered up my leg, growing ever tighter.

Twisting in the serpent's grip, I fixed the iron sights of the crossbow on the writhing shadow beneath me. In the darkness of the water, I could see almost nothing, and the creature was shaking me too violently to take proper aim.

Trust your instincts, John's voice said in my ear. I could almost feel his hands on mine. *Don't overthink it. Just aim it like a camera.*

Taking aim as best I could, I squeezed the trigger.

The bolt released from the crossbow, cutting through the water like a harpoon. Something big shrieked under the water and the grip loosened around my calf. In the next instant, the flailing tail smacked my ribs and I flew through the water, bobbing up on the surface.

Gasping for breath, I fled to the floating slab of wood nearby and managed to drag myself atop it.

Behind me, the water churned as Llorona thrashed her tail and moaned in pain. I saw red eyes open beneath the water, and a brief glimpse of something finned and black, like a big fish, before she broke the surface.

Then she rose in the form of a naked woman, her body now gaunt and rotted. She came up screaming, her mouth impossibly huge, lined with inhuman fangs.

In that moment, as adrenaline coursed through my body, I had never felt more afraid. The fear brought both intense focus and a strange sense of detachment. Time seemed to slow as Llorona floated closer.

I knew, in that moment, that it was over. I'd already fired my only bolt; the rest had sunk to the bottom with John. Her madness had won, as it had won over a thousand lives before ours, and there was nothing I could do.

Then I looked at my leg, and realized: I did have *one* more bolt, didn't I?

As the wooden box rocked beneath me, I leaned back and cocked the crossbow with its rusty crank. Then I reached for the last bolt—the one still buried in my thigh where John had shot me.

Just touching it sent waves of pain through my leg, but pain was no concern now. Gritting my teeth and biting back a scream, I wrapped my fingers around the cold iron bolt and wrenched on it, but it was buried too deep, the barbs of the arrow hooked in my flesh. It took several wriggling tugs, each jerk darkening my wet jeans with fresh blood till the bolt came free with a ripped-Velcro sound.

Weeping, I shoved the bolt in the groove of the bow, chunks of my own muscle and bloody sinew still clinging to the broad arrowhead.

She was coming on fast, her dagger-teeth bared, as I leveled the bow with her open mouth for my last shot.

Then the vast tail swept up from my side, smacking me. I sprawled down on the rocking box, the crossbow falling from my hands.

"*No!*" Reaching for the crossbow, I lost my balance and tumbled off the wooden box, barely clinging to the side as it bounced.

Beside me, the crossbow sank rapidly. If I'd lunged for it, I could have saved it. Could have taken my last shot at Llorona.

But something else caught my eye, floating behind the bow. It was a doll, her hair blackened and burned away, her rubber skin scorched and disfigured—but I recognized her, and my eyes widened.

Instead of the bow, I reached for Rosita.

As La Llorona bore down on me, I raised the doll above my head.

"*Sanctum, por favor!*"

Llorona's snake-teeth snapped shut and her eyebrows rose in what must have been surprise. Fresh blood welled from her empty eye sockets, which were now fixed in the doll's direction instead of mine. Slowly, she drifted back, giving me a bit of space as she surveilled this new threat.

With my free hand and my last strength, I wrenched myself back onto the big floating box. For the first time, I noticed the colorful, medieval-style coat of arms painted on top of the box, and realized what I was floating on.

A few yards away, La Llorona shrieked, and the foul wind of her breath made me wince back, afraid. I clutched the drowned girl's doll and kept praying, to my friends, to everyone who'd been lost to this monster.

"*Please!*" I cried. "*Give us sanctum from the restless dead!*"

Before me, Llorona inched closer. Behind me, her tail lashed the water. All around, skeletons bobbed amid dolls and debris, loosened from the soil under the ruined island.

"I know you can't find peace while her curse remains," I shouted. "So please, help me now, I beg you!"

For the sake of the friends I'd lost, for the sake of Don Julio, the drowned girl, the spirits of the island—and for *her* sake, Doña Marina herself, the betrayed and misunderstood mother of a whole new race—for all of them, I intended to break the curse of La Llorona, no matter what it cost.

Llorona shrieked at me again. She was inching closer and closer in the water, trying to approach, but still warded off by the doll in my hands.

"Please," I appealed to her. "We are *all* your children. Don't you know that by now?"

She gnashed her teeth, snapping like a dog, mere feet from my face. I could smell the rancid death flowing from her ravenous mouth, foul as a tomb. Shielded only by the doll, I stood my ground.

"We've suffered enough," I cried, "and so have you!"

I could feel the doll's power waning, breaking under the will and madness of Llorona. The monster was leaning ever closer, lashing the water with its tail like an angry cat.

Standing tall on the wooden box floating beneath me, I faced her down.

"Come on," I growled, starting to grin. "I'm gonna give you back what they took from you, Marina."

Then I tossed Rosita aside.

"So come and get it, you *bitch!*"

Llorona's black eye sockets widened and her mouth opened in a horrible grin. Instantly she saw her opening in the absence of the doll. The tail flashed down from behind and Llorona lunged, her teeth gnashing down at my head.

But I was already leaping away, throwing myself into the water as Llorona's tail smashed the box beneath me.

And the coffin broke open.

Chapter 34: A Mother's Love

Falling from the coffin, I submerged, and quickly lost sight of the light. My wounded leg felt numb, clumsy and useless as wood. I didn't think I could swim back to the surface. I wanted to let myself sink, deeper and deeper, into the bottomless abyss.

John was waiting for me, and Miguel, and Larry. And Mom, too.

But then I thought of *you*, Dad, waiting back home. I thought of how worried you must be. How guilty you'd feel if I didn't return. It gave me strength, for the moment.

To my surprise, I felt the bottom of the canal at my feet. With my one good leg, I kicked off from the bottom and paddled back to the surface, ignoring the pain.

As I came up, I saw the monstrous form of Llorona, hunched over the coffin she'd smashed open trying to crush me.

Two child-sized skeletons slid out of the splintered coffin, bundled in rags.

For what seemed like forever, La Llorona simply stared at the bodies, her razor teeth still bared, her eyes still empty holes, her hair flying back around her like wild serpents.

Slowly, her mouth shrank, becoming human, her lips full and red. Her wet dark hair fell in lustrous curls over fair shoulders and full breasts. Tilting her head, she drifted closer to the two tiny skeletons. As the desiccated cloth took on water, the bundles started to sink.

Llorona raised her arms under the water, gently pulling the bundles in toward her.

A shockwave pulsed through the water, and a sudden bright flash made me wince, shielding my eyes.

When I looked up again, La Llorona and the children's skeletons were gone.

In their place stood Doña Marina, in her true beauty—weeping and holding her children, a laughing boy and a pretty girl, twins by the look of them. Marina pressed her forehead to theirs, tears streaming down her cheeks as she wept.

For the first time in centuries, Doña Marina wept in joy, not sorrow.

Turning away from me, Marina drifted away across the debris-scattered lake, speaking softly to her babies in her Aztec tongue. Slowly, they sank beneath the waves, and the vision faded like mist before the morning sun.

Grabbing a piece of board from the broken coffin, I pulled myself up onto it with my last strength, gasping.

I was alone, floating amidst the smoldering wreckage of the sunken island. Melted dolls bobbed past, mingled with dozens of half-rotten skeletons—victims of conquest, murder, madness. The chaos had dredged up all the bodies from the bottom of the lake, like worms after rain.

Yet even among the dead, I felt strangely at peace. I was starting to bleed out from the hole in my thigh, and with that came a kind of complacency; but more than that, I knew all these spirits would find peace now, at last.

They could rest—but I couldn't. Not yet.

It would have been easy to give in to exhaustion and pain, to lie back on my own piece of floating coffin and rest for just a little while; but a distant voice in the back of my mind kept telling me if I didn't move now, I'd be dead.

I think it was your voice, Dad.

And I *didn't* give up. I want you to know that.

I pulled myself to the edge of the board, dipped my hand in, and started to paddle—not away, but deeper into the fuming debris where the island had been. There was something there I needed.

As I picked my way through the smoking wreckage, I scanned the canal, searching amid the bodies and dolls floating on the surface.

Even as I watched, the waters were growing still again, calm. The bodies were starting to submerge, returning to rest, this time forever. They could all rest now, knowing no one else would fall to the curse of La Llorona.

Up ahead, the roof of Don Julio's half-collapsed barn still thrust up like an iceberg from the bottom of the canal. Some of the trees, too, were still standing, ringed in places by rotting boards and other remnants of the broken island.

Lifting myself up on my piece of flotsam, I raised a hand to shield my eyes and look around.

Then I saw it, floating amid the plastic doll heads—a bright blue backpack bobbing on the surface, the strap looped over a low branch in one of the remaining trees. There were still dolls pinned in the tree above it.

"The whole world could sink," I rasped, remembering what John had said about his dry bag, "and this baby'd still be floating."

Paddling closer, I reached out and grabbed John's bag.

One of the dolls fell off the tree, like rotting fruit, landing practically in my hands. I looked down into its glass eyes—the only feature left in a face burned black—then I tucked the doll under my arm with John's backpack.

Slowly, I drifted on my board up to the roof of Don Julio's sunken barn. There, I pulled myself up onto the creaking, slanted wood beams, and rolled over on my back, gasping, trying to catch my breath.

Gathering my strength, I made myself sit up and open John's waterproof bag. The plastic had fused together in places, but sure enough, the contents were still dry.

I mended my leg as best I could with John's belt as a tourniquet and the last of the gauze from the first-aid kit. My pant leg was completely red from the knee down. I'd lost so much blood already, I didn't think I had much more to lose.

I looked out over the empty space where the island had been. Aside from the barn's rooftop, only a few trees still stood, strung with half-burned dolls.

By then, the sun was coming up. It was Wednesday, I realized, October 31. All Hallow's Eve, the start of the *Día de Muertos*, when children make altars to invite the dead back to visit.

Here, the dead were leaving instead, submerging again. The dolls were dispersing, floating away into the marshland to either side, where insects hummed, and birds fluttered among the trees.

There was little left in John's pack. The flashlight, towels, and much of the rest were missing. The food, of course, was long gone. The water bottle had only a swig, which I chugged greedily.

In the front pocket, I found the MP3 recorder I'd let John borrow to record his thoughts when we first arrived. I played the one recording he'd made. The tinny voice sounded alien against the soft, nature sounds.

When I heard John's voice, tears started flowing again.

"Hey, Carmen. Just recording my experiences. Really loving it so far. Can't even piss in private with all these dolls watching you."

I laughed a little through the tears. In the background, I could hear pee hitting dry leaves. Further off, I thought I heard Miguel's voice, shouting something. John must have recorded this on the very first day, when he slipped off the trail to relieve himself.

"Yeah, I'm coming," he called. Softly, to the recorder, he added, *"You owe me big time, honey. Next vacation, we're doing Football Hall of Fame."*

The recording ended abruptly. I sat there, rocking and weeping over the recorder. Then I hit play again, listening to the last time I'd hear him say my name.

"Hey Carmen. Just recording my experiences…"

I stopped it. Hit play again. Stopped it. Hit play again.

"Hey Carmen… Hey Carmen…"

"John," I moaned.

Sadness overcame me. I rolled over on the groaning roof and curled in a fetal position. Pain radiated through my leg, which now felt oddly cold, almost tingling.

"I'm sorry," I sobbed. "I'm so sorry."

Beside me sat the burned doll that had fallen from the tree when I grabbed John's backpack. Its rubber eyelids were scorched away and the glass eyes stared at me from its cracked and wrinkled face.

As I looked at it, my tears subsided into sniffling. The sight of the doll watching over me gave me comfort.

"You'll protect me, won't you?" I whispered.

Then something *cracked* beneath me and I startled as the rooftop shifted. A fissure split through the middle of it, boards prying apart down the seams. Startled, I grabbed the doll and John's backpack and rolled off into the water.

As the barn finished falling apart, I climbed onto a piece of flotsam and struggled to paddle away, fighting the pull of the structure sinking behind me.

In a moment, the barn was gone. The other debris had sunken, too, leaving no trace of the island at all.

It was over. The Island of the Dolls was gone.

Still I held onto the burned doll, tucked under my arm.

"All gone." I looked down at the doll, my sight blurry with tears, and forced a smile. "But you'll protect me."

With its eerily wide eyes, the doll stared back in silence.

I took my final look at the place where the island had stood, then turned and paddled away.

Like I said, I tried to get away. Don't think I didn't try, Dad. For the better part of the morning, I struggled down the choked and leech-filled waters, heading what I thought was north.

But my leg was hurt bad, and I didn't know the way. It was all I could do to even hold onto the board.

And I still heard the crying, however far I paddled.

I can hear it now, God help me.

It's in my head, now, as much a fixture there as my own thoughts. But I know that's all it is. It can't be real, I know it.

It wasn't long before I gave up paddling. My body just didn't have the strength. The best I could do was lie on the board, float down the canal, and pray for a *trajinera* to pass and save me.

As my hopes grew thin, I took out this audio recorder to tell my story. My confession.

The batteries must be almost dead, now. I'm glad it lasted long enough. Glad *I* lasted. Maybe I'll put it up in a tree, above the water. Someone will find it there.

I hope it'll survive. I hope it finds its way to you, Dad.

I'm so sorry I won't be coming home. Me, or John, or Larry, or Miguel. I'm so sorry to everyone I hurt with my recklessness. My ambition. Only now do I see the *Muñecas* project never mattered. Mom always loved me, anyway.

You were right about that, Dad. A mother's love is a powerful thing. A bond that transcends even death...

[Static interference]

...hope you love me, still. You, and Mom...

[Interference; audio quality deteriorating]

...light keeps blinking. The batteries are done. I'll have to stow the recorder somewhere they'll find it. I see a grove of trees up ahead, I think. It's getting hard to see, and the water's cold. So cold...

[Unusual static; possibly human whispers]

...can hear her again. *Why* do I still hear her? God, do you hear it, or am I losing my mind?

It's not just her, either. There are others with her, now.

[Wind or static; indistinct sounds; children's laughter?]

...hoped I was dreaming, but I don't think it's a dream. Don Julio was right. She can't forgive. Can't move on.

[Very unusual wind or static; indistinct laughing or weeping?]

I don't think she'll let me go, Dad. Do you hear it?

Do you hear the crying?

I think... oh, God. Wait. I see something. It's not just a tree grove up ahead. There's land, and—

And there's something in the trees.

Oh my God. No. *No!*

[Loud wind, splashing]

—they're in the trees. They're everywhere. But it can't be. I saw them burn! I saw them all burn!

[Wailing wind, static]

—the dolls! Oh, God.

The dolls!—

[End of Transcript]

Afterword

The search for Carmen Benitez and her friends is still active today. Her father leads the search in cooperation with the Banks-Lee Detective Agency. He has established the Find Carmen Foundation and offers a $10,000 reward for anyone with information leading to her whereabouts.

The best way to help is to get the word out. Please share Carmen's story with your friends and family. The more people know, the better the chances that we'll uncover more information about the Island of the Dolls, the *Muñecas* Project, and the legend of *La Llorona*.

Consider reviewing this book at your favorite retailer or book review site. Even just a few words can go a long way to raise awareness for this important issue.

You can also join the A.E. Hodge Email Newsletter and receive:

- News on the Search for Carmen Benitez
- Notification of New Book Releases by A.E. Hodge
- Exclusive Promotions and Bonus Content
- No Spam, Ever!

www.aehodge.com/mailinglist/

www.findcarmenfoundation.com

ALSO BY A.E. HODGE

SO DAMN BEAUTIFUL

Roses Are Red, Violets Are Blue
One Day Very Soon, I'm Coming For You

When beautiful, obsessive psychopath Christian kidnaps her young son, single mother Meredith Banks sets out alone on a desperate vigilante quest into Christian's dark world, a surreal nightmare of human trafficking, murder, and madness.

The further she steps outside the law, the less hope she has of turning back. Pitted against the cops, a crime syndicate, and Christian himself, Meredith must unravel the deadly secrets of Christian's past—and resist the compulsion of his hypnotic smile. Failure will cost Meredith her son—but finding him may cost her soul.

READ ON FOR AN EXCLUSIVE PREVIEW!

Now, a special sneak preview—scenes from
SO DAMN BEAUTIFUL: THE LONELY ONE
Book 1 of **SO DAMN BEAUTIFUL**

* * *

By the time I reach the office, breathless and clutching a lukewarm McCoffee, it's almost ten o'clock, another sunless morning in Midtown Detroit. In a half-assed attempt at hiding my lateness, I slip through the back door of the Law Offices of Spector & Krunk, Attorneys at Law.

The sight of my reflection in the hallway mirror makes me wince—my long red hair, still wet from the shower, is drying into a mess, and my green eyes look drab without makeup. My purple blouse is wrinkled for lack of ironing.

My unusual height makes it hard to sneak into the office unnoticed, and I'm forced to smile and wave at the older woman working reception. Her eyes slide from me to the clock on the wall with disapproval.

When I reach my tiny two-walled cubicle, I set my knock-off purse under the desk and sit down. Invoices and documents pile up in my black plastic "To-Do" bin, but I ignore these. Like my tardiness and my frumpy appearance, work couldn't concern me less right now.

I turn on my computer, sip coffee nervously, and start to research my son's latest ailment.

Pinworms are small white roundworms that live in your upper digestive tract. At night, the female pinworms crawl out of your ass and expel their eggs while you sleep. The eggs make you itch, and when you scratch yourself you get the eggs under your nails, and then in your mouth, and thus back in your guts—the circle of life. According to Google, it's one of the most common parasites. Over forty percent of the human population has or has had a pinworm infection. Most probably don't even know it.

A trace of sandalwood cologne penetrates my concentration, and I turn to see the office intern, Christian, leaning casually against the gray wall of my cubicle. He wears a light blue Oxford shirt, perfectly fitted and tucked, no blousing. His dark hair's long, but neat. When I look up, he moves in closer, eyeing my computer screen. "No solitaire this morning?" he observes.

I've been so pre-occupied, I almost forgot about Christian. Today is his last day in the office. "Do you know what a pinworm is?" I ask him.

He lifts an eyebrow. I motion him closer and he stands behind my faux-leather chair to watch my computer screen while I play an online video taken by a microscopic medical camera. The video shows hundreds of worms crawling on the glossy red walls of someone's intestines. Christian sums it up perfectly: "Nasty."

"But harmless. Almost always harmless." I smile cheerlessly. "You could have them and not even know it."

He looks a little concerned for me. "Is that so?"

"Sorry," I say, realizing what I'm talking about—and who I'm talking *to*. "It's just my son has these things. Here I am this morning, trying to work the damn coffee machine, and Troy comes in and says his *turd has a tail...*"

Christian smirks. "How is he?"

I shrug. "He still wanted to go to school." I sigh and shake my head. "I should've been washing his bed sheets more often…"

"He probably *caught* it from school," Christian assures me. "Those shit-holes are incubators for disease."

I mistrust Christian's smile; that damn cocky smile. "I'll start washing his sheets every week," I say again.

Hoping vaguely that he'll leave, I swivel back to face my computer. The worms greet me on the monitor and I feel a pang of nausea as I close the web browser. The desktop background on my PC is a tranquil image of the sunset over the Mediterranean. My husband used to take photos for calendars before he died. I always thought this photo was his most beautiful.

Behind me Christian says, "They were talking about us in the break room."

* * *

Still I say nothing, only clench the faux-leather steering wheel in a death grip and drive. Instinctively I know I have to get control of this situation somehow. They always say not to go with the kidnapper. You never go along with the kidnapper, no matter what.

I can feel the pistol in my waistband, pressing uncomfortably against my hip.

He leans forward so he's right behind me. I can almost smell the mint on his breath. "Can I just say I find this side of you a turn-on?" he says, in his gentle baritone.

After what they did to me in Room 213, this is more than I can take. My eyes immediately tear up as I drive. "Shh," he consoles me, stroking my hair. "Here, pull into that McDonalds. I want to show you something."

In the same gentle, coercive voice, he urges me to the dim edges of the parking lot, beside the dumpster. Trash spills over onto the pavement, teeming with flies. Christian asks for the keys from the ignition and I hand them over without resistance. My heart is pounding as I wait for the right moment. I still don't know if he's armed.

He gets out of the back, comes around and opens the passenger door. He has to ease his legs in around my backpack on the passenger side floor, and this slows him down—my only chance.

Even as he climbs in next to me, I wrench the handgun from behind me and point it straight in his face.

Across the barrel of the gun he looks at me almost shyly, wearing a small smile. His long hair parts neatly down the center. His hand is hidden in one of the pockets of his black leather jacket.

"Don't move, motherfucker," I growl. My back is pressed to the door and the gun is only inches from his face.

He sighs slowly. "Good seeing you again, too. You look like hell. What did they do to you?"

He starts to reach toward me, as if to touch my face. I press the tip of the gun to his forehead to shove him back. "Put your hands up, slowly," I say. He doesn't move. "Get your hand out of your pocket! Now!"

His smile is almost sad. "You think I want to hurt you? I don't want any of this. All I want is to love you."

"I'll shoot you, Christian," I whisper.

"I believe you would," he whispers back. "But you know what's funny? I feel closer to you now than ever before. After watching you, seeing how you coped. You're such a good mother. And you're just like me! Driven by a primal urge, some evolutionary compulsion. Even willing to kill to get what you want."

This is like a knife to my belly. Willing to kill? What does he mean by that? I start to sweat in worry for my son. "It was an accident," I say, shakily. "I didn't mean to kill them."

"Shh, it's okay. I *like* that you did it. It shows what a good mother you are. You'll stop at nothing to find Troy. Isn't that right?"

"Yes. That's right." The gun trembles in my hand.

"Then do it," he says.

I stare at him, not comprehending. His smile never wavers. He turns slightly, raises his free hand very slowly, and points a finger at his own forehead. I let him do this, too surprised to react.

"Do it," he says again, in his eerily calm voice. "Shoot me." His smile widens almost imperceptibly. "And never see your son again."

* * *

About A.E. Hodge

Wizard of weird A.E. Hodge is a writer of horror, dark fantasy, and other thrilling fiction. He is the author of *Spoiled Lunch and Other Creepy Tales* and *So Damn Beautiful*.

Hodge has an official website at **www.aehodge.com**. You can also follow him on Facebook (A.E. Hodge) and Twitter (@FictionFugitive).

Visit www.aehodge.com for the latest releases and more!

WWW.AEHODGE.COM